After All

Alan Johnson

AFTER ALL
Copyright ©2017 Alan Johnson

ISBN-13:   978-1544114170
ISBN-10:   1544114176

*While some readers of AFTER ALL will be tempted
to assign the characters, situations and places
to actual people, experiences and locales,
they do so from the recesses of their own memories.*

This story is complete fiction.

*The characters and their interactions with each other,
reside only in my mind, and do not now, nor have they ever existed
in reality.*

*Some actual locations and historical events are referenced only to
lend an air of authenticity to the narrative, and
I have done my best to reflect the history accurately.*

*None of the events related in the story actually happened
the way they are portrayed in the pages that follow.*

Acknowledgements

The story that follows is fiction and is a complete fabrication drawn from the fantasy world that I visit (or that visits me...) from time to time. Actual historical events have been intertwined in the narrative to convey a sense of the time and the conflict that we experienced in the late 1960's, and to lend an air of realism.

From an early age, I have created alternative scenarios to explain the inconsistencies we all encounter in our lives. I truly believe God granted me this gift to allow me to maintain my sanity.

I will forever be indebted to friends who have given encouragement to continue writing this story. My sincere thanks goes to Fran Goddard, Julia Reedy, Kim Hicks, Peggy White and Carol McKenzie who read early drafts and gave me the benefit of their insight, telling me where I went wrong.

And a very special thank you goes to Cindy Moser for her artistic perspective in the creation of the cover picture for this book. Cindy captured perfectly what I envisioned.

And finally, I thank those who have granted me what I consider to be one of the highest honors that can be given—to be called a FRIEND. This story is dedicated to you.

...Alan...

Other books by Alan Johnson:

WHEN FOREVER'S OVER

Following publication of WHEN FOREVER'S OVER, which was the initial offering in the story of Cubby, Danny, Will, Amy and Mary Beth, I received a great deal of feedback that the dialect in which that book is written, was somewhat difficult to read. A critic with a publishing house in Chicago even suggested that I issue a 2nd Edition of the book, deleting the dialect that I heard in my head as I wrote.

So, to facilitate the reading, I have "changed my ways" and written the majority of AFTER ALL using (my version) of proper English. I did attempt to preserve the phrasing and tempo of our way of speaking here in the mountains of East Tennessee. And I simply had to keep the dialect in place where direct quotes occur in dialog between characters. I will forever maintain that the unique way we speak, and twist the language to our own ends, is beautiful, and to my mind, well worth preserving.

I have re-edited WHEN FOREVER'S OVER, changing the body of that book to a more standard (*i.e.*, proper English) style, and will be offering a 2nd Edition of that book to make reading it easier.

And for any readers who are curious, and want to know the "rest of the story," take heart. Mid-way through my writing of AFTER ALL, the story for a third and final book in this series took form. I have already begun the task of making notes and outlining the story, running dialog and situations through my head.

So, as we used to hear on the old TV shows, *stay tuned…*

I sincerely hope you enjoy this offering.

ALAN JOHNSON

PROLOGUE

Nothing ever came easy for Paddy Leary. Of course, he brought a lot of it on himself, but he never got any breaks. Getting a fair shake out of life just didn't happen.

About a week after we started our sophomore year in 1967, Paddy stepped just inside the door of our homeroom, leaned up against the doorframe with his hands buried deep in the pockets of his jeans, and waited. He was escorted by Principal Webster who handed a wad of papers to Mrs. Pinson, our home room teacher. She adjusted the glasses on the end of her nose and took her time looking through each of the pages before she motioned for him to find a seat, turned to the class and told us "Mr. Leary" would be joining us. But Paddy just stood there looking at us for a minute, hands still in his pockets, till Mr. Webster poked him on the shoulder.

We should've known right then, things weren't going to turn out for the good.

We could all tell right off that the new guy was older than the rest of us, since he had a two day beard stubble on his cheeks. For the most part the rest of the guys were just shaving every other day, whether we needed to or not. Except for Will Boyd, that is. Will was growing a full set of whiskers by the middle of our freshman year.

That morning, ole Paddy slid down in a desk seat and sat there the rest of the period, never making another sound. After the bell rang at the end of the class period and while we were getting our books and stuff ready to go to the next class, a few of us went up to him to introduce ourselves, and kind of give him a welcome.

I stuck out my hand and told him my name was Cubby James. Paddy got a smirky grin on his face and asked, "Cubby? Like the kid on Mickey Mouse Club?"

I could feel my face getting hot, and just nodded as Danny MacMahan elbowed me over to the side and stepped up. But when Danny told his name, Paddy got a weary look on his face.

"MacMahan? You any kin to Sheriff MacMahan?"

I could see Danny's shoulders square up and his eyes narrow a bit.

"Yeah. Rocky's my big brother."

Paddy stared back at him for a second of silence, before he shrugged his shoulders and said, "OK."

He didn't have much time to think on it, because Amy Higgins, who was in her own mind, the self-appointed leader of our class, shoved Danny out of the way and stuck out her hand.

"You any kin to the sawmill Leary's?" Amy asked, pushing her glasses up on her nose, and cocking her head over to the side.

"Might be…" was all he said.

Time was running out on us, and we had to get a move on to get to second period class, so that was about all that got said that morning. We only had five minutes between classes, and that short exchange near about took it all up. We all told Paddy we'd talk later, and headed out of the room.

But later never came that day.

Trying to be neighborly, and since we wanted to know more about the new guy, me and Danny looked for Paddy at lunch. But he was nowhere to be found. I even looked outside the smoker's door, at the side of the school building, where all the kids that had the craving went to light up, to see if he was there.

That was the way it was with Paddy. We figured out pretty quick that he had no intention of staying in school, and every time he spotted an avenue of escape, he took it. Ole Paddy purely couldn't be penned up.

Even when the Truant Law would catch up to him, and make him come in, Paddy made it real clear he didn't want to be there. On the days he came, we'd see him in the morning, but generally by afternoon, he was AWOL again.

When he was at school, he was mostly quiet, watching the rest of us from a corner, so quiet we'd almost forget he was there. But then something would set him off and he'd do something that would get him out of class, and into the Principal's office.

The different personalities in our class, all thrown together and stirred up, made us kind of different, almost unique. Or at least we thought we were a special bunch. We were always into something, but nothing we ever did was too bad because we were all afraid it'd get back to our folks and we'd be in more trouble at home than we were at school.

But that wasn't the case with Paddy. He didn't give a rat's ass who thought what. In the time he was with us, he dumped his books in the trash cans, tore up the stenciled homework assignments the teachers gave out, threw paper wads at the blackboard when the teachers had their backs turned, and flat-out refused to answer any questions that the teachers put to him. And when he got forced to say something, he'd mostly give a completely smart-ass reply.

One time, when Mrs. Henderson, the guidance counselor, put her trash can outside her door for the janitor to empty, Paddy sighted in on it as he waltzed down the hall, planted his size 10 motorcycle boot in the side of the can and kicked it near thirty feet down toward the library door, scattering trash all over creation.

The final straw came the middle part of October, about six or seven weeks after Paddy first came to be with us. We were in homeroom on a Thursday morning and Mrs. Pinson had us scoot our desks back on each side of the room, closed the window blinds, turned off the lights and started the projector to show us a movie.

That morning she was showing us a Civil Defense film about how we could lay down in a ditch, or sit on our ass and put our heads between our knees and cover our eyes, and by doing that, we could survive a nuclear attack, if the Russians decided to nuke Oak Ridge.

I reckon, doing those kind of things might have been OK for folks that were living a-ways away from ground-zero. But the thing about it was, we were close enough to Oak Ridge, depending on how many mega-tons the bombs were, and how good the Russian's aim was, if we didn't get burnt to cinders in the fire-ball, we were sure to get the full effect of the radiation. So no matter what happened, if the bombs got dropped, our asses was grass.

Well, that morning they'd just got through the credits saying the movie was made by the Civil Defense folks, when Paddy figured he'd just about enjoyed all he could stand. He reached out and sneaked Mary Beth Rivers' science book off of her desk, opened it up and fanned out the pages, flicked off the top of his Zippo lighter, spun the spark-wheel with his thumb, and set fire to the pages. Then he rared back and threw it across the room, over toward where me and Danny were sitting.

I recollect it reminded me of the story we'd read in English class about the Phoenix bird, burning across the sky. For a few seconds, it was actually sort of pretty, with the book covers flapping on both sides of the flames, like the Phoenix's wings.

But then we realized if we didn't move—and move fast— we'd most likely become fuel for the fire, and we all took to scooting desks out of the way real fast, and diving for cover. The burning book hit the floor and skidded up under the asbestos wrapping around the radiator pipes that ran along the bottom of the wall.

Somebody went out in the hall and came back with the fire extinguisher, pulled the pin and hit the book dead-on with a short blast that put the fire out, and sent little black pieces of burnt book pages floating all over the room.

The alarm got pulled and the whole of Lincoln High School poured out of the building to watch the fire trucks and police cars that started pulling up. I don't know who it was that told, but shortly after that we saw Mack Stephens, one of Rocky's Deputies at the Sheriff's office, putting Paddy in the back of a County Cruiser with his hands cuffed behind his back.

Rocky had to send Paddy down the mountain to the Blount County Jail in Maryville, because he was just seventeen at the time, and Andrew County didn't have any place to keep a juvenile. Blount County kept him in a separate cell there for a few days while they figured out what to do with him. Me, Danny and Will wanted to go see him, but none of us were sixteen yet, and so didn't have a driving license, and we weren't able to talk anybody into driving us.

The next week, Paddy was brought back to the Andrew County Courthouse and he stood up in front of Judge Watson, the Magistrate that was sent to hear the case. We didn't know it before, but ole Paddy had already done some time in a juvenile facility before he'd ever got to us in Lincoln. So, after a lot of pleading by his defense lawyer, and a lot of thinking and praying on everybody's part, Judge Watson gave him a choice.

Since Paddy was turning eighteen the first week in October, he could either go to juvenile jail, or he could join up with the Army.

Paddy's Daddy told the Judge he was washing his hands of him, because he couldn't do nothing with him. Paddy for sure didn't want to go to back in juvie, so they set about getting things fixed so he could go to the Army.

We didn't see nor hear any more of Paddy after that, and apparently the lawyers got it all set up so he could enlist.

The next time we heard anything about him was just before school was out at the end of our sophomore year. Amy came into school one morning waving a letter she'd got with a Fort Knox, Kentucky return address. We didn't know it, but her and Paddy had been writing back and forth to one another since he'd been gone.

In the latest letter, he'd written to tell her his unit had just got their orders. They were being shipped to Viet Nam.

ONE

———

The best I recollect, 1968 pretty much sucked.

The country was in a tar-baby war on the other side of the world, and it looked like every time we tried to do something to end the thing and bring our boys home, we just got stuck on something else, and the killing and maiming just kept getting worse. Folks here at home were protesting all over the country, and laying the fault for the war on the soldiers that were just doing what they were being told to do by the know-it-all Generals and politicians. There was nothing right about any of it.

Here at home, them that thought they were better than other folks, because of the color of their skin or where they were from, or what schools they went to, were fighting to keep other folks down. There wasn't any way to deny there was a difference in how some folks were treated in a lot of places. Them that had, were trying to hang on to it, and keep them that didn't have, from getting it.

There was nothing fair about it. It simply wasn't what we thought America was about when you got right down to it.

Beginning in the spring of '68, we started killing our own. First it was Dr. King and not long after that Bobby Kennedy was gunned down. A lot of people looked to those two as leaders. They saw something that wasn't right, and they were trying to do something to fix it. A lot of folks thought those two could make things better. When they died, it seemed like the conscience of the country died with them.

Everything looked to us like it was coming apart at the seams. And here in the mountains of East Tennessee, we watched and waited to see what was going to happen next.

Our piece of paradise here in the mountains, was the small town of Lincoln, the County Seat of Andrew County, a little section of mountain land we thought the rest of Tennessee was trying to forget. Around the time the north and south squared off in the 1860's, the folks that lived here decided they didn't much agree with the rest of the state on the subject of secession. So, apparently not realizing they were doing the same thing they were opposing, they declared that they were forming a new county and leaving the state. They pledged their allegiance to the Union side of the conflict, and then laid low for the next four years, hoping nobody would pay 'em much attention.

They must have done a pretty good job of it, because nobody much bothered with any of 'em, and folks here for the most part, carried on with very little interference from either side. The fact that they'd carved out a part of the mountains that was so remote and hard to get in and out of, pretty much kept 'em isolated from the rest of the world. And to be honest, a lot of us liked it that way.

Just before the turn of the century, somebody realized that the timber that covered all the hills and hollows, was worth a fortune. So they laid railroad track around the sides of the mountains to haul out load after load of hardwood they'd cut.

For a while, Lincoln became a bustling center of commerce. But once the government started tucking back land for the National Park, the logging business pretty much played out, the trains stopped running, and we settled back down to the sleepy little town where we were all raised up.

Me and several other guys, all right around the same age, lived on Depot Street, one street over from the main street of the town. The street was named for the old train depot that was several blocks east of where we lived. The depot building had been abandoned for a while, but the shell was still there.

My given name was Aburn James, after my Great-Great Grand Daddy, but nobody actually knew it, because everybody called me Cubby. That was the nick-name my Daddy hung on me when I was a baby, and to tell the truth, I was right proud of it.

My best friend was Danny MacMahan, who lived across the street and one house down from my house. We did most everything together, but we were as different as night and day. Danny was a thin, wiry kid, almost ten months older than me, but I was always about thirty pounds heavier and three or four inches taller. And while he was generally tanned, with dark hair, chipmunk cheeks and big ears that were a MacMahan trademark, I had freckledy fair skin and strawberry-blond hair that you could spot a mile away.

Will Boyd lived three houses down from Danny on the same side of Depot Street, and the three of us threw in together on most everything we did. Will was so bow-legged he could carry a nail keg between his knees, but he was quick as a cat, strong as an ox, and as honest as the namesake of the town. He had a head full of dark, wavy hair and clear blue eyes that made all the girls look twice at him, and later on, when we actually got interested in girls, having Will around came in pretty handy.

There were a couple of other boys, some older and some younger, that lived on Depot Street. But till Will's family moved to a small farm just outside of town, the three of us were together in most of whatever messes we could get into. Not that we could get into much. Lincoln was so small, we couldn't get in too much trouble without the whole town knowing about it.

When we were young'uns, it didn't matter too much. But later on, after Danny's big brother Rocky, came back from his hitch in the Army and won election to be the High Sheriff of Andrew

County, we pretty much had to be on our best behavior. Either that, or we had to be really sly about what we did.

Rocky was something of a legend in our neck of the woods. He was one of those guys that whatever he put his mind to, he most always wound up being the best at it, and folks around took notice. That was especially true when it concerned girls, and Danny did his best to carry on that legacy. Or at least he tried, since he fancied himself as a real ladies man.

Being close in age and growing up on the same street, us guys stuck together like brothers, and early on, we didn't much have any reason to be messing around with any girls. But that kind of changed when we started in first grade. It was then that we got to know two girls in particular, who more or less fit right in, and became part of the group.

Mary Beth Rivers actually changed right before our eyes from the skinny, talky little girl we started in first grade with, to being pretty much the gold standard for the fairer sex. With her shoulder length brown hair, big brown eyes, and curves in all the right places, Mary Beth turned out to be a real looker, and I reckon every guy in school must have made a play for her attention at one time or another.

Truth was, I personally thought Mary Beth was just this side of flat out dangerous. I'd seen her turn her smile on some unsuspecting guy, to get 'em to do her bidding. I'd witnessed her batting her eyelashes and swaying her hips back and forth, and watched dang near grown-up boys melt in their tracks. Mary Beth was kind of like a flame for a bunch of male moths—sort of irresistible.

Early on, Danny took a shining to Mary Beth, and for a while it looked like they were destined for one another. But it didn't take long before Danny got the wandering eye, and put a torch to that relationship. After that, Will and Mary Beth took up with one another, and from all accounts, it looks like they might just be a match for the duration.

Mary Beth's best friend, Amy Higgins was the other girl that fell in with us—though there were times all of us guys wondered why. Amy was cute and all, with a round china-doll face and short brown hair that flipped out at the ends. And she was shapely enough to get her fair share of second looks. But she was dang near blind as a bat without her glasses, she had an annoying habit of talking on and on, and she was the bossiest person I've ever known. Amy had an opinion about everything, and wasn't a bit shy about letting everybody in earshot know what it was.

For some reason, I was able to tolerate Amy more than most. Fact was, I really didn't pay much attention to whatever it was she was spouting off about most of the time. And over the years, the two of us came to more or less depend on one another. When she needed somebody to go with her to the Methodist Church youth get-togethers, she'd call me, and when I needed somebody to go with me to the Baptist stuff, I'd call on her.

From time to time, I wondered if maybe Amy and me might get together and be a little more than just friends. But after being around her, and having to listen to her go on and on over something that most likely didn't amount to a hill of beans, and never would, I came to realize the two of us would probably just kill each other if we had to be together too much.

Kids in the '50's were born in a time when things were going good. Ike was President, folks that wanted to work were working, and it appeared that things back then were more simple—happier. Or at least that's the way we thought it was.

But around 1958, about the time we started first grade, it seemed like things started to unravel. America was stunned when the Russians launched Sputnik, and beat us to the punch on getting into space. We watched the news in '62 when President Kennedy told us about the missiles in Cuba threatening us with nuclear war. And when he sent out the Navy to blockade and shut it all down, we took a step closer to what we thought was the end of times.

Then in November of '63, the Principal at Lincoln Primary, interrupted classes and put the radio broadcasts out of Dallas on the intercom, and we heard the news flashes telling us the President had been murdered. We watched the caisson bearing his casket, and the rider-less horse. And our hearts broke as the President's son John-John, saluted the procession on the way to his father's final resting place.

We watched news reports of battles fought half-way around the world, as legions of helicopters brought American soldiers into hot LZ's, and then returned to take 'em out, bandaged and bloodied. We watched as the politicians and Pentagon brass allowed things to go from bad to worse in Viet Nam.

While our childhood faded behind us, we watched more and more of our future being sent overseas, and we saw the body count of the dead and wounded rise higher and higher. We saw pictures in the newspapers, in magazines, and on TV of the fighting and dying.

And we watched the boxes being unloaded out of the transport planes, covered with red, white and blue flags.

TWO

———

While the rest of the world was coming unglued, here at home our bunch was trying to figure out what the hell we were doing, and where we fit in the whole mess.

When we were little kids, me and the guys kept our sights on playing sports, fishing in the creeks, scuffling and wrestling around, and doing the kind of stuff boys do. We didn't have a whole lot of use for girls. But all that changed when Danny got the honey britches for Mary Beth. I guess all of us took another look at the opposite sex around the time we became teenagers.

I was probably a little slower on the uptake than Danny and Will were. I reckon our sophomore year in high school was the year I turned the corner.

Since I totally sucked at math, I'd put off taking Algebra my first year. But I knew I couldn't put it off forever, so I signed up to take it my second year with Kenny Bolt and a bunch of other freshmen. Kenny was the back-up quarterback on the football team, and was one of the younger guys that lived on Depot Street with us.

On the first day in class, I got assigned the seat in front of Carrie Ann Mallory. Now, I'd been around Carrie Ann at school and church socials and such, but really hadn't paid much attention to her. She was just another one of the girls that lived in town.

But when I looked at her that first day of class, Carrie Ann had changed—and I mean, really changed. She'd traded in her long blond curls for short, straight locks that framed her face and had bangs that hung over beautiful emerald green eyes. A sprinkle of light freckles dotted across her perky nose and all but disappeared in the glow her smile. She smelled of honeysuckle shampoo with a hint of baby powder, she had curves where they were supposed to be, and had gorgeous legs that went all the way up to the cutest fanny I'd ever seen.

I had a hard time keeping my eyes to the front, and kept turning around to say something to her, or give her papers, or any reason I could think of. Kenny thought me and Carrie Ann might get along pretty good, so he kept on me for a couple of weeks to ask her to one of the dances. Things kind of happened that threw us together, and I reckon it just took off from there.

Truth be told, it wasn't long before I fell for her like a big ole tree in the woods. But for some reason, she didn't feel the same way I did, and couldn't make up her mind about me. We courted for a couple of months, but then Carrie Ann called it quits with me about the same time Danny put the torch to his relationship with Mary Beth.

I flew solo for a few months, till we were at a spring football scrimmage and I got my bell rung. When I came to, the first face I saw was the cute student-trainer from Walland's football team, holding an ammonia cap under my nose.

Angel Burke was short and sassy with long dark hair that hung to the middle of her back. She carried herself with an air of confidence that you could see in dark eyes that seemed to look directly into my heart, and she had a nose on her beautiful face, that looked to me to be slightly crooked.

From the first time I saw her, I was completely smitten, and with a little help from Amy, I managed to start a long distance relationship with Angel—and danged if I didn't fall head over heels for her. At first, we courted over the phone mostly, getting to actually be with one another at the prom that year, and then with Danny's help, sneaking off to the drive-in a few times.

The problem was, Angel was looking for something a little more permanent than I was, and dang it—I just wasn't ready for that. I thought we were both too young, and things moved way faster than I could tolerate. So I had to do one of the hardest things I'd ever done, and this time it was my turn to call everything off.

I still thought about Angel a lot. I had really strong feelings for her, and I reckon I always would. Angel was special to me, but...

The thought of Carrie Ann—the sound of her voice, the way she smelled, the warmth of her when we'd hold each other—was stuck in my head. Or maybe she was stuck in my heart. Wherever she was stuck, I couldn't get rid of the thought of her.

So, at the start of my junior year in '68, when I found myself in Biology class with Carrie Ann, and I saw her blond bangs and green eyes, and I smelled the honeysuckle and baby powder—I purely couldn't help myself, and I felt myself tumble over the cliff all over again. We started talking, and before long, the old feelings returned, and things went right back to the way they were before.

The first few months of my junior year with Carrie Ann were glorious, until we ran into all the whoopla with the Boy Preacher at the Prophet's Church, the Revival and the all the mess that resulted from that, and at the dance after the football game with Lanier, Carrie Ann "dumped my ass again," as Danny so delicately put it.

The way I figured it, by the first week in October of '68, I'd been in and out of love three times—twice with the same girl. And now, I was flying solo again.

Amy told me once she thought I was in love with being in love. I hated to admit she might be right, but the way things kept going for me, I was beginning to think she might be on to something.

But in mid-October, we were still in the middle of football season. And as Will kept having to remind me, more often than I wanted, we didn't have time for me to be feeling sorry for myself.

After the first time I'd split with Carrie Ann, I really got pretty pissed with myself, and I took out all my frustrations on whoever happened to get in my way on the football field. I visioned they were the cause of all my problems, and found I purely enjoyed hitting whoever was available. It might not have been the most right-thinking thing to do, but it sure made me feel better.

Coach Quarters called it playing with "reckless abandon." I didn't care what happened to me, or anybody else. The simple matter was, hitting somebody on the football field felt good. And it was what we were supposed to be doing anyway. I could take out all my aggression on the field, and not get in trouble, so it worked for me.

In spite of the fact that my personal life had pretty much swirled down the toilet, we'd been having a fairly good year on the football field. With five more games to go in the season, our record was three wins, one loss and a tie.

The next team on our schedule after Lanier in '68 was Happy Valley, and we blanked them, 28 to zip. Their school was a lot smaller than ours and being honest, it wasn't a fair fight. But a win was a win, and we started thinking we were on a roll.

The next week we played Walland, on their field. I dreaded it since Angel was still their trainer and it was most likely I'd probably run into her. If I did see her, I had no idea what to say.

I still felt real bad about the way things had ended with us, and I couldn't blame her if she hated my guts. I actually still had feelings for her. Every now and then her face, or the sound of her voice, or the feeling of a wet nose, would pop into my head, and I'd get all achy feeling inside.

As it turned out, I didn't have cause to worry. That Friday night, Angel was nowhere to be found—and I guarantee you I searched the Walland sideline every chance I got, hoping to catch a glimpse of her. Later on, I heard from Amy that Angel had stayed home sick that night. I'm sure she was actually sick and didn't stay home because of me.

I reckon thinking about Angel must have distracted me. In the game with Walland, I missed blocks, messed up the snap to Kenny a few times, and overall played a crappy game. But apparently I wasn't the only one, because we got our asses handed to us, 21 to 7. Kenny scored our only touchdown on a busted play when everybody on our team went right, and he reversed out and went left on a three yard run.

The next week, we finished out the last Friday in October at Tallassee and then hosted Wildwood on the 1st of November, putting two more "W's" on the board. That left us with a trip to Oak Creek, our cross-county rival, for the last game of the year, on the second Friday in November.

But before we could load the bus for that fight, there was a national battle to settle.

On the first Tuesday, following the first Monday in November of 1968, the entire country loaded up and went to the polls to vote for President.

Running on the Republican side was "Tricky Dick" Nixon, who'd beat out a couple of pretty promising candidates to be the party's nominee for the job. The movie actor turned Governor, Ronald Reagan, gave a rousing speech at the convention after he'd made a run for the nomination himself. Reagan impressed a lot of people, so folks on the Republican side were feeling pretty good about the party's future, no matter what happened on this election.

If ole Tricky Dick was able to get himself elected, he was promising to straighten out the country, and put an end to all the protesting and rioting and such, restoring law and order. He said he'd give us new leadership, deal with the war in Viet Nam, and let us get back to living again.

It surely looked like he might make a good choice, what with his experience as Ike's Vice-President. But winning wouldn't be a cake-walk. Even though the Democrats were all split up, they were still a force to be reckoned with.

After Bobby Kennedy was killed that summer, most of the Democrats looked to Hubert Humphrey, who'd been LBJ's second man. But not all of 'em. A lot of the Kennedy people went over to Senator Eugene McCarthy, and the news reports kept telling that the southern states might go for George Wallace, who'd decided to make a go for President on a third-party ticket.

The country looked to be torn apart between Democrats and Republicans, and between different leaders on both sides. And Election Day, would probably come right down to the wire when the people went to the poles to decide.

The smoke started to clear some when the Democrats nominated Humphrey to be their candidate. But when the whole country saw their convention in Chicago dissolve into a bunch of protesting and head knocking, a lot of voters started thinking a law and order President might be just what we needed.

Candy Roberts, who was the leader of the Andrew County Republican Party, recruited me and Danny to work putting up Nixon-Agnew posters and signs. So when I wasn't at football practice, and I could pry Danny away from whatever girl he was courting at the time, me and him would load up a stack of signs and hit the road with a staple gun. We did pretty good putting up posters all over our end of the county. Of course, while I was working for

Mr. Roberts, I kept on the lookout, just in case his daughter Linda, came around.

Linda Roberts had graduated the spring before, and even though she was several years older than me, to my mind, she was the most beautiful creation God ever made. She had blond hair, a smile that could brighten all the dark corners of the world, and blue eyes you could get lost in. And the Lord topped all that off with a body that had curves in all the right places. There was no doubt that I lusted after her something terrible.

From the time they'd set up the town, Lincoln was pretty much Republican territory and folks who were of the Democrat persuasion went across the ridge to Oak Creek. But there was always some opposition lurking in the corners of both places.

At Lincoln High School, the opposition came in the presence of Wally Lawson. In the run-up to Election Day, he was loud and proud to be supporting Humphrey and the Democrat ticket, and he let everybody in hailing distance know about it.

Wally joined us at Lincoln High in our freshman year, coming in from one of the smaller primary schools out in the county. He was a bully and a blow-hard. Wally was one of those guys that when you first met, looked like he'd be a tush-hog, standing over six foot and weighing in at some over two-hundred. He used his size and his big mouth to intimidate the kids that didn't know him. But it didn't take us too long to see he was all talk, and had no desire to back up anything with any action. We tried to get him to join us on the football field, but he wanted no part of it.

We'd already held the county election, and put Danny's big brother Rocky, back in office for a four year term as the High Sheriff, so that Tuesday the national election was the only thing of consequence on the ballot. And once Huntley and Brinkley started reporting the results coming in from the states, it was obvious it was going to be a squeaker.

The fat lady didn't sing till early on Wednesday morning and final results showed Tricky Dick with a very narrow lead in the popular vote. But he won the big states that he needed to give him a whopping win once it went to the Electoral College delegates.

Now we just had to wait a few months for him to take the oath of office, and we'd see if he could keep all the promises he'd been making during the campaign.

THREE

———

The games with Tallassee and Wildwood were both home games, and the tradition was for the Letterman's Club to sponsor a dance in the school gym after the games. But after Carrie Ann cut me loose at the dance after the Lanier game, I didn't have much interest in going.

The walk home after home games, up the hill from the dressing room past the gym, was tough on me. In my mind's eye, I imagined everyone dancing and having a good time. And I tortured myself with visions of Carrie Ann in the arms of some ass-hole, swaying to the music that blasted out of the open windows. Danny and Will tried to get me to the dances, but once they saw how I felt about it, they laid off.

The week of practice for our last game of the '68 season was the hardest we'd ever had. Coach Quarters was constantly on our case to run the plays better, and hit harder. It seemed like he was in a real tizzy over something, but danged if any of us could figure it out. We'd been running the same plays all year, and thought we'd about got 'em down pat, but Coach had his drawers all up in a wad over something.

On game day, when school let out, the team went to the dressing room to make sure our pads and equipment were ready, pack it all up, tape ankles and such, and wait for the time to board the bus. While we waited, Coach generally walked around and talked to us, making sure we had our minds right.

But that Friday, he stayed in his office, finally coming out to give us a talk just before time to load the bus. Coach stood in the middle of the room and we all circled around him. He looked each one of us in the face, and took a deep breath before he started.

"Guys, you've worked really hard this year to get where you are, an' we're 6-2 an' 1 because of it. You've faced some pretty stiff competition, an' you've done well. I'm really proud of ever'thing you've accomplished.

"I've been coachin' here for five years now, an' I've watched ever' single team become fine young men. I'd like to think I've had a little to do with that.

"Tonight is gonna be our last game together this season... an' it's gonna be my last game as your Coach."

He stopped and got a deep breath before continuing.

"I've been offered a job at a school up in Johnson City, an' if I'm gonna stay in coachin', there's no way I can pass on this chance. I want you to know I'm never gonna forget you guys. You've all meant the world to me.

"There waddn't any good time to tell you... but I want you to know that tonight, you're playin' for the honor an' the glory of Lincoln High School. You're not playin' for me—you're playin' for you.

"Tonight you're gonna go to Oak Creek, an' show the whole county what you're made of. Tonight you're gonna show ever'body what winners look like."

With that he turned and walked back to his office. For two or three minutes, not a one of us moved. We looked at the floor, or the ceiling. We sat in the stinky dressing room, silent and stunned.

Coach was right. We all knew what had to be done. Over the last three years I'd been on the team, he'd taught us how to play the game. He'd taught us how to fight through a tough time. He'd taught us how to win.

The bus ride to Oak Creek was silent, and the only sound heard was the rush of the wind past the windows, and the rumble of the motor, as the bus driver switched gears going up and down the hills and around the curves.

Everybody on the team was thinking about what we had to do as we rode out the Oak Creek Road, past the Ridge Top beer joint, around the curve above Leary's Sawmill, and down the other side of the ridge to Oak Creek. By the time we pulled up to the school, we were all itching to get out of the bus and get on the football field.

The stands on both sides were full, and it was a fine night for football. The sky was clear and the air was November cool, just enough so you could see your breath. We took the field like it was our own, determined to prove to the world that Coach Quarters was right about us.

Oak Creek won the toss and deferred to receive in the second half, so we lined up to take the opening kick-off. When their kicker's foot hit the ball, all our guys on the front line, took a couple of steps back, formed a wedge and started looking for somebody to hit.

Will took the kick on our 15 yard line, checked for a running lane, and ran it straight up the middle of the field, all the way to our 40, to set us up for the first series. It truly, was a wonderous thing to see.

The first play from scrimmage was 32 Blast, another play up the middle, and Will got the ball again, hit the hole fast, going right off my right butt-cheek, and caught the Oak Creek linebacker stunting the wrong way. He zipped through the line like his tail was on fire, and was dang near to the goal line before their safety finally tripped him up on the 10. The bleachers on the visitor's side went crazy and all you could see was a blur of red, white and blue shakers.

The second play was a sweep around the left side. This time Kenny kept the ball and mortally flew around the end. The play was a thing of beauty, with everybody blocking down on the line, Will leading the ball carrier, and kicking out on their defensive end to open up the side line. Score a quick 6 for us, and with the point after, having run only two plays from scrimmage, we were ahead 7 to nothing.

The rest of the game went pretty much the same way. The line opened holes you could drive a truck through, and our defense shut down most every try Oak Creek made when they had the ball. We gave Coach Quarters a grand send off for his last game with us, beating our cross-county rival by 35 points that night.

But it wasn't just for Coach. Deep down, we all knew Coach was right. We did it for ourselves too.

With the end of the Oak Creek game, our third year of football ended, and for a week or so, having the extra time on our hands took a little getting used to. We still talked about football, especially in sixth-period athletic study hall, replaying every game we'd played that year. And we all did a lot of guessing about next year.

Me and Will discussed it, and we were pretty much in a quandary about what would happen to us without Coach Quarters. He was the only football coach we'd ever had since we started playing, and getting used to hearing somebody else holler at us, and figuring out new plays and such, worried us. But Coach told us he was going to finish out the semester till Christmas break, so we didn't have to get too worried till after first of the year.

We had a few weeks to finish out 1968, and there was a lot of things to do before we could start the New Year. First up, came Thanksgiving, when I got the chance to stuff myself when my family got together at my Mamaw's house, and then do it all over again when I'd go over to Danny's and help the MacMahans get rid of their leftovers. And following close after, was Christmas.

Always before, when school let out for the holiday, I slept in and pretty much rested up. But that year, Mr. Parker caught me looking through the albums in the record rack at the Five & Dime, and asked if I'd work playing Santa Claus for him at the store.

Truthfully, I was needing to make a little money for myself, and sitting around listening to little kids tell what they wanted for Christmas, sounded like it would be right up my alley. I agreed on it, and got everything set up to start the week school let out for Christmas vacation. Mr. Parker set me up with a red suit and fake beard, and we figured out a place in the back of the store where he'd set up a chair for me to sit in. Things looked pretty good to finish out the year.

But I had one other special thing happening. Right around the middle of the month I'd be turning sixteen. It was the magic birthday when I could finally get my driver's license, and cut the strings that'd kept me tied to everybody else.

FOUR

———

The last full day of school before Christmas break that year was my birthday—on Friday the 13th. We had to go in the next Monday for a few hours to pick-up grade cards, and stay just long enough so the County could charge the state for a full day, but since we weren't there long, I went ahead and set it up with Mr. Parker to start the Santa Claus gig for Monday afternoon.

I'd got my learner's permit back in September, and me and Dad had been going down to the parking lot at the school to practice driving. I started out on the big Ford station-wagon that Mom drove, since it had an automatic transmission. But once I got the basics down, we switched over to Dad's Corvair, and I learned to drive a four-speed manual shift. And a couple of times, when we'd get out on a back road, and nobody was around, Danny let me have a turn driving his Chevy that had the shifter on the column. So come December, I felt like I was pretty well ready.

The state driver's test people came to the Sheriff's Office in Lincoln a couple of times a month to give the driving test, and their next trip up the mountain that month fell on the 20th, a week after my birthday. The extra week just gave me a little more time to worry over it.

I rode in to school with Danny that Monday to pick up our grade cards, and afterward he dropped me off at the Dime Store so I could make my first appearance in the Santa suit. The fake beard was itchy, and the elastic strap that ran around the back of my head to hold it on rubbed a raw place on the top of my ears. But there was a right-smart bunch of kids that lined up to sit on my lap and tell me all the stuff they wanted and I "Ho-Ho-Hoed" my way through for a week.

A little before 1:00 on Friday, I put up a sign saying Santa had to go feed the reindeer, slipped back into the back room to change clothes, and went up to the front to watch for Dad. Directly he pulled up and I hopped in for the ride down to the Sheriff's office.

When we walked in the door at the Jail, big Mack Stevens, one of Rocky's Deputies, grinned real big and gave me a thumbs-up. I guess he could see I was nervous when I wrote my name on the sign-in sheet, my hands were shaking so.

First up was the written test, and I sweated that. I had to guess at one of the questions that asked who went first when a bunch of cars got to an intersection at the same time. I'd asked Danny about it earlier, and he told me whoever had the biggest car went first. But I was pretty sure that wasn't right.

As soon as I finished the written test and took it to the desk, the lady doing the driving part came around the counter looking over the papers on her clipboard, and motioned for me to head out to the car. It was a fairly cool December day, but I could feel the sweat rolling down my sides.

The testing lady's name tag over the green pocket-flap of her tan uniform shirt said: S. LAMB. She was older, probably in her 30's—a tiny little woman, with short brown hair and big brown eyes. I was still nervous and I reckon it showed, because she told me not to worry—this part wouldn't take long.

I was pretty sure I had the basic driving stuff down, all except for the parking part. I'd practiced parallel parking over and over, getting it right about half the time. So if I screwed up anything, I figured that's what it would be.

As we walked out the door, I spotted Danny, Amy, Will and Mary Beth, sitting on the grass across the street. None of 'em would look at me, but I could see their grins as we walked to the car. I couldn't figure out what they were doing there, and I had a bad feeling about it. Then when I opened the car door, they all stood up and clapped and whistled.

I could have killed every single one of them.

I tried to ignore 'em and settled in behind the steering wheel. Miz Lamb could see how red-faced I was, and she reached over, patted me on the knee and said, "Just drive honey... Don't pay 'em no never mind."

I pushed in the clutch and turned the key to get the car started, remembering to reach up and adjust the rear view mirror before I put the shifter in reverse. Then I slowly let out the clutch and backed out of the parking space onto the street in front of the Jail. I'd kept the windows rolled up trying to keep out the cold, but we could still hear the ass-holes cheering as I shifted to first and drove down the hill—away from my adoring fans.

When we got to the next street, Miz Lamb told me to take a right and drive around the block. I raked the gears a little shifting into second, but I remembered to put on my turn signal and come to a dead stop at the stop signs. After I made four right-hand turns around the block, she told me to pull back in to the same parking spot I'd just pulled out of—and that was it.

Miz Lamb got out of the car, walked back in the Jail and left me sitting there. I turned the ignition off and followed her, but just before I got to the door, I turned back toward the street and, shielding it from anybody else's view, threw my support group a bird.

I didn't know if I'd passed or not till Big Mack gave me another thumbs-up and a grin. At the desk, Miz Lamb handed me my temporary license and said they'd mail the permanent license from Nashville in a couple of weeks. Apparently, I'd worried about the parking part for nothing.

The 'fan club' had scattered by the time me and Dad got outside. He let me drive back up to the dime store where we switched places and he went back to work. And now that the 'reindeer were fed,' I put the red suit back on, "Ho-Ho-Hoed" for the kids, and finished out the day. But I kept my billfold in my pocket all afternoon, with the folded temporary license paper in it.

Later on that night, Dad let me take the Corvair to get Danny for a ride down to Wilson's, the restaurant where we all generally hung out. I felt like I was on top of the world.

After I dropped him off, I pulled in the driveway at the house a little after 10:30, and sat in the car for a while fiddling with the radio, setting the buttons to the rock-'n-roll stations we could get. For a second, the thought crossed my mind to go over to Carrie Ann's and take her for a ride.

But it was just a thought, and it was an early night because Santa had to work the next day.

FIVE

Getting to the magic age of sixteen, and getting my driver's license felt like being set free. It's hard to explain, and there weren't any words that could tell the feeling of finally being able to go wherever I wanted. Not that there was any place I really wanted to go to, but just being able to go was enough for the time being.

Being sixteen also meant I was that much closer to the next magic number—eighteen—when I'd have to fill out the registration form for the draft. And from the way things appeared to be going, that wasn't anything to be looking forward to.

But I had two more years before I had to worry too much about it, and with some of the promises being made by the politicians, and some of the things Nixon had been saying since the election, it looked to me like folks were working hard to get us out of Viet Nam. Least-ways, that's what we were all hoping for.

On Christmas Eve business at the Dime Store slowed to a trickle and Mr. Parker closed up early. Most folks had already finished their shopping, but there was always a few stragglers, and I worked the Santa thing right up to the end. About 4:00, I changed out of the red suit, got my final pay check, a pat on the back and heard the door lock behind me.

The wind coming out of the north-west was chilly, and with the sun dropping behind the ridges, I had to zip my coat and put my collar up to keep out the cold as I walked home.

Instead of cutting back onto Depot Street, I decided to walk through town and then cut down on Oak Lane, which was the closest cross street off Main to my house. The stores were mostly closed and I window shopped the clothes at Leon's Dry Goods store as I poked along. Farmer's Drug Store was one of the few that was still open, and I waved at Billy Taylor as I passed by. Billy graduated high school about the same time as Rocky and Brad. He'd gone on to make a Pharmacist and then come back home to work for Doc Farmer.

When I got to the edge of downtown, I saw that Danny's Daddy had already shut down the service station, and I could almost smell all the food cooking in the MacMahan's kitchen. A few cars passed me by on their way home from work or coming in from a last minute shopping chore, but there wasn't much going on. I was about the only one still out.

I'd already bought presents for my family, mostly from the dime store, so that part was done. But I remember feeling awful lonely since there wasn't anybody special to buy for.

Last year, I'd bought Carrie Ann a sweater and a silver necklace, and really looked forward to Christmas Eve so I could see her face when she opened the packages I'd wrapped. This year though, it would just be family.

A little before 8:00, I got in the station wagon with Mom and Dad and rode to the church for the Christmas Eve candlelight service. I met up with Danny and promised him I'd see him the next day so I could tie any neck-ties he might get for gifts.

After Preacher Mason did a short 'thank you' sermon and we had the Lord's Supper, Danny skee-daddled in a hurry to take his presents to Jenny Wilton. He and Jenny had been keeping time pretty regular, and I reckon he'd forgot all about Mary Beth, which was a good thing, since Will was probably over at her house giving her the presents he'd got. And as far as I knew, Amy and Randy Taylor were still seeing one another pretty steady.

It looked like I was the only Lone Ranger in the bunch.

On Christmas morning we got up and opened the gifts that were wrapped and stuck under the tree. I got the usual assortment of underwear, socks and sweaters—then Dad handed me a little box. When I shook it, it rattled, and when I opened it up, inside was a set of car keys.

I looked expectantly at Dad, hoping against hope… thinking maybe… until he started talking…

"Cubby, the car's not all yours yet, but I thought you oughta have your own keys. We're still gonna have to share for a while, but I'm lookin' for another car, an' after I get it, the Corvair will be yours to drive."

I got the standard lecture about being a careful driver and all, but it was worth it. Having to share wasn't hardly as good as having a car all to myself, but I guess it was the next best thing. It was like a promise of things to come. So I was pretty tickled when I went out the door, car keys jingling in my pocket, ducked under the limb of the maple tree in the front yard, and headed over to Danny's.

Sure enough, he had two new neck-ties laying on his bed when I went in his room, so I flung 'em around my neck, stood in front of the mirror, and tied while we talked. We'd both gotten about what we'd expected for Christmas, with the exception of the future promise of me getting Dad's car. When I showed Danny the keys, we started right off figuring out how to make a few changes.

The Corvair wasn't a hot rod or anything. It was just a stock, '65, two-door model with Willow Green paint and a four-speed shifter on the floor. But with a little help, we thought it could really make something. We visioned a set of Chevy wire hubcaps with 3-prong spinners, and eventually some raised white-letter tires. And as soon I could get some extra money together, we'd put in an 8-track tape player and extra speakers so we could get the music going.

I didn't stay too long, since Danny was going over to Jenny's, but in the short time I was there, we did a lot of dreaming.

I might have felt a little lonely, being as how I'd be spending the rest of the day all by myself, but I had lots of things to think about as I walked back across the street to my house, and Danny drove off in his Chevy.

SIX

———

On New Year's Eve I went over to Mary Beth's for a party she was having, but it didn't take long to figure out everybody there was pretty much paired-off, so I left early before Carrie Ann and whoever she was with got there.

I drove around for a while, winding out the six-cylinder engine on the long straight-away coming toward town on the Oak Creek Road, getting the speedometer up over 75, and then down-shifting before I started into the curve.

The Corvair wasn't much off the line, but once I figured out the feel of the weight of the motor in the rear end, I could skid it around curves at a lot higher speed than Danny could in his Nova. There'd been a lot of talk about that car being dangerous, but really it was a matter of how it was driven, and truthfully it wasn't any more dangerous than any other car that was on the road.

On New Year's Day, me and Danny met a few others in Will's basement and played poker while we watched Arkansas beat Georgia in the Sugar Bowl. We played 'gut poker' where you had to match the pot if you stayed in and lost the hand, and even though we had a limit on the bets, some of the pots got up near eight or ten dollars.

Ole Danny, bless him, pretty much sucked at cards. For the life of him, he couldn't figure out about betting in turn, or bluffing, or even the rank of hands. By the time the game was over, I wound up with most of his Christmas money and had a good start on paying for the wire hubcaps I was thinking about.

The big talk on the first day of school in the new-year was who we'd be getting to replace Coach Quarters. There hadn't been any announcement over Christmas vacation, so we figured they were going to surprise us when school started back. But on the first day back, that wasn't so.

When we walked in the room for sixth-period athletic study hall, Principal Webster was standing behind the desk. Since Danny didn't have any kind of filter on his mouth, and generally said whatever happened to pop in his head, he came right out and asked Mr. Webster if he was going to be the new coach. All he got was a sneer and a quick, "*NO!*" before he told us to get our seats.

Talk in town was that they were having a hard time finding somebody to accept the job mid-way through the school year. We were still a couple of months away from time for spring practice, so we didn't get too worried about it. But with the athletes we thought we had and the promise of a good season for our senior year coming up, not having a coach kind of put a hitch in our gitty-up.

Me and Will were especially hoping for a good season, since it might give us a chance to go on and play college ball. And there was always the possibility that we might get at least a partial scholarship that'd pay for some of the school. So, for that reason alone, the coming-up year was getting more and more important the closer we got to it.

When we came to school the third week, talk was buzzing all over about the new teacher. Word was that the new guy was somehow 'in-law kin' to one of the school board members.

Despite what our guidance counselor, Mrs. Henderson, thought, we weren't all that stupid, and we started putting two and two together. So we weren't too awful surprised when we walked into sixth period study hall to find a scrawny little guy with big black rimmed glasses standing behind the desk. My first impression was that he looked like Mr. Peepers.

Once the bell rang and we'd all got in a seat, we watched as he walked around, crossed his arms and leaned back to prop his butt up on the edge of the teacher's desk at the front of the room. Problem was, he was just a little bit too far away, and had to jerk his feet back quick like, to catch his balance and keep from falling in the floor.

The whole room started snickering while he recovered himself, and finally matched his backside to the desk top. But then things got quiet when he started talking, in a high-pitched, nasal voice that pretty fair matched his looks.

"My name's Mr. Little."

He paused—for some kind of effect, I reckon—and looked over the room.

"I'm gonna be teachin' Health for the rest of this year. An' I'm gonna be the new football coach."

All of us football players started looking at one another. When I looked over at Will, we both mouthed the thoughts of the whole team, at the same time:

'…Oh shit…'

Getting a new coach wasn't the only thing that happened that day. Right after the noon hour, Richard Milhous Nixon was sworn in as the 37th President. Aside from us wondering what the hell kind of name 'Milhous' was, at least part of the country was looking forward to some changes from the new leadership. But everybody was sure the new administration had their work cut out for 'em.

The whole country was divided up over something and nightly news broadcasts didn't give anybody a chance to forget about it either. Government sources did their best to deny it, but stories were coming out about the killing of civilians along with the enemy soldiers, and the thought of it was adding fuel to the fire of the anti-war movement in the country.

I'm not real sure how anybody thinking straight could ever believe there was any such thing as a clean war, where the only casualties were the soldiers fighting for their cause. History taught us it just wasn't possible. Innocent civilians always got caught in the crossfire. That's the way war had been since the beginning. But the people who wanted us out of the war were using everything they could to convince the rest of the country they were right.

It was hard for us to believe our side was purposely targeting civilians, and if it was true, it was sure to come out. If American boys had to fight, we did it as honorable as it could be done. Purposely putting innocents in the line of fire wasn't our way of doing things, and it was something they couldn't just sweep under the rug.

The stories and pictures about all the protests over the war, and what was going on in Viet Nam were like a low rumble of thunder, rolling on and on across the mountain ridges, and echoing through the hollows and valleys. There was no way to escape it.

The war troubles were continuously with us, and anything that didn't have to do with the war was a welcome break.

The last of January, at the end of the news they showed a short clip of the Beatles playing live for fans from the roof of their recording studio in London. The camera fixed for a second on Paul, which pretty much put to rest all of the rumors that he was dead, and all in all, it looked like all the fans that were there had a high ole time of it.

And we always had the continuing adventures of Danny MacMahan's love life for entertainment.

The best word to describe Danny I reckon, was 'unsettled.' One minute, he was head over heels afflicted with one girl, and the next, he had his eye on some other girl, wondering if she might be the one for him.

Thinking about it, 'unsettled' might not be the right word. Stupid-Crazy was probably better.

The object of his attention that winter was Jenny Wilton. Jenny was one of the girls we'd come up through the primary grades with, and there was no question she was cute. Standing about five-six with shoulder length brown hair and matching eyes that sparkled when she smiled, she was no doubt a looker. And Jenny had a way of making you think you were the only person in the world when she talked to you. To my mind, I thought she needed to put some meat on her bones. But apparently Danny liked skinny girls, and he was right taken with her.

But same as when he was courting Mary Beth, it seemed like he just couldn't be satisfied with a good thing. One minute, he and Jenny would be walking arm in arm through the halls at school, or sneaking a kiss behind the lockers, and the next minute they'd be screaming at one another. Generally, I could tell from his mood, whether they were on good terms or on the outs. But that wasn't always the case.

Several times he'd pick me up to go riding around, like we did whenever the spirit would hit us. Always, the first thing I'd say when I got in the car was to tell him I didn't want to be going out to Jenny's house.

I'd no more than get that warning out of my mouth when he'd start denying any intention of going to Jenny's. We'd ride out the Oak Creek Road for a couple of miles, and then turn around in the Ridge Top parking lot, which was our usual route. But dang near before I could get the radio adjusted to clear the static, and get half-way through a second cigarette, I'd catch him turning onto Cedar Lane where Jenny's house was.

"Danny, I told you I waddn't goin' out to Jenny's house…"

"I just got one thing to tell her, an' we'll be on our way."

"Dammit. You say that ever' time, an' ever' time I get left sittin' in the car, listenin' to the radio."

"What're you gripin' about? I always leave a pack a-cigarettes. An' most times Tammy comes out to keep you company." Then he'd grin and look over at me. "Ya know, Tammy really likes you Cubby…"

And by that time he was pulling in the driveway.

Tammy, was Jenny's little sister. While she was 'cute-in-training,' with big eyes and brown hair that brushed her shoulders, she was just a freshman. I'll admit the attention she paid me was flattering, especially since I didn't have anybody else paying a lot of attention to me. But I really didn't have any interest in Tammy, and I had no intention of leading her on.

Paying attention to anybody you weren't interested in, was a dangerous thing to be doing about that time, because most everybody—especially the girls—had their minds on the prom that was coming up.

Since Amy was the one that got all trained-up on "proper prom puttin' on" last year, she was the lead dog for getting it all together for the seniors in '69. And it was really a perfect fit for Amy, since she dearly loved telling everybody what to do anyway.

The first organization meeting was in January, and of course, she gathered up the usual suspects to be on the Prom Committee, and added a few more for helpers. The regulars included me, Will and Mary Beth, and since we were over all the fireworks between Danny and Mary Beth, and her and Will looked to be the perfect pair, she brought in Danny and Jenny on the team.

It wasn't like I was all that interested in being on the Prom Committee since I was thinking about blowing off the whole thing anyway, but being in on the planning did get us out of class some. So for that, I was willing to sit through the meetings while she talked, and take a few orders from Amy. Over the years, I'd got pretty good at blocking out her voice anyway.

Amy got to hand-pick some of the sophomores so they could learn "proper prom puttin' on," like we all had done last year. And hopefully the new bunch would absorb enough to do a bang-up job on the Prom next year when we were seniors. Over my protests—which she didn't pay a damn bit of attention to—Amy picked Carrie Ann to be one of the sophomore worker bees.

The prom was set for the first Saturday in May, and Amy held planning meetings once a week, all during February and March. Me and Will tried to stay in the back and not volunteer to do anything, so for the most part, the two of us kept pretty much under the radar.

And hiding from Amy gave me a chance to avoid having to deal with Carrie Ann. It wasn't because I was mad at her or anything. Truth was, I didn't trust myself being around her.

Carrie Ann was just something I couldn't shake off. But then I really didn't have to worry too much. It looked like she was keeping time pretty much regular with Virgil Corkran, the heir to the Corkran Funeral Home business. So I don't think me being around bothered her none at all.

Come the second week in March, we were really thankful that Amy hadn't assigned us anything much to do on the prom. Spring football practice was fixing to start.

SEVEN

In sixth-period study hall, me and Will had tried to pump Coach Little about what kind of offence and defense he was intending to run. The only thing we'd ever had any practice on was Coach Quarter's system, so if Coach Little was going to be changing things up, we wanted to know it. But all he'd say was, "I'm workin' on it boys. You'uns can learn it all when we start spring practice."

On Monday, the cold snap that started the first of March was still hanging over the mountains, and we were hoping it would be the last gasp of winter that year. As soon as the bell rang, signaling the end of school, the football team filed into the dressing room in a drizzle of cold rain, to draw the equipment we'd be needing for the next four weeks. The managers had just finished handing out shoulder pads and were starting to fit helmets when Coach Little blew the whistle that was hung around his neck, and told us to get a seat.

We got settled in and he proceeded to hand out a stack of mimeographed papers with "X's" and "O's" and scribbles all over. Once we got a chance to really look the papers over, me and Will looked at one another again, and repeated the same thing we'd said a couple a-months before: "…Oh shit…"

For the past three years, we'd been a power football team, taking Coach Quarters philosophy of 'three yards an' a cloud a-dust' as gospel. And with the personnel we had, that was pretty much the kind of football we had to play. Most of us were fair size, and pushing people around was what we were best at. Under Coach Quarters, if we couldn't physically manhandle the other team, we got our butts beat. We'd always trained to hit harder and run longer than any of the other schools that were on our schedule. But it looked like that was about to change.

Coach Little cleared his throat, pushed his glasses up on his nose, and started talking in his squeaky, high pitched voice.

"OK guys. From what I've heard, you'uns have had to run over the other teams you been playin'. But that ain't the way we're gonna do it on my watch. We're gonna play smarter'n the other guy. So as of right now, we're gonna start from the beginning."

He held up a football, so we could all see, and continued.

"This here's a football."

And from there, it all went downhill.

For the next hour, he lectured us on what football was all about, how he was going to out-think our opponents, and how he intended to do it. That day, we never put our pads on, and never took the field. We left with instructions to study over the papers he'd given out, and come back the next day ready to learn the new plays.

For the next four weeks, we went out on the practice field and ran pass play after pass play. The guys that played end last year were changed over to wide receivers, and the half-backs got sent out in the slots. Line split was dang near a yard wide, and looked to me like we were giving a wide open invitation for Kenny and the other backs to get their killing.

But being football jocks, and loving the game, we were willing to give it a try and by the middle of the third week, the plays were at least starting to look like they did on paper.

Problem was, we really weren't the quickest bunch. And Kenny, bless his little heart, didn't have the strongest arm. He was good for a quick-in pass, or a play-action toss out in the flats for at most fifteen yards. But asking him to drop back and throw thirty or forty yards downfield on a regular basis, flat-out wasn't going to happen.

And taking the splits in the line that were almost three feet required us to be able to close that gap in a hurry to stop a pass rush. From tackle to tackle, we averaged about 220 pounds each. We all thought we could hold our own in a head-to-head match-up with a decent defense. But there weren't any of us on the line, quick enough to close a three foot gap between us.

More and more, we got the feeling that things were swirling down the crapper, and a few of us that were going to be seniors went to Coach Little and told him so. But coach kept saying to give it a chance and we'd see—he was for certain sure it'd work.

On our last day of spring practice, coach set it up for us to go across the mountain and scrimmage at Seymour. So on the first Friday in April, we loaded the bus at the beginning of sixth period, and headed out.

We spent two and a half hours that afternoon getting our ass whipped so bad, it wasn't funny. The defense actually held their own, and they were able to stop Seymour's running game for the best part of the day.

But offensively, we pretty much sucked.

Just like we thought, the line couldn't close the gaps from the git-go, and the Seymour defense players poured through as soon as I'd snap the ball. Somebody with a different jersey was in our backfield ready to bust whoever had the misfortune to have the ball, generally with no more than a brush from our guys. Because of the pressure, Kenny spent most of the day either running for his life or at the bottom of a pile. And when he could get a pass off, it wasn't anywhere close to being on target.

The scrimmage was a complete disaster, and when we got back on the bus, Coach Little sputtered and screamed at us for the whole first half of the ride home, saying we "waddn't worth nothin'." He was completely blind to the fact that his offensive system might have a little responsibility for the mess.

The way I saw it, football and life was a lot alike. You don't always get to choose what it is you've got to work with. So you take what you've got, use the best parts to do what you need to do, and go from there.

In our case, we had a sizable bunch of guys on the line that could push the other team around and open holes to run through. And we had backs that were fast enough to carry the ball through those holes, and strong enough to carry a few of the other team along with 'em, gaining yardage on most every play.

We weren't quick, and we didn't have a wealth of receiver talent, not to mention that Kenny sure didn't have a Broadway Joe Namath arm to throw with. But we were fairly strong, and we all liked to hit. When you got right to it, we weren't bad at playing smash-mouth football, and we didn't have the people to play it any other way.

Thank God, spring practice was over and we had a few months to convince Coach Little to make the changes that needed to be made. But if we couldn't get him to change, the fall season—our senior season—was going to be a long one.

EIGHT

———

While we were in the process of screwing up our football team, the world kept right on turning.

On the same day we started spring practice, James Earl Ray, the guy they said killed Reverend King in Memphis the year before, pleaded guilty to the murder.

The FBI and the Memphis Police claimed he did it all by himself, but I kept thinking there was something fishy about the whole thing. One lone nut, escaping a dragnet like what was put out for him? And he didn't just escape from the net they cast out in Memphis. This "lone gunman" as the news kept calling him, all on his own, got clean out of the country, finally getting caught in England. Something just wasn't adding up.

Later on that same month, President Nixon announced in a news conference that he was going to end the war in Viet Nam and bring all of our boys home sometime in 1970. He didn't exactly say how he was planning to do it, but just him saying it out loud gave us guys that were getting closer and closer to draft age, a little hope. The simple fact that somebody was at least thinking that way, I reckon, was a good thing.

On the first weekend in April, college students across the country went out to protest the war. They marched and carried all manner of signs, and some even burned their draft cards. I reckon the politicians in Washington must have taken notice of it, because the next Friday, the President said the prospects for peace in Viet

Nam were better now than they'd ever been. We all hoped he knew something that we weren't seeing.

On the following Wednesday, Sirhan Sirhan, the guy that shot Bobby Kennedy, was sentenced to death. Closing that chapter was a good thing, but bringing back all the memories just made us think about how things might have been different if he'd gone on and won the election.

Closer to home, Amy was keeping the prom planning right on schedule. While me and Will were trying to figure out which way was up on the football field, ole Amy had set up committees and given out marching orders for what to do. It looked to us like she had it all running like a well-oiled machine.

Since we wouldn't be needed till later on when spring practice was over, Amy put me and Will down to be on the Decorating Committee. All the others got assigned to one of the others she'd fixed.

There was the Advertising and Invitation Committee that had to do all the posters and stuff, and the Entertainment committee that was responsible for getting the band lined up. Then there was the Food and Refreshment Committee, and she'd even named a few to a Set-Up and Clean-Up Committee.

And something else she did, was make sure that me and Carrie Ann weren't on the same committee. Amy might have been a hard-ass on a lot of things, but she knew where my head was when it came to Carrie Ann, and she took care of me on that.

I got to thinking if the Generals at the Pentagon could get their heads out of their ass, and let Amy organize the goings on in Viet Nam, she'd probably have the war won and all the soldiers home in a couple of months. Looking at it all, I have to admit, I was right impressed with her.

April that year was pretty typical, with rain showers popping up in the afternoons. We were on the downhill side of our lessons, getting ready to finish out the year the last of May, and with the weather like it was, we didn't have any problem staying late for a prom planning meeting. But as we got closer and closer to the first Saturday in May, the pressure started building.

Since we were juniors, we wouldn't be having to walk in the traditional promenade from town to the school, that'd been going on for years. But being juniors, we were expected to be at the prom—especially those of us that were part of the bunch that was putting on the damn thing. And that meant, we were supposed to be there with a date.

I'd looked around at the possibilities, and truthfully, I didn't see anybody I wanted to go with. Amy had arranged things so Angel could be my date last year, and I had to admit, that worked out pretty good for a while—till I put a torch to that relationship. And the way things looked to be going, it didn't look like Carrie Ann was in my future. I even thought about asking Jo Lee Clark, but I assed around long enough, and she got asked by one of the other guys.

Will would be going with Mary Beth, Danny had Jenny, and last I heard, Amy still had a hook in poor ole Randy Taylor, the guy from Walland that she'd conned into taking her out. So the way I had it figured, I was getting down to either asking little Tammy Wilton, or just blowing off the whole thing.

And that was about what I'd decided to do—till two Saturdays before prom night.

That Saturday afternoon, I was at home watching "Rocky & Bullwinkle" cartoons, when I heard somebody beating on the back door. Mom had gone to the store, so I thought at first she was needing me to carry in groceries. But when I opened the door, Amy busted in, flung her arms around me and buried her face in my chest, crying.

No… that ain't exactly right. She wasn't crying, she was wailing. I'd never seen her so torn up, and truth be told, it scared me.

While she hung on for dear life, and soaked the whole front of my T-shirt, I did my best to calm her down, asking what had happened to upset her so. After a good five minutes, I finally got her walked into the den, and sat her down on the couch. I got in front of her on the ottoman and held onto her arms, watching the tears drip off the bottom of her glasses, and we sat there for a few minutes till the sobs turned to occasional sniffs.

"Tell me what's wrong, Amy, an' if it can be fixed, you know I'll help you fix it."

She finally took her hands away from her eyes and through the tear tracks on her glasses, looked straight at me. I reckon she'd figured out we were the only ones in the house, because she didn't whisper.

"The son-of-a-bitch called an' said he was in love with somebody else…"

I was pretty sure she had to be talking about Randy, since he was the only guy she'd ever dated, and for some reason, suddenly I got all protective feeling.

"What happened?"

She sniffed and reached over on the side table next to the couch for a Kleenex.

"Oh hell… I don't know… I just know I ain't got nobody now…" And that set off another round of blubbering.

I slid off the ottoman, sat next to her on the couch, and put my arm around her shoulder, trying to think of something to say.

"You're gonna be OK Amy… It ain't the end of the world… Of all the people that oughta know—I know…"

We just sat there for a while, with her face wetting my shirt sleeve… and I held her… and let her cry it out.

After a few more minutes, she started calming down again.

"Cubby, I'm really sorry I came over here an' dumped all this on you. But you're the only person I thought would understand…"

I reckon she was right on that account.

After that, her old self started taking over, and she started talking. And very un-typical for me, for some reason, I actually listened to her. A lot of it was plain ole feeling sorry for herself, but after a little while, she started to slow down, and leave some quiet between her words. Her head was still laying over on my shoulder and I still had my arm around her, when she reached up and blew her nose on the tear soaked tissues she still had in her hand.

"I guess me an' you are 'bout in the same boat now, not havin' anybody. An' it really don't look promisin' for the future… for neither one of us.

"Cubby, I tell ya what. If neither one of us finds anybody by the time we're 20, we'll just get married an' go on with it. Whatta ya say…?"

What could I say…? When we were little, I'd thought about me and her. Growing up, we'd always ask the other to go to the church socials, and skating parties, and such. There weren't any expectations really—just two good friends.

And it wasn't like I had any big prospects for *my* future either. So, I thought… what the hell…

I must have thought for a second too long, because she moved her head off of my shoulder, turned and looked up at me. From the look on her face, I could see she was thinking maybe I was going to reject her too. But when I told her that sounded like a fine plan to me, she laid her head back down and I felt her relax a little.

We sat quiet for a few minutes and she blew her nose again. And then a thought came to me.

"Amy… Uh… What are ya gonna do about the prom?"

"Oh, shit..."

I gave it a second, and took a chance.

"Ya know, I still hadn't asked nobody to go with me. Whatta ya think about me an' you goin' together, like when we 'uz kids? No obligations, of course—till we're 20 an' still unattached, that is..."

She thought about it, and after a few seconds I felt her head nod on my shoulder. She sniffed big and I heard her whisper, "That'll be OK with me."

NINE

———

Amy didn't stay much longer after that. Once she got calmed down, and got the dried tear stains off her glasses, I made sure she was OK and then escorted her to the door before Mom got back from the store. Amy still wasn't the happiest person in the world, but at least she'd stopped all the weeping and wailing.

There wasn't anything on TV worth watching that night, and Danny and Will were both out on dates. So after supper, I took the Corvair and drove around. Nobody I wanted to see was at Wilson's Restaurant, and I didn't feel like hanging out at the jail, like me and Danny had done since Rocky got elected to High Sheriff. I made a few passes through town, and even drove by Carrie Ann's once. I saw that the front porch light was on, so figured she was out with somebody.

After a while, Lincoln got tiresome and I wanted to get away. So I turned the radio up and headed towards Maryville, listening to WNOX, and thinking about how everything was so screwed up.

After I crossed over into Blount County, I slowed way down and looked as I passed by Angel's house. I don't know what I was hoping to see, since it was a good bet she was out on a date too, being it was Saturday night and all. But, I looked anyway.

Ole Amy was right—as usual. After all was said and done, the future really didn't look all that promising.

The Generals and the politicians that were running things looked to be hell bent to keep us in a war half-way around the world, without any idea of what they wanted to do or how they were intending to finish it up and get the guys home. And the war in Viet Nam wasn't the only thing that had everybody torn up. If you listened to the news, it looked like the whole country was choosing up sides.

The young folks didn't like the old folks. White folks and black folks were at odds with one another. City folks and country folks were having words... Democrats and Republicans... men and women, boys and girls—hell, even cats and dogs were still fighting. It didn't appear that anybody could get along!

And right here in Lincoln, if we didn't talk some sense into Coach Little, it looked like the coming up football season was going to be a total disaster. And right then, getting coach to change his mind, wasn't looking good.

Our personal lives were a mess too. We all pretty much had to tip-toe around Danny and Jenny because nobody ever knew whether they were on or off. Amy and Randy were split up, and I couldn't hold on to a girl for nothing. As it stood now, Will and Mary Beth were the only ones that looked like they had it together.

I don't know why I was so protective feeling over Amy. I did think of her as a friend, and truth was, I considered her to be one of the best friends I had.

But Hell... she'd deviled me every chance she'd got since we were young'uns, and there were times I wanted to strangle her. But for some reason, hearing that Randy had hurt her and made her cry, made me want to find him and whip his ass. I didn't like seeing her hurt, and I reckon that's what made me go and ask her to the Prom.

Now that I had a little time to think about it, everybody in school was going to think it was a pity date. They all knew how me and Amy fought one another. Most everybody thought I was an idiot anyway, since I'd got my ass dumped twice by the same girl, so I really didn't give a crap what anybody thought of me. But I didn't want anybody thinking we were going to the prom together because she couldn't get anybody else.

Amy deserved better.

I saw Danny at church the next morning, and we sat through the sermon, watching from the balcony where we usually sat. I didn't say anything to him about Amy's situation, and sure didn't tell him I was going to take her to the Prom.

Later on that afternoon, I heard the rumble of the Cherry Bomb muffler on Danny's Nova pass by the house, and I made my decision. I went in the hall, picked up the phone and dialed Amy's number. She picked up on the third ring and I took a deep breath.

"Amy… Have ya changed your mind about yesterday?"

"'Bout what?"

"'Bout us goin' together to the Prom..."

"No… Have you?"

"No. But I had it on my mind last night. You know ever'body at school knows us pretty good an' they know we're kinda at odds a lot of the time. I don't want nobody thinkin' we're goin' together outta pity…"

"Yeah… I thought about the same thing."

"So… Whatta ya think about us makin' sort of a practice run an' goin' to see a movie this comin' weekend. It'd sorta be like a test run. An' we could make sure ever'body knows about it. That way, maybe they'll think we're startin' somethin', an' goin' to the Prom together won't look so sudden an' all."

The line went quiet for a few seconds while she thought about it, but then she allowed that it was probably a good idea. Amy said she'd tell Mary Beth and a couple of the other girls, and she told me to tell Danny and Will about the "date." She reasoned that everybody liked a good rumor, and this one ought to spread like wildfire.

By the time we finished talking, she'd taken over the planning of it all, and taken complete ownership of the idea.

I thought it was a good idea... And I was right glad she thought of it.

TEN

—————

I rode in to school with Danny on Monday, and 'casually' mentioned that I'd talked to Amy over the weekend and found out that her and Randy had broken up. Then I dropped the bomb on him and dang near caused him to hit a telephone pole when I told him that I'd asked her out.

"On a date...? Hell Cubby... I'll give you two 'bout a hour bein' together before you're both tryin' to kill each other."

I kept my mouth shut for a while, as if I was thinking about it.

"Maybe... Ya never know..." And I left it there.

I couldn't tell him the whole story because I knew very well he'd blab it all over school. So I fed him just enough to make him wonder over it, and I reckon Amy was doing the same thing with the girls. Sure enough, by third period, the rumors were flying.

At lunch period, after I got my tray, I spotted Amy sitting at a table over next to the wall, and I walked over and sat across from her. I could feel the eyes of everybody in the cafeteria on us as I leaned forward and whispered so she was the only one that could hear me.

"Is ever'body lookin'?"

"Yep."

"Reckon we need to touch hands or somethin'?"

"Hell no... Just talk to me."

"What about?"

"Oh shit… You're dumber 'bout this than you look."

"Don't get all pissy with me Amy. We both need to make this look good."

"Oh, alright."

She leaned back then and gave me a smile that everybody in the room could see. And about that time, Will and Mary Beth pulled out chairs, set their lunch trays down, and joined us.

Amy asked me out loud, so they all could hear, what we were going to do Saturday night. It flashed through mind to say we ought to just go to a motel, but then checked my mouth right quick because I figured she'd probably kill me later. So I said I was thinking about going to see a movie at the walk-in theatre in Maryville. She allowed that sounded good to her, and we moved on to other things. But out of the corner of my eye, I could see Will and Mary Beth listening to every word, and giving one another looks like they couldn't believe what they were hearing.

We minded our own business the rest of the day, but as soon as Danny dropped me off at the house, I ran to the phone and dialed Amy's number. She must have been sitting right on top of it because she answered on the first ring.

"I think we pulled it off, huh…"

"From all the questionin' I got, sure looks like it."

"Did anybody ask about you an' Randy?"

"Yeah. I told 'em we just agreed to take a rest, an' that me an' you had talked about goin' out for a while."

"An' they bought that?"

"I guess… Nobody asked me nothin' else. So I guess they did."

"So, what's next?" To be honest, I really didn't know how to act the rest of the week. But it was for sure that Amy had it all planned out in her head, so I waited to see what my part was going to be.

Amy had it figured that we didn't need to appear too friendly, just go on like we'd always acted toward one another. But we did need to decide about what we were going to do on the 'date' that we'd set for Saturday. I told her I was serious about going to the movie in Maryville, and she agreed that'd be fine with her.

I'd seen in the Sunday paper that a new movie with James Garner, *Support Your Local Sheriff*, was coming out, and I dearly loved a good western. But Amy nixed that idea right fast, saying that a musical staring Shirley McClain, *Sweet Charity* was playing. When she said it was a musical, I wasn't too happy, but I figured I could gut it up and tolerate it—with a lot of popcorn.

On Wednesday afternoon, we had one of the last planning meetings for the prom, and as usual, Amy ran it like a machine, barking out orders and making sure everybody had their jobs down. There wasn't any argument as she read down her list of jobs and asked for reports to be sure we all were doing what she told us to do. We were only there for thirty minutes and everything was said and done.

I'd walked out of the room where we were meeting and was bent over getting a drink from the water fountain while I waited for Danny, when I heard Carrie Ann's voice behind me.

"I heard you an' Amy are datin' now… I'm happy for you Cubby. I hope it works out."

I stepped back and looked directly into the emerald eyes I'd fallen completely in love with. I couldn't think of anything to say, so I just stood there like a wooden Indian. But there wasn't any way she could have missed the thump, thump, thump of my heart beating.

As Carrie Ann stepped past me, I caught the scent of honeysuckle. Then she leaned over, got a drink from the fountain, and I watched her walk away.

The rest of the week went by way too fast, and before I had a chance to get a good breath, it was Saturday. I'd made it up with Amy that I'd pick her up at 5:30, we'd get a hamburger in Maryville and catch the early movie. That way, we could get back home before 10:30 and make it an early night.

Saturday morning I got up and spent a couple of hours washing and cleaning up the Corvair, mainly because I didn't want to listen to Amy complain about it. After that, I got cleaned up myself and about 5:00, drove to MacMahan's Shell to fill up. Danny was leaned up against the Coke cooler, and when he saw me, he pushed his ass off the cooler and walked over to the pump island.

"Hoo-wee! Did you shine up your car just for Amy?"

"Gimme a break Danny."

"You're seriously goin' through with this, huh."

"Come on Danny… If you give her a chance, Amy ain't so bad."

He just shook his head and hollered over his shoulder as he walked to his Chevy, "I want a full report tomorrow. I'll come by an' pick you up for church?"

I got a five dollar bill out of my billfold to pay for the gas, then got in the car and headed to get Amy. It didn't take but about ten minutes to get to her house and when I knocked on the door, her Mama hollered for me to come on in. She was standing next to an ironing board, told me Amy was almost ready, and asked if I wanted anything to drink. I told her no, but I wouldn't have had time anyway because right then, Amy walked into the kitchen.

She actually looked pretty good all cleaned up, in jeans and a pale yellow blouse, and her brown hair held back with a butterfly shaped barrette. It looked like she'd even cleaned the lens of her glasses because I could actually see her eyes. She took me by the arm and pulled me toward the door, telling her Mama we'd be back early, and I followed her out.

Amy was uncharacteristically quiet during the drive through town, and didn't say a word till I turned onto the road heading to Maryville.

"Are you OK?" I asked.

"Yeah... Why?"

"You just ain't said nothin'... Are ya sorry we're doin' this?"

"No... Are you?"

"No..."

Things stayed kind of quiet and we listened to the radio till we got to the county line. Out of the blue, she piped up and said she hated that things didn't work out with me and Angel, and again with me and Carrie Ann. I more or less agreed with her, and told her it was a shame about her and Randy too, and I saw her nod her head out of the corner of my eye.

She waited a couple of seconds, and then started in again.

"Cubby...? I know you're not really wantin' to do this... an' I want ya to know, I really appreciate it..."

I hesitated only a second before I lit into her.

"Alright Amy... We're gonna stop this shit right now. Me an' you are friends... Hell, I reckon we're 'bout as close a-friends as boy an' girl can be. We been friends since we 'uz little. An' we'll be friends forever. Friends do things for one another. I ain't datin' nobody right now, an' you ain't neither. We both need somebody to go to the Prom with. An' tonight... this is about two friends goin' to see a movie... OK?"

I heard a soft OK, an' she reached out an' patted me on the shoulder.

The rest of the night went pretty smooth. We talked about school, and what all everybody else was up to. We got a hamburger at the Dairy Dip Drive-in and then drove over to the walk-in movie at Midland Shopping Center. *Sweet Charity* wasn't as bad as I'd made it out to be in my mind. Shirley McClain was actually kind of cute, and the large popcorn made things really tolerable.

By the time we got back in the car to head home, we were both laughing and joking, and things were pretty much back to normal with her talking on and on, like she usually did. We even sang together on some of the songs that WNOX was playing that night, and I have to admit, I was having a pretty enjoyable time.

I down shifted to turn into the street to her house and pulled into the driveway, stopping behind her Mama's Chrysler. I turned off the ignition and turned the key on over to the left so the song on the radio could finish. Then I pushed in the knob to cut the lights, and everything around us went dark, except for the glow of the radio on the dashboard.

Both of us sat there for a few minutes, not knowing what to do next, and listened to the Beach Boys sing *Don't Worry Baby*. Then Amy turned in the seat towards me, and softly said, "Cubby, I really had a good time tonight."

I told her I'd had a good time too, and turned towards her, reaching my arm up on the back of the car seat. I reckon she must have thought I was making a move because she reached out and put her hand on my leg, turned her head toward me and leaned in a little.

Well hell… I did what came natural. I scooted closer, put my right arm around her shoulder, bent my head down… and I kissed her.

It'd been a few months since I'd kissed a girl, and I was hoping I hadn't forgot any of the lessons I'd learned the summer before, sitting on Mary Beth's front porch with Peggy Cannon. Now, I might have been a little rusty, but it all came back to me pretty fast.

Our lips touched, parted slightly and I tasted the salt left over from the popcorn we'd shared, as our tongue's slightly brushed. After a few seconds, it was over and I moved back a little so I could look at her. She still had her face tilted up at me, and her eyes stayed closed for a few seconds, before she leaned back in the car seat.

"I guess the gossip was 'bout right…"

"What gossip?"

"Word was that you were a pretty good kisser… An' that waddn't half-bad."

"Half-bad…?"

I couldn't let it go at that, so I pulled her a little closer, leaned back down and our lips met again. When I did, I reached around her waist with my left arm, and I felt her hand move up my leg—stopping just short of the prize.

And again, I did what came natural. I moved my hand up and cupped her breast… but then I realized I really didn't know what I was expected to do next—and I don't think she had any idea either.

When the kiss ended, we both sat there, with our hands still on each other, and I looked past the lens of her glasses, into her eyes, and she looked at mine. We were so close together that I could feel her breath on my face.

Then, as if on cue, and without a word said, both of us moved our hands away from the other and sat back in the seat. We waited a respectable few more seconds, both thinking about how close we'd come, and then we reached for the door handles, got out of the car and walked slowly to the door. When we got there, Amy turned to me and looked up.

"Are we still friends?"

"Yeah… really good friends, I'd say… An' I reckon we always will be." I could see she was thinking about something.

"Remember… If we ain't found nobody by the time we're twenty, it's me an' you."

"I remember…"

I reached around her waist and interlaced my fingers, and she put her arms around my shoulders and we stood there hugging one another for several minutes. I guess we both just needed to feel the warmth of another person.

With her head on my shoulder, I heard her say again that she'd had a good time, and I told her I did too. Then Amy leaned back and looked up at me. Still with our arms around one another, we kissed one more time.

When it ended, she reached for the door and I turned back to get in the car, looking at my watch as I walked down the driveway. It was just a quarter till 11:00.

ELEVEN

On the way to church the next morning, Danny quizzed me about the night before, but all I'd tell was that me and Amy had a good time. And the next day at school was more of the same.

Me and Amy had talked about it, and decided we'd play this right on through and keep everybody guessing. We took every opportunity to meet in the halls between classes, lean close and whisper things, reach out and touch one another, and we did it with a smile on our faces. Just knowing it had everybody torn up was enough to keep a grin on our faces.

Between all the play acting, and doing all the stuff for the Prom, it made the week fly by. On Friday, Amy had the last meeting of the Prom Committee, went down her checklist to be sure everything was done, and then gave us our last orders.

When the meeting was over, me and Will walked to the gym to check on the decorations. Since Wednesday, a bunch of us had worked every afternoon, putting up streamers, blowing up balloons, setting up tables for the refreshments, and fixing places to take pictures, and such. I have to say, the ole gym looked good, and me and Will agreed we were ready.

The next morning, I washed and cleaned up the Corvair again, and drove down to the florist to pick up Amy's corsage. And I made sure my clothes were neat and pressed and my shoes were all shined up.

I had to pick Amy up around 3:30 so we could be the first ones in the gym. Generally the seniors started coming in from their promenade around 6:30, and Amy wanted to get there early to be sure everything was ready.

At 3:00, I checked my reflection in the mirror for the last time, and judged that I didn't look too bad. I'd rented a white dinner jacket and black pants to go with the traditional white shirt and black bow tie. And I had my shoes so shiny, you could see yourself.

At the appointed time, I knocked on Amy's back door. Her Mama led me to the den, but I didn't have to wait more than a minute. When Amy walked through the door, I dang near swallowed my gum.

She really did look nice. The baby blue sleeveless dress with scoop neck, fell just below her knees and matched shoes that had just enough heel to be dangerous. Her hair and make-up were just about perfect, and I couldn't hardly believe it was really her.

I fumbled pinning the corsage of white roses to her dress while her Mom was taking pictures. Finally she reached up and did the pinning herself, and then she pinned a red rose boutonniere on my lapel. We stood for one last picture, headed out the door, and high-tailed it for the school.

Jimmy Dawkins, who was the lead singer of the *Jim-Tones*, was already there, talking to the guys in the band. Amy had put Jimmy in charge of the entertainment, and he booked *The Air Notes*, the same band that had played at last year's prom. While the band got all their equipment set up, Amy went about checking everything else, and I did my best to stay out of the way. The way I looked at it, the decorations were still up, so my job was done.

I was hoping to find a corner to hide in, but Amy didn't hardly see it that way. I got the job of being her gopher. I took off my coat, hung it over the back of a chair and followed her around, moving this here and checking that there, while she marked on her list.

The rest of the prom planners straggled in over the next couple of hours, including Danny and Jenny. I was right proud when Danny got there since he was in charge of one of the things most dear to my heart—the refreshments.

Carrie Ann was on the clean-up committee, so her and Virgil didn't get there till around 6:00. Virgil was wearing a black suit that I guess he'd borrowed from the funeral home. But when I saw Carrie Ann, I had to catch my breath. She was totally beautiful in a peach colored dress that contrasted and brought out the color of her eyes and for a second I got all fluttery feeling inside.

But she wasn't none of my business—so I busied myself doing other things.

Since Amy had temporarily run out of things to order me around on, I went with Danny to the cafeteria kitchen to get the punch bowl. He'd met up with some of the other refreshment bunch that morning and mixed the punch in a big pot, so all we had to do was dip it out in a big bowl that had a chunk of ice in it, and wheel it to the gym.

By the time we got back, they had the rest of the eats all spread out on the tables. There was chips and onion dip, cookies, brownies, little hot dogs in some kind of sauce, and a whole platter full of country ham slices on little-bitty biscuits. It all smelled delicious and by 6:00, I'd decided to make claim to the ham and biscuit platter. But I saw Amy give me the evil-eye while I was sampling the chips and dip, so I backed off—but not too far back.

A little before 6:30, the first of the seniors from the promenade started coming in. They stood around and talked while the rest of their class arrived, and a few started eating. So I figured it was OK for me to start sampling. After all, somebody needed to check everything out.

Right at 7:00, I saw Amy standing over by the refreshment table. She set her brownie down, looked at her watch and gave Jimmy the high-sign to get the band started. So far, it was all clicking like clockwork.

For the next hour, we had a grand ole time. It was a beautiful night, the weather was perfect, the band was great, and the biscuits and little hot dogs really hit the spot. The whole place was laughing, and dancing, and everybody was getting really loose and relaxed, and having a good time.

I even got Amy to put her papers down, and dance with me—including a couple of slow dances. We did it right too, snuggling up close to one another. Ole Amy seemed to be really getting into it and I was surprised how relaxed she was. It looked like things were going great.

At the end of the first hour, *The Air Notes* took a ten minute break. And it was about then that the wheels started coming off the buggy.

The band no more than got the announcement made that they were taking a break, when I heard Danny's voice over everybody else, coming from over next to the spot we had set up to take prom pictures. I turned to see what was going on and saw folks start running in that direction. And I saw Mr. Franks, who'd drawn the short straw again to be the chaperone, moving fast from his spot at the door.

By the time I got there, Danny was standing over Wally Lawson, with his fists bunched up, and Mr. Franks was holding him around his waist. I took hold of Danny's arm and pushed him to the back corner, and some other guys picked Wally up and took him the other direction to separate the two.

Jenny was trailing along behind me and Danny, and the only thing he'd say was, "I ain't puttin' up with this shit no more!"

Just before we got to the bleacher seats in the corner, Danny jerked his arm away from me. He turned, glared at Jenny and told her if she was going with him, she'd better come on. Then he stomped out the door and headed for the parking lot. Jenny looked at me with a shit-eating grin on her face, and then turned and followed him out the door.

There was no stopping him, and I knew it. When Danny MacMahan got his mind set, there wasn't anything to be done about it.

By the time everything got calmed down, *The Air Notes* had started playing again. I scanned the gym trying to find Amy, and finally spotted her sitting in the third row of the bleachers, behind the refreshment table, munching on a brownie. I walked over and sat down next to her, expecting to get my ass chewed out, but she just stared at the lights behind the band that kept turning different colors.

After about a minute she noticed I was there. She smiled funny like, put her hand over on my leg and said, "Ya know Cubby, ole boy… you sure look awful cute tonight…"

When she looked up at me, I saw that her eyes behind her glasses were bigger then saucers.

"What the hell's wrong with you?"

"Ain't it a great prom…?"

"Dammit Amy… Have you been drinkin'?"

She looked at me with the same shit-eating grin I'd just seen on Jenny's face, and leaned her head over on my shoulder.

"OK Amy, just sit here an' don't move. I'm gonna go find you a coke or somethin'."

I stood up and had to grab her and sit her upright to keep her from falling over onto the bench. When I thought she was steadied, I stepped down the bleachers, and walked over to get a coke off of the table. I waved Mary Beth over while I was pouring the drink in a cup and asked her if she had any idea what was going on with Amy. She didn't know but said she'd take the drink and check on her.

I was standing in front of the refreshment table, trying to figure it all out, when Peggy Cannon came up to get some punch. Since Peggy was one of the seniors, I'd seen her come in with Jimmy Martin from the promenade walk, and dang near slobbered on myself. She was drop-dead gorgeous in a black, silky dress that was just tight enough to show off all her assets.

"What's all the whoop-la about Cubby?"

"Damned if I know… Where's Jimmy?"

I looked around, but couldn't find his face in the crowd.

"Went to the bathroom. I think he's gonna be a while…"

About that time, *The Air Notes* hit the first chords of the song, *To Love Somebody* by the Bee Gees. It was a really good slow song, and all of a sudden, I wanted to dance.

But Peggy was faster on the draw than I was.

"Would Amy get mad if I danced with ya?" she asked.

I turned and saw that Mary Beth and Amy had their heads together, and then turned back and looked at Peggy. Really, there wasn't any decision to make.

I took her by the hand and we walked in amongst all the others that were on the floor. She put her arms around my shoulders and I wrapped mine around her waist. Peggy snuggled up close and we moved with the music, hips swaying back and forth, stepping in time to the beat.

When the song was over, we leaned back away from one another, and I took both her hands in mine, and looked in her beautiful brown eyes. I was going to tell her I appreciated the dance, but again, she beat me to it.

"Thank you Cubby."

Then before I could move, she leaned forward and right there in the middle of the dance floor gave me a quick kiss—right on the mouth.

She grinned and said, "For old time's sake."

Then she turned and was gone.

TWELVE

———————

Still wondering what had just happened, I walked back over to check on Amy, scratching my head. By this time, Will had joined Mary Beth, and when he saw me coming, he got up and stepped down out of the bleacher seats meeting me at the edge of the gym floor.

"You figure out what's goin' on?"

Will shook his head, looked back at the girls, and took me by the arm, walking me to the back of the gym, away from everybody else.

"I don't know. She says she ain't had nothin' to drink, 'cept the punch. I asked to see if maybe she took somethin' to take the edge off, but she swears she didn't. Ain't no question, she's higher'n a Georgia pine, but we can't figure out how."

"Well, the punch ain't spiked. I been drinkin' it all night an' the only thing it's done for me is make me pee."

"Somethin's goin' on. Have you noticed how ever'body's actin'?"

We both looked around us. There wasn't anybody staggering around or anything like that, but I had to agree, it sure seemed like everybody was a little looser and more relaxed than they usually were.

"It don't look like anybody's wiped out or nothin'. I think Amy's the worst off."

I looked at my watch and saw it was almost 9:00, and the band would be taking another break pretty soon. We still had a couple more hours before the prom was over, and if everybody stayed till the end, maybe whatever it was would wear off and there wouldn't be any problem getting them all home.

I looked back over at the refreshment table and saw there was still plenty of stuff to eat, and reasoned if we kept everybody fed, they wouldn't be leaving to eat elsewhere. But with Danny gone—and it didn't look like he was coming back—somebody had to make sure the all the snacks kept coming.

I told Will that, and he agreed we'd have to take over the management of the refreshments. We walked over to check on things and saw there was still plenty of chips and dip, a couple more pots of little hotdogs and even another tray full of the little biscuits and ham. The cookies and rice-crispy squares were starting to get sparse, but we still had some left. It looked like the only thing completely gone was the brownies.

We decided we'd be able to make it till the end, and started to walk back to where Mary Beth and Amy were sitting, when Will grabbed my arm and leaned in to whisper.

"One more thing Cubby… Uh… I think you need to be real careful tonight when you take Amy home."

"Why's that?"

"Well… whatever's got into her has got her all fired up, an' I don't know why, but it sounds like she's got the hots for you. If you ain't careful, you're liable to get lucky tonight."

He had a grin on his face, but I could tell by his voice he was dead serious about it.

"Aw, hell… Come on, let's go see if we can figure this out."

As we got close to where they were sitting, I heard Mary Beth ask Will if he'd talked to me, and I saw him nod his head. I sat next to Amy and leaned forward to look in her face.

"Amy, tell me the truth… Have you taken any medicine or pills of any kind?'

She shook her head and just smiled at me. Then she leaned in close, like she was about to whisper something in my ear… but instead, she put her hand over on my leg, and kissed me on the cheek.

"I saw you dancin' with Peggy…" She laid her head on my shoulder. "Tell ya what big boy… Let's me an' you take a walk out to the parkin' lot an' I'll show ya a few things…"

I heard Will say, under his breath, "I told ya so…"

I knew good and well, I was probably going to hate myself later on, but I took her hand off of my leg, held it, and looked right at her.

"Amy… You know I love ya dearly…" and I saw her nod. "An' I want ya to know that under the right circumstances, if I believed that was what you really wanted, I'd smoke you like a big cigar… But somethin' ain't right, right now. Me an' you been too good-a friends for too long, an' I want us to keep bein' friends. If I took advantage now, I'm pretty sure that'd be the end of it. It ain't what I want to happen, an' I think when you get your head back on straight, you're gonna know it ain't what you want to happen."

I saw Mary Beth relax a little out of the corner of my eye, and Amy just stared at me a second before she spoke.

"Cubby… you're a real ass-hole, ya know it?"

"Maybe right now, but you're gonna thank me later—I think…" For a few more seconds, she just looked at me.

"Well shit. If we're not gonna screw around, I'm gonna get somethin' to eat. I'm starvin' all of a sudden…" That said, she started to push off of the bleacher seat, but I grabbed one arm, Mary Beth grabbed the other, and we sat her back down.

"You just keep your seat. I'll get it…"

"OK. But be sure to bring some more of those brownies…"

"They're all gone. But I'll get some other stuff…"

And then it hit me like a semi-truck… I didn't want to believe it, but it was the only explanation for everything.

Somebody spiked the brownies.

For the next couple of hours till the dance was over, Amy and most of the other kids at the prom, ate enough snacks to choke a horse. By 10:00, she was starting to steady up some, and it looked like most of the others were too.

I thought some activity might sober Amy up faster, and I even got her out on the dance floor several times. I did make the mistake of dancing a couple of slow songs with her, and on one, she ran her hand down my back, squeezed my butt, and scared the shit out of me. But other than that, we didn't have any more fights, the food held out, and right around 11:00, The Air Notes played the last song of the night, a right good rendition of The Beatles *That Boy*.

I was a little concerned about trying another slow number with Amy after she'd massaged my ass right on the dance floor. But everything went OK and we got through it.

Will told me him and Mary Beth would be sure the clean-up bunch got started, then he gave me another warning that I needed to be careful getting Amy home, and he sent us on our way.

I got her in my car, and asked her all the way to her house if she was OK, or did I need to go back and get Mary Beth to come help her. But Amy swore she was OK.

We pulled into her driveway and I ran around to help her out, and walked her to her back door. When we got there, she turned and threw her arms around my neck and buried her face in my chest. We just stood there for a few minutes.

"Cubby… You're really not a ass-hole… I 'preciate you bein' a gentleman." Then she looked up at me, grinned, and whispered, "But you really missed your chance…"

With that, she pulled my head down to hers and kissed me. And while she had my head spinning, she moved her hands down till they rested on both cheeks of my butt, and squeezed.

Then, as soon as it started—it ended. She turned, opened the door and started in the house, with one last order: "We'll talk tomorrow."

THIRTEEN

I pulled out of Amy's driveway and headed straight to Danny's house, but his car wasn't there. And it wasn't at the Jail, or at the school, or at Jenny's house. It was like the boy disappeared from the face of the earth.

Me and Will had agreed that we needed to keep things quiet about our suspicions, till we could get with Danny and try to figure it all out. Marijuana laced brownies was the only thing that explained why everybody was acting so funny. And that explained why every bite of the refreshments disappeared. Anybody that ate the brownies, got the munchies.

Laced brownies explained Amy's condition too. When she got nervous, she'd eat. And everybody knew how much she liked chocolate. After I had a chance to think about it, every time I saw her at the first of the prom, she had a brownie in her hand. Best I could figure, she probably ate four or five of the suckers. I recollected that I only saw one tray of brownies, so more than likely, nobody else ate more than one or two. If that was the case, Amy probably got the biggest dose.

Since Danny was in charge of the refreshments, he ought to know who brought the brownies—but we had to talk to him first. And if anybody else figured it out, word was sure to get out and Rocky and the County Law would get involved. If that happened, most likely we'd all be in trouble.

I drove around till about 12:30 looking for Danny but never did find him. My last trip was back to the school to check with Will and Mary Beth, but when I pulled in the parking lot, the lights were all off and all the cars were gone.

There wasn't anything more I could do, so I went home and went to bed.

I'd already decided to blow off church the next morning and about 9:00, I dialed Danny's number. Mrs. MacMahan answered, said Danny was still in bed, and I told her I really needed to talk to him, so she got him to the phone.

"Hello…"

"Get 'cha britches on. I'll be there in five minutes. Meet me on the front porch. We gotta talk." And I hung up.

It didn't take five minutes for me to walk out the door, duck under the limb of the maple tree and walk across the street, so I stood on the porch for a minute before Danny opened the front door. His hair was sticking up on the back of his head from sleeping on it, and he still had on his pajama top with his jeans.

"Where the hell did ya go last night? I looked for ya ever'where…"

"Aw shit, Cubby. I couldn't…"

"No… Don't say nothin' here. Go get your keys. We gotta ride an' do some talkin'."

He looked at me a little funny, but I reckon he could tell I wasn't fooling around.

"Is it Amy…? Oh hell, what happened?"

"No, it ain't Amy… Well, it's sorta Amy… Go get the keys an' I'll meet cha at the car."

Danny went back in the house to get his stuff, change out of his pajama shirt and smooth down his hair while I walked around to the driveway where his Chevy was parked. Five minutes later we pulled out on the street, drove through town and headed out the Oak Creek Road.

While we rode, I filled him in on what all happened after he left the prom. When I told him me and Will had it figured that somebody had laced the brownies with marijuana, he dang near ran out of the road. He said he didn't eat one, but Jenny did, and he thought she'd acted a little funny after that. But he didn't have any idea who brought the brownies.

By his recollection, brownies weren't even on the list of refreshments that we were supposed to have. He remembered seeing a tray full when we brought the punch in from the cafeteria kitchen, but didn't really pay much attention, thinking somebody must have just brought 'em in.

About 10:00, we stopped back by Wilson's and I went in and got a couple of egg and bacon sandwiches. While I waited, I used the pay phone to call Will. He hadn't gone to church either, so I told him we were coming to get him.

Fifteen minutes later, Will got in the Chevy and we went over the whole night one more time. Best we could figure, if it was marijuana laced brownies, nobody got sick, everybody got home, and all the evidence got eaten up. And from what me and Will saw, Amy was most likely the worst off of anybody.

When the subject of Amy came up, I saw a big grin come on Will's face.

"Well… Did ya get lucky last night?"

I answered that one real fast. "Hell no! You an' Mary Beth both heard what I told her. If I'd done anything with her in the shape she was in, when she got her senses back, she'd-a cut my nuts off. An' I'm really right partial to that part of me.

"An' besides, by the time the prom was over, she sobered up enough to realize what was goin' on, so I reckon I missed my golden opportunity."

Since all the stuff with Amy happened after him and Jenny had left, Danny had no idea what we were talking about, so we had to explain the whole thing to him. And that bought up questions about him leaving in such a huff. So we talked about that, and I was right glad to get off the subject of me and Amy.

Danny said Wally had been trying to make a move on Jenny for the past week, and as far as he could see, she hadn't really done anything to discourage it. So right before the band took a break, Wally came up and asked Jenny to dance. Danny didn't take too kindly to it, words were exchanged, and Danny decked him. Simple as that.

After they left, he and Jenny drove to Maryville to get something to eat, and rode around till he took her home around 11:00. Then he said he rode around by himself till about 1:00 in the morning.

The three of us agreed, if what we thought happened was what actually happened, we'd probably hear about it from somebody. If they thought they'd pulled it off, they were sure to brag about it. And we were all in agreement that the whole thing could have been really dangerous. But now it was all over, since nobody got hurt, and that might be what made folks at the prom a little "happier" this year—we decided it was a case of no harm-no foul.

Our best bet was to keep our mouths shut about what we thought, and see if anything more came of it.

Mary Beth and Amy would have to be told, but the fewer people that knew, the more likely we'd be able to keep it secret. As far as we knew, the three of us were the only ones that thought we'd put it all together. Keeping it just between us for the time being, was the best thing we could do.

Will said he'd swear Mary Beth to secrecy and it'd be my job to convince Amy to keep her mouth shut.

AFTER ALL

After I got a chance to think about it, it occurred to me that I wound up with the hardest job in the whole mess.

FOURTEEN

———————

I held off till around 2:00, trying to figure out what I was going to say. But finally I gutted it up and called Amy. She sounded a little sheepish, but said OK when I told her we needed to talk and I was coming to get her.

She was waiting on her carport when I pulled in the driveway, and typical Amy, as soon as the car door shut, she started talking.

"Cubby, I guess I owe you an apology. I don't know what got into…"

But I cut her off right there, before she got another word out.

"For once Amy, shut up an' listen to me… First off, you ain't got nothin' to apologize for. The way we figure it, there waddn't nothin' that happened that you were responsible for…"

I laid out what me and Will and Danny thought happened, and while we rode through town, we talked our way through the whole of the night. Amy agreed with Danny that brownies weren't on the refreshment list, and like him, she thought somebody just threw 'em in at the last minute out of the goodness of their heart. She also confirmed that she ate a bunch of 'em, but she couldn't recollect exactly how many since a lot of things about the night were pretty fuzzy in her memory.

After hearing everything we'd been able to piece together, her first reaction was to get madder'n hell, and declare that she was going to launch a full investigation. But I pointed out to her that would bring in Rocky and the law, and Danny would be square in the cross-hairs of that, since he was the one she'd put in charge of the refreshments. That thought calmed her down fast.

Then the old organizing, analyzing—and paranoid, Amy took over, and she started going down the list, trying to figure out who might have wanted to ruin her, and ruin the prom. But she didn't get any further in the guessing game than the guys had earlier. There simply weren't any obvious suspects. Whoever laced the brownies had been really slick about it.

Amy got real quiet and I thought she was still thinking. When I looked over at her, she had her head down, and I got afraid she might be crying. But when I started to say something, hoping to ease her mind, it was her turn to stop me.

"No Cubby… I was just thinkin' how good a bunch of friends I've got… To take care of me an' keep me from makin' a complete fool of myself… An' then to take over an' make sure the rest of the prom went OK an' ever'body was OK to get home when it was over…"

She stopped again for a few seconds before continuing.

"An' what I was startin' to say when I got in the car… I think I do need to apologize to you… Things are a little fuzzy, but I think I really put you on the spot, propositionin' you an' all."

I knew when it came out of my mouth, it probably wasn't the most Christian thing to say, but I just couldn't resist.

"It's OK Amy… What you done for me later, really made up for ever'thing…"

I glanced over and saw her face turn beet red and her mouth drop open a little. I reckon it's the first time she ever opened her mouth and no words came out.

"Did I…?"

"Oh, you was wonderous. You done things that I'll dream about for years…"

She buried her face in her hands, an' all I heard was a soft, "Oh, shit."

I'd played it about as long as I could... and besides, I couldn't hold it in any longer, and I busted out laughing. When she finally realized I was leading her on, she lunged at me from her side of the car, and hit me on the arm.

"Hell Amy... Nothin' happened, 'cept gettin' my butt squeezed... That was nice, but I was a little disappointed I didn't get the grand prize."

Well... that pissed her off even more, and she launched into beating on my arm again.

She finally got calmed down, and we got back to talking about the prom and the spiked brownies. I convinced her that we had to keep our mouths shut, not saying anything to anybody, and hope whoever did it was so proud of themselves, they'd start talking about it. Once I got her promise to keep it all just between us, and say it so I believed her, I turned the car around and headed back to her house.

We sat for a few minutes in her drive way, listening to Blood, Sweat and Tears singing *God Bless the Child* on the radio, then I walked with her to the door. When we got there, she turned and hugged me... and I hugged her back.

"I owe ya Cubby..."

"Damn right ya do..."

With her head still on my shoulder, I heard her ask, "Did you really say, if it was another time an' place, you'd smoke me like a big cigar?"

"Yep... Just might collect on that debt someday. Ya never know..."

I reached up, pulled her head to me, and kissed her on the forehead.

"Friends...?" I asked.

"Yeah... Good friends."

She went in the door, and I headed home.

There was only about a month of school left, and our next chore was to work the graduation ceremony, and help shove the seniors of 1969 out the door. The five of us that were in the know, sure enough kept our mouths shut and our ears open, hoping we'd hear somebody say something or start bragging about what they'd done. But nobody said anything that ever got back to us.

Tuesday night, Walter Cronkite announced on national news that American planes had started carpet-bombing parts of Cambodia, the country that was right beside Viet Nam. It was a serious expansion of the war that Tricky Dick had been telling us he was getting us out of, and it set dang near the whole country to screaming.

Nobody could figure out what the hell was happening. Nixon got elected saying he was going to get our boys home, and we'd have 'Peace with Honor.' But instead, it looked like they were opening up another front. If the man could lie about this, what else would he lie to us about?

After that, news on the war just got worse. Correspondents with the national networks who were in-country with our troops sent back stories about a fierce battle with the North Regular Army and the Viet Cong over a place called Ap Bia Mountain. For the next ten days, they kept up reports detailing the number of soldiers killed and wounded trying to take the hill. Fighting was so fierce and the slaughter so bad, they took to calling the place 'Hamburger Hill.'

After all the prom whoop-la got over with, me and Amy went back to the way we'd always been before—kind of like friendly combatants. Except both of us felt like if either one really needed the other, we'd be there. Least-ways that was how I felt.

The days started to get warmer, grass started to green-up and the little buds that came out on the trees, turned into little leaves. The laurel and dogwoods began to bloom and the hills and hollows all around us came back to life. Springtime in the mountains was a wonderous time of the year.

I checked with the hardware store where I'd worked the summer before, but they allowed there wasn't enough work to hire me for the summer, even for part-time. I asked around a couple of other places, but there wasn't anybody hiring.

Jobs were getting scarcer than hen's teeth, and a lot of people were out of work. The logging and lumbering that had been a big part of our local economy, had slowed down to a trickle.

The government stopped a lot of it, while they looked at adding more land to the National Park and the tree-huggers were protesting and filing injunctions right and left, to stop the cutting and land clearing. Sewing factories that were once on every corner, were closing down and laying off. Most of 'em had owners that lived away from here, and word was they were shipping work overseas where they didn't have to pay the workers so much or fight with the unions.

Personally, I was torn over it. I dearly loved the mountains, and the wild part of the forests that covered the hills. Seeing it cut down and destroyed was like cutting off a part of me. And being pretty much a capitalist, I could understand business trying their best to cut their costs down. But doing all that came at a cost to the folks here at home that depended on work to pay their bills and raise up their families. There just wasn't anything fair about any of it.

Before we turned around, May was over, and we finished out the last day of school. That night David Brinkley sounded disgusted when he announced that U.S. and South Vietnamese troops had withdrawn from Hamburger Hill. After ten days of some of the hardest fighting of the war, and hundreds of casualties—the Generals just walked off and left it all.

The national news outlets weren't the only ones disgusted. Protests were going on all over, and no matter how we looked at what was happening, none of it made sense any more.

On the last day of May, we found ourselves back in the gym handing out graduation programs. I watched as Peggy Cannon walked across the stage to get her diploma, and I was as proud of her as I'd been for her drop-dead gorgeous cousin the year before.

Since we were juniors, we did the organizing and supervising this year, and got to boss the sophomores like we were bossed last year. So much had been going on that I hadn't paid much attention to who all the sophomores were—but of course I knew Carrie Ann was one of 'em.

During all the setting up for the graduation ceremony, I did my best to keep my distance from her. I'd been burnt twice by her, and she'd made it pretty clear she was looking for something other than what I had to offer.

But it didn't matter. I still dang near fell all over myself every time I got around her. For some reason, I couldn't help it.

After the graduation ceremony was over, the kids on the committee stayed to get the gym straightened up, and I ran smack into Carrie Ann while we were folding up the chairs. I said hi, and she said hi… and then both of us just stood there for a few minutes, and looked at each other, till finally she broke the stalemate.

"Are you an' Amy still goin' out?"

I figured she was just trying to be sociable, but I couldn't reason why she'd be interested.

"Naw… We both figured it was a lot better to just be friends."

"I'm sorry things didn't work out for you. I kinda know how you feel… things not workin' out, that is. Nothin' seems to be workin' out for me either. Are you workin' at the hardware again this summer?"

"No. They're not hirin', so I guess I'll be gettin' a few yards to mow an' do odd jobs for folks."

"Hmmm... I'll call you if I hear of anybody that needs anything done." We stood there kind of awkward, for a few seconds and I could feel myself falling into the emerald pools of her eyes...

She started to turn away, but stopped and looked back at me. "Well... I'll probably see you around..."

All I could do was watch as Carrie Ann folded the last chair in the row, leaned it up, and then walked away.

FIFTEEN

————

Even though I hadn't been able to get a summer job lined up, I really wasn't too worried about it. For folks that wanted to work, there was plenty to do, as long as you didn't care to ask for it. I started asking a few people in town about mowing and cleaning up for 'em and it wasn't long before I'd lined up several things to keep me busy.

Danny worked at his Dad's gas station again, and I figured if things got really slow for me, I could try to get some pick-up work at the station, doing whatever nobody else wanted to do. And then there was pick-up work on the farms all around, hauling hay or helping work the tobacco patches.

I wasn't going to get rich, but I figured I could make enough to put gas in the car and keep some jingling money in my pocket for dates—if I ever found anybody to go out with.

Early on in June President Nixon met with the President of South Viet Nam on Midway Island to talk about the war. I reckon he was trying to get all the protesters off his back since he'd started out saying he was going to get us out of Southeast Asia, and have "peace with honor." But then he went and bombed the shit out of Cambodia, who we weren't supposed to be fighting.

Anyway, ole Tricky Dick had the balls to tell that he was intending to withdraw 25,000 troops out of the war zone by August, saying that his "Vietnamization" plan was working and it wouldn't be long before we'd be turning over the war to them.

Hell… Nobody knew whether to believe him or not.

We had a few bright spots in June. CBS introduced a new show called "Hee-Haw," that joined "The Beverly Hillbillies" in poking fun at us.

I have to admit, it was right entertaining. They did corny skits, and sang and picked some pretty good country and gospel music, and the girls that popped out of the corn patch were kind of cute. For an hour most folks forgot the shape the country was in, and had something to laugh about.

But then, the news brought back all the confusion over the war when they announced that North Regular Army and Viet Cong troops had re-occupied Hamburger Hill.

It purely didn't make any sense. Our boys—the future of our country—just doing what they were told, taking orders from some idiot that was most likely far away from the blood and the smoke— dead, hurt, disfigured—all for nothing. All the pain and dying. And the generals just walked off and handed it back—for nothing.

The whole country ended June of '69, pretty much confused and pissed-off. It was coming real close to being too much to tolerate.

July was, as usual, hotter'n hell. The 4th that year was on Friday, and Lincoln did their traditional parade through the seven blocks of downtown. The band led everything off, followed by a few hay wagons towed by tractors and pick-ups that the churches had decorated. Then came a few police cars and fire trucks with horses and riders bringing up the rear.

The horses were always the worst part to my thinking. For the rest of the weekend, the whole town smelled like a barn, and we had to watch to keep from stepping in the horse crap, until the next rain came to wash it all away.

That weekend was one of the times Danny and Jenny were on the outs, and Danny talked me into riding over to Pigeon Forge to see the fireworks. The little wide place in the road on the way to Gatlinburg was making a last ditch effort to promote their one attraction, other than Trotter's family style restaurant.

"Rebel Railroad" had opened a few years earlier trying to capitalize on the still simmering hostilities between North and South. They had a real steam engine locomotive that did a turn around the park and at one point in the trip, blue coated Yankees would mount a cavalry attack on the train, and all the kids got to shoot cap-guns at 'em.

Since my heritage was blue-coated, I wasn't so thrilled with it, but I had to admit the show was right entertaining. And to celebrate the 4th, the park was advertising a fireworks show that for some reason, Danny was all thrilled about.

I wanted to ask Will, Mary Beth and Amy to go with us, but Danny told me they were all busy, and the two of us were on our own. We got there about 6:00, got one of the last parking spots in the upper lot, and headed straight to the line for the train ride.

The inside of the train car was hot, and filled with kids holding either Rebel Flags or the cap-guns they'd handed out for the coming fight.

I wondered what would happen if I declared my allegiance to the North, staged a mutiny on the train car, and let the Yankee raiding party win for once. But then I figured that would just get us thrown out before we could see the fireworks, so I dropped it. Mainly I just sat back and enjoyed the breeze that blew in the windows of the passenger car that gave a little relief from the hot July afternoon heat.

Once the trip around the park was over and we stepped off the train onto the station platform, I discovered why Danny was so insistent on just the two of us making the trip. Standing at the back of the platform I spotted Lisa Coulter—and with her, looking cuter'n a bug's ear, was Angel Burke.

I could have killed him.

Lisa was a friend of Angel's that we'd fixed Danny up with last year so I could meet Angel at the drive-in movie. I had no idea he and Lisa were still in contact with one another, but knowing Danny, I really shouldn't have been surprised.

Since there wasn't anything else I could do, I followed along behind Danny as he walked up to Lisa, leaned over and kissed her on the cheek. Danny took her hand, turned to me, and with a grin I wanted to slap off his face said, "We're goin' to get somethin' to drink… An', uh… I think you two have some talkin' to do."

Hand in hand, they walked off toward the concession stand, and left us standing there.

Angel looked up at me and for a second, I got completely lost in her eyes.

"I'm sorry about this. Lisa didn't tell me she was comin' to meet Danny."

"Don't be sorry… Danny didn't tell me what was goin' on either. But now we're here, I'm not a bit sorry about it."

The platform emptied out as the train loaded for another run around the park, and the big steam engine belched black smoke and blew the whistle, chugging out of the station. The roof-cover over the platform, made for more shade than other places, so me and Angel found seats on a bench and did exactly what Danny had told us to do.

We started out asking about each other, how school was going, and generally talked about anything we could think of that didn't have to do with what had happened between us before. I'd forgotten how easy it was to talk to Angel and I realized I missed hearing the slight nasal tone of her voice.

Even though she acted as if she held all the cards, I could tell from her occasional glances to see what my reaction was to something she'd say, that she wasn't as sure of herself as she wanted me to believe. More than once, I wanted to reach out and touch her, and tell her everything was alright, and she was somebody special.

Most likely, I was the one that put the doubt in her mind to start with…

After a while we ran out of general conversation things to say, and for a few seconds it got quiet. We both knew that eventually, neither of us could avoid the elephant in the room, so I took a deep breath and started it off.

"Angel… I'm really sorry about what happened between us. You're really somebody special, an' you didn't deserve to be hurt like that. But, I…"

"Don't say anymore." She reached up and put her fingers on my lips to stop me. After a second, she moved her hand and looked away.

"It most likely waddn't all your fault. I guess I just pushed a little too hard… but I thought I'd found what I wanted. An' I guess I thought you'd just go along with it." She paused and thought for a second.

"Yeah… It hurt… But I have to take part of the blame."

Now, I couldn't stop myself… I reached out, took her hand and turned so I could look in her eyes.

"Angel… I care a lot about you. I felt it the first time I met you, an' no matter what might happen between us, I most likely will always care. I have no idea whether it's love or not… but I'm willin' to give it another try to find out, if you want to…"

She looked directly at me for several seconds, trying to confirm whether I was being sincere or not, before she spoke.

"If you want to, I'd like to try again too… but, slow an' easy this time… no pressure."

I felt her squeeze my hand, and we sat back on the bench and looked out at the mountains around us. We sat together through the late afternoon, ignoring the crowds of people coming and going on the train platform. To tell the truth, I lost all track of time, I got so wrapped up in her.

Along about dark-thirty, Danny and Lisa finally reappeared. When Danny saw that I was holding Angel's hand, he got a huge "told-ya-so" grin on his face.

"Well, I see you two got your talkin' done. I knowed if I could get you together, you'd figure it out. Now, let's go find a good spot to watch the fireworks."

That night, we watched the rockets explode in the sky overhead, and when it was over, I held Angel's hand and we walked to the lot where Lisa's Ford was parked. As Angel opened the car door, she stopped, reached and put her arms around my neck, and gave me a hug. Then, as if it was an afterthought, almost hesitantly, she kissed me good-night, and they drove off.

Slow and easy…

Danny was all grins on the way back to Lincoln. The boy was right proud of himself, and he told me so about every fifteen minutes. He talked the whole way back, but it was more or less a one sided conversation because I was all tied up in my own thoughts.

For some reason, I kept feeling like I'd done something wrong.

SIXTEEN

————

At some point between the train ride and the fireworks, I'd asked Angel about going to the movie in Maryville the next Saturday. Since we were older now, and it was OK for her to date, we didn't have to sneak around to see each other.

This time, I'd be picking her up at her house, and that meant I'd have to meet her Mom and Dad. I didn't think they knew about our "secret" meetings at the drive-in, but I was still a little worried. Considering what happened the year before, meeting Angel's parents face to face, wasn't something I looked forward to.

I kept the feeling that something was wrong the whole week, but danged if I could figure out what it was. Come Saturday though, I drove to Walland and pulled in her drive-way at 5:30.

Angel answered the door and took me in to make the introductions. Her Mom was nice enough, but Mr. Burke had a right stern look on his face when I shook his hand, and he told us both she had to be home by 11:00. After that, we didn't piddle around any, and Angel rushed us out the door.

We talked and laughed and sang along with the radio on the ride to Maryville, and after a quick bite to eat, we saw the new John Wayne movie, *True Grit.* Somewhere between the popcorn and holding hands in the dark theatre, whatever it was that had been deviling me, more or less disappeared. I had a good time just being with her, and as far as I could see, she was having a pretty good time too.

Angel had trimmed her hair a little since we'd dated before, but it still hung just over her shoulders, and framed her dark eyes and long lashes. The slightly crooked nose that had occasionally surfaced in my dreams, was still as cute as I remembered. Whatever it was I was worried about, purely drifted away from me.

I kept an eye on my watch to be sure I got her home on time, and at 10:15 we pulled back into her driveway. Since we were there with time to spare, Angel stuck her head in the door to let her Dad know we were back and told him we were going to sit on the porch for a spell.

It was a clear summer night, and at first, we just sat in the swing, listening to the sounds of the hills around us. Every now and then, a car would pass, heading toward the mountains or going back toward Maryville, but otherwise the only sound was the creaking of the swing chain and the singing of the katydids.

We snuggled as close as we could and I put my arm around her shoulder as we listened quietly to the hoot of a barn owl somewhere in the distance… and waited.

"I had a good time tonight, Cubby."

"Me too."

I pulled her closer, she turned her head towards mine, and after I quickly glanced at the front door to be sure we didn't have an audience, we sneaked in a kiss for a few seconds.

I'd gotten a quick kiss from Angel after the fireworks the week before—but this was different. It was the kind of kiss you could feel all over. It was the kind of kiss you remembered.

And when it was over, with a flick of her tongue, she licked the tip of my nose, then sat back and grinned at me. I still thought it was a little strange, but there were some right pleasant memories attached to that surprise nose lick. And to be honest, I kind of liked it.

She settled back in the crook of my arm, laid her head on my shoulder, and we talked, softly so that we were the only ones who could hear.

I asked her about going out again the next weekend, but she told me she couldn't because she was going on a church trip. But she said she'd give me a call when she got back and we'd set a date. I was a little disappointed, but since we were doing this "slow and easy" there wasn't a great lot I could do about it.

Along about 11:00, we got off the swing and walked to the door. She turned to face me, put her arms around my waist and tucked the top of her head under my chin. We stood like that for a minute, before she looked up, inviting another kiss... and of course, I obliged.

After the kiss, and one more hug, she opened the door and started in... but at the last minute, Angel turned back, smiled, and winked at me.

At least I think it was a wink.

Sunday morning I met up with Danny at church, and we listened to the sermon—or better still, we acted like we were listening. He kept trying to find out how the date went, and I had to keep shushing him before the whole balcony turned around to see what we were talking about.

When Preacher Mason said the last "Amen," we scooted out of the balcony and headed for the Chevy. To satisfy his curiosity, and get him to shut up about it, I told him everything was cool—no, I said it was better than cool—between me and Angel. He grinned big at that, and he was still grinning when I got out at the house and he drove off.

After Sunday lunch, I called Angel and we talked awhile. She told me her church trip the next week was to Washington, D.C., something they'd been planning for months. A bunch of kids from

Methodist Churches all over the district were going, and they'd chartered a big bus to take the whole group. They were leaving on Friday afternoon and wouldn't be back till the next Tuesday.

I allowed as how there were a lot of museums and history to see, and said I thought it'd be a really nice trip. Being pretty much a history nut myself, I was actually a little jealous. But I told her to have a good time, and to call me when she got back.

After we hung up, I sat for a minute thinking about her. There was still something that kept eating at me, but I couldn't put a finger on it.

I could close my eyes and see her long dark hair and her dark eyes that seemed to look deep into my heart, and could at times, pull it right up in my throat... and I could feel myself falling. I could almost hear the sound of her voice and feel a slight dampness on the end of my nose... and I had to remind myself over and over about the "slow and easy" part.

I wasn't off the phone to Angel ten minutes when it started ringing again. I hoped it was her calling back, but when I picked it up, before I could even say hello, I heard Amy's scratchy voice.

"Whatcha doin' right now?"

"Not much..."

"Can ya get the car? If ya can, come an' get me... I need to talk to somebody, an' I reckon you're elected..."

I told her it shouldn't be a problem and I'd be over in a minute. Typical Amy, she didn't say 'bye' or anything. I heard a click and the line went dead.

When I pulled in her driveway, Amy was standing out on the carport, looking at the fluffy clouds that were building up from the south-east, over the tops of the ridges. She didn't even let me get the motor shut off... just plopped her behind in the seat and gave me the command to "Drive."

We hadn't even got backed out of the driveway when she started in.

"Hell Cubby... I don't know what I'm gonna do... I signed up to go on this trip with the church youth group... paid my money up front an' ever'thing... an' now I find out Randy's gonna be goin' on the same trip...

"What am I gonna say? How can I ride on the same bus all the way through Virginia with the son-of-a-bitch after what he did? What am I gonna do?"

I damn near wrecked.

"Church trip...? On a bus...? Amy... is this trip goin' to Washington, D.C?"

She looked over at me. "Yeah, the Church's been plannin' this for months. They're loadin' a big charter bus an' pickin' up kids from a bunch of other churches... an' I've already paid my deposit an' ever'thing... We're supposed to leave Friday...

"I don't know what to say to Randy... I don't want him thinkin' I've been sittin' around thinkin' about him... I thought about tellin' him me an' you were still datin'... Whatta ya think on that?"

I hadn't had a chance to talk to Amy for a couple of weeks, so I had to fill her in on how Danny had got me and Angel together at the fireworks show, and how we'd decided to give it another try, but this time we were going to take it "slow and easy," and see what happened.

I told her from what I could figure, Angel was going on the same trip. So, I told her in no uncertain terms that she was not to tell anybody that me and her were dating. Sure as the world, Angel would hear it, and that would most likely put an end to everything.

I turned onto the Oak Creek road to cruise the same route that me and Danny usually took, and I noticed Amy got real quiet, so I looked over at her. She had a funny, smirky grin on her face, and I asked her what the hell she was smiling about.

"Well, shit… This trip might turn out to be all kinds of fun."

"Why's that?"

"Carrie Ann's goin' on the trip too… Hell, I might just get us all together an' we could form a 'Cubby Club,' an' compare notes, since we've all been out with ya…"

The vision of my hands around her throat flashed through my mind. But then I thought… 'Nah, Amy owed me… she wouldn't do that to me…

Would she??

SEVENTEEN

After threatening to set her out in the Ridge Top parking lot, I finally got her to promise she wouldn't be chartering any "Cubby Club" and talking about me. But when she promised, she kept a really smart-ass grin on her face.

I was a little worried over what might happen if all three girls got their heads together. But I convinced myself I was just being paranoid, and I was pretty sure that girls didn't talk about guys like that. Least ways, I didn't think they did.

I called Angel a couple of times that week before she left on the church trip, and I made it a point to stay away from Amy. To tell the truth, I was kind of scared that if Amy thought I was worried about her getting together with Carrie Ann and Angel and talking, she'd do it just to spite me. So I figured my best bet was to be cool about it.

Laying in the bed at night, trying to go to sleep, I ran through all my memories of the time I'd spent with Angel, and the times I'd been with Carrie Ann. I really couldn't think of anything really bad that I did or said. It was a damn good thing none of 'em could read my thoughts, or I'd have really been in deep shit. But to my recollection, I never really acted on anything I might have been thinking.

So, the best I could remember, there actually wasn't anything too awful bad they could talk about even if they did get together. Least ways, I didn't think there was anything.

That Saturday was hotter than the third ring of hell, and by the afternoon, when I got finished mowing the last yard that day, the only thing I could think of was a cold shower. Which was probably what I needed anyway.

By 6:30, I was properly cleaned up and sitting in one of the back booths at Wilson's, with a hamburger, fries, and two large, cold Coca-Colas, looking forward to a quiet night. I'd just taken the first bite when Danny waltzed in and sat down in the booth across from me. He never said a word. Just reached out, took a big French-fry off of my plate and stuck it in his mouth.

"I thought you'd be out with Jenny, or Lisa, or somebody?"

Trying to talk and chew at the same time, he shot back at me. "Hell, if you'd call me ever' once in a while, you'd know what I was doin'." He reached for another French-fry, but I stabbed my fork at his hand and he jerked it back.

"Well... Why ain't-cha out with one of 'em?" I asked as I picked the hamburger up. Danny saw I had both hands occupied, and quick as a raccoon, grabbed another fry.

"Too much pressure. I figure I've pretty much wore 'em all out, an' they need a rest this weekend."

It was hard to grin with my mouth full, but I gave it a try.

"You're so full-a shit, your ears are turnin' brown. Waddn't nobody'd go out with you, huh...?"

He gave me a go-to-hell look, waved the waitress down and ordered a burger platter and we hashed over the state of the world for the next hour.

It didn't take too long for Danny to ask why I wasn't out with Angel. So I filled him in about the church trip she was on, and how Amy was going on the same trip.

Then I backed up a little, and told how Amy'd called all worked up because Randy was going on the same trip, and she wasn't sure how to deal with him. I still thought the odds were pretty even that Amy would whip Randy's ass before they got back, but Danny figured she'd just hide from him the whole time.

Danny got real interested when I mentioned that Carrie Ann was going on the trip too, and that Amy had threatened to get her and Carrie Ann and Angel together for a "Cubby Club" meeting so they could compare notes about me, since at one time or another, I'd been out with all three of 'em. But I told him I threatened to leave her big ass up at Ridge Top, and made her promise to keep everybody separated.

When I said that, I heard him give a low whistle and when I looked over at him, he was shaking his head at me.

"Don't tell me you're trustin' Amy to keep ever'body separated? Cubby, you really are dumber'n you look. You know as well as I do, Amy's meaner'n a copperhead. She'd like nothin' better'n to fry your ass with both of those girls... Hell, there's a good chance none of 'em will speak to ya again after this... But that kinda brings up the reason I come lookin' for you...

"I got a call from Carrie Ann a couple-a nights ago. She started in talkin' about some stupid stuff at school that didn't make a whole hell of a lot of sense. But it didn't take long to get around to what she called about—you."

"Ah, bull-shit..."

"I ain't kiddin' ya. Carrie Ann thought she was bein' real sly about it, but she was wantin' to know if you was goin' out with anybody..."

He picked up the squeeze bottle of ketchup and squirted a stream all over his fries, and then sat there rearranging each one of 'em on his plate, saying nothing, till I couldn't stand it anymore.

"Well hell... What'd ya tell her?" He tried to hide it behind his napkin, but I could see the grin on his face as he wiped the ketchup dribble off of his mouth.

"Oh... I didn't think you give a shit..."

"Dammit Danny! What'd ya say?"

"I told her you was goin' out ever' now an' then. But that I thought ya still had a thing for her... I did tell her she damn near blowed her chance with ya, dumpin' your ass at the dance last year like she done. But I told her when school started, she might just get another try.

"You oughta think about it, Cubby... Askin' her out again. I really think you an' her was meant for each other..."

I sat there, completely bum-fuzzled for a minute.

"Wait a minute... You're the ass-hole that pulled the big conspiracy to get me an' Angel back together? What was that all about?"

"Ole buddy, I hate to tell ya, but you was actually just a means to a end. I needed a reason to call Lisa, an' since you'd been mopin' around for the last few months, I figured gettin' you an' Angel talkin' again might be a good reason to call her... An' it worked, didn't it?"

I leaned over the table, and looked in the booth seat next to him, and he asked what I was looking for.

"You ass-hole... I thought since you're playin' Cupid, maybe you'd brought your bow an' arrows with ya."

EIGHTEEN

We rode around till about 9:30, smoked a few cigarettes, cussed Amy a whole bunch, and talked about everything and everybody. The subject of Angel or Carrie Ann didn't come up again, but taking what Danny had said, he'd given me a lot to think about.

There wasn't any doubt that Carrie Ann still had a hold on me. Every time I smelled honeysuckles, I thought about her. Every time certain songs came on the radio, I thought about her. Every time I saw a girl with blond hair, or green eyes, or freckles across her nose, I thought about her.

Hell... truth was, I thought about her a lot. And I reckon, when I told her I loved her last year... I meant it.

But she'd made it pretty clear she didn't feel the same way about me. She'd already broken up with me twice. And I didn't have any intention of being her yo-yo.

But I still thought about her, and I still dreamed about her, and I still wanted to hold her close.

Then there was Angel. When we were sneaking out to be together before, it was a wonderful thing. Yeah, I guess things got out of hand and she got a little carried away. But there wasn't any question about whether she cared for me or not. Angel cared so much, it was scary.

And I really did care for her. And I thought about her a lot too... her long black hair... her dark eyes that crinkled up when she smiled, and her slightly crooked nose… the feel of her arms around my shoulders… the taste of her lips when we kissed… and the strange little lick of my nose. There wasn't any doubt in my mind— Angel was special. In fact, she was so special there was every possibility I loved her too.

Then I remembered that after the church trip was over, it was also entirely possible that neither one of 'em would ever speak to me again.

It was a terrible feeling to know Amy could be holding my entire future in her hands.

That night, Apollo 11 went into orbit around the moon. Before the rocket blasted off from Cape Kennedy on the Wednesday before, the guy from Mission Control said if everything went right, our astronauts would take the first step on the moon. It looked for sure that we were finally going to beat the Russians to it this time, and the whole country was glued to their TV's to see it happen.

On the national news that Sunday, NBC announced that Teddy Kennedy, Jack and Bobby's little brother, had been in a car wreck up in Massachusetts, and a girl had got killed. The details were kind of sketchy, but it looked like the bad things that kept finding that family, just kept on coming.

Later that night, most of the country stayed up late to watch Neil Armstrong step off of the ladder from the lunar module, and through the crackle and the beeps of the long, long distance radio transmission, heard him say, "That's one small step for man… One giant leap for mankind."

Our guys walked around on the moon, posed for pictures like a bunch of tourists, left the Stars and Stripes, and headed back home. On Thursday, their spaceship made a perfect re-entry into the atmosphere, and splashed down in the ocean, close enough to get picked up by a U.S. Navy Carrier. They did indeed, make us all proud.

That same afternoon, the bunch on the church trip to Washington came home too. I made a point to not be anywhere close to the church when they unloaded, since I didn't want Amy or Carrie Ann either one thinking I had any interest. But the suspense was killing me. I didn't have any idea if Angel and Carrie Ann had met up and talked… And what Amy might, or might not have done, was a total toss-up.

I finally got up enough nerve to call Amy about 9:30 that night, but her Mama said she came in worn out from the trip and was already in bed. And my call to Angel's house got the same answer.

Were they both really that tired? Or just not wanting to talk to me? I really didn't know what to do. But the way I looked at it, the only way to handle any problem was to face it head-on, and that's what I decided to do—tomorrow.

I started work early the next morning, but by mid-afternoon I'd done all I could do in the heat. I went home, did the cold shower thing again and drank about a gallon of water. I was tired, but I still had to know what happened on the trip.

Amy's line was busy when I called her, but when I dialed Angel's number, her Mom picked up on the third ring, and got her to the phone.

"Hello…"

"Hi Angel… How'd your trip go?"

"Oh, Cubby… It went great... I thought you were gonna call last night?"

"I did… But you were already in bed."

"Sorry, I didn't get the message."

Maybe I was imagining things, but she sounded a little distant.

"I was wonderin' if you might wanta go ride around tonight? I'd really like to see ya."

"I'm still pretty tired. Can we make it tomorrow night?"

"Oh… OK. How 'bout I pick you up about 6:00 an' we'll get some stuff and drive up in the mountains for a picnic?"

"That'll be fine. I've got a lot to talk to you about."

I heard Mrs. Burke say something in the background, and Angel said she had to go and she'd see me tomorrow. Then she hung up, and I got a terrible sinking feeling in my belly.

I was still sitting with my hand on the phone when it rang.

"Cubby… Are ya busy tonight?" Amy's voice was low and whispery over the phone line.

"No."

"Good. Come an' get me."

"Now?"

"Hell no, not right now. Come about 5:30 an' we'll go get a hamburger."

"OK… What happened on the trip?"

"Not now… We'll talk tonight."

The phone clicked, signaling that she was finished talking, and I sat there with the receiver in my hand till the off-hook reminder started buzzing in my ear. A little voice in the back of my head was telling me everything was fixing to fall apart. And I still had almost an hour to worry over it.

NINETEEN

I left the house early with the feeling that a sword was hanging over my head, and drove around to kill some time and try to work it all out in my head. Right at 5:30, I pulled in Amy's drive way, and turned off the engine. But before I could get out of the car, Amy came barreling out of the house, skipped across the drive way, got in, and grinned big at me.

"Let's go. I'm starvin'."

Since I was always hungry, I backed out of the driveway and pointed the Corvair towards Wilson's Restaurant. I'd decided I was going to have to be patient and let her do the talking, because if she figured out I wanted information out of her, there was no telling what she'd make up. And besides, she liked to do most of the talking anyway.

"Cubby, have you ever been to Washington? It's a beautiful place, an' there's people ever'where, goin' somewhere an' doin' somethin'. Ever'body looks like they're real important, an' they're all dressed up like they're goin' to church all the time.

"An' the buildin's are huge. We went to see the Capitol an' got a tour, an' we saw the Smithsonian museums, an' the White House an' the Treasury buildin', an' the FBI buildin', an' the Supreme Court an' all sorts of places. My favorite was the Library of Congress. You'd-a loved that place, there was books ever'where.

"One afternoon, we went over to Arlington Cemetery an' looked at the Eternal Flame on Kennedy's grave, an' saw the Unknown Soldier monument an' all the crosses that's there.

"An' on the way back home, we stopped at Mount Vernon, where Washington lived…."

I was afraid not to listen to her, because I thought she might say something important at some point. I didn't block her out like I usually did. I just let her talk—all the way to the parking lot at the restaurant. She quieted down when we got to the door, but just till we found a booth way in the back, away from everybody else.

After we put our order in, and while she was sucking some Coca-Cola through a straw, and couldn't talk with her mouth full, I reached across the table and took hold of her wrists, looked straight through the lens of the granny glasses into her eyes, and asked her, straight out, "Alright Amy… Tell me what happened?"

She swallowed the Coke she'd sucked up, leaned forward in the seat, and started in again.

"Cubby, you wouldn't believe it. When Randy got on the bus, he walked straight to where I was sittin', an' sat down right next to me. At first, when he started talkin', he wouldn't look at me, like he was embarrassed or afraid or somethin'. But he said right off he realized he'd messed up, an' he was sorry for breakin' up with me.

"He said he got scared that we were gonna get too involved—can you believe that? Gonna get too involved?

"Then he looked right at me an' said that he'd been miserable ever' since, an' that he couldn't think of anything else but me… Can you believe it??"

NO… I couldn't believe it. There she sat, with the keys to my entire future! And all she could think of was that damn fart-head Randy!!

I took a deep breath to calm myself, counted to ten, and made a conscious effort to not reach up and slap the shit out of her right on the spot. Then I started... slow, and soft.

"Amy... I'm really happy for ya. An' I hope you an' Randy have a long life together. But right now, I don't give a cracker's crap about you an' Randy... I need to know if Angel an' Carrie Ann talked."

It took a second or two for it to register in her tiny brain, but she finally figured out what I was getting at.

"Well, how the hell am I supposed to know? I spent the whole time with Randy."

"Damn it Amy... You were supposed to be watchin' out for me... You promised me you'd be sure to keep 'em separated."

She saw how torn up I was, and sat back in the booth while the waitress set our plates on the table.

"I'm sorry Cubby... I just thought you'd be happy for me..."

"I am... But I called Angel a little while ago, to go see her, an' she put me off till tomorrow night. Said she was too tired to go ridin' around."

"Well honey, she probably is tired. I'm wore out myself. But after I blubbered all over you when Randy broke up with me, I thought I needed to tell ya the good news... an' let you know that you're off the hook to marry me later on."

I rearranged a couple of fries on the plate with my fork, stabbed one that was dripping ketchup, and put it in my mouth.

"Cubby... I'm sure they talked to one another, but they didn't have time to have no big, long conversation. An' I know there waddn't no cat fight between 'em. More 'n likely, your name probably never came up."

I salted my fries again, and reached over to her plate for the onion slice she'd taken off her burger and added it to mine. Amy continued to make comments, trying to make me feel better while we ate. But I didn't have much of an appetite, and I still felt like there was something hanging over my head, waiting to drop.

We paid our check and got back in the car, but as we started to pull out of the parking lot onto Main Street, I had to wait for a tan Pontiac to get past us.

"Who was that?"

"Where?" Amy leaned up and looked left and right.

"Drivin' that tan car?"

"I didn't see. Why?"

"I swear that looked like Paddy Leary... Is he back in town?"

"Not that I know of. I never heard anything from him about comin' back here."

I'd started to pull out onto Main Street, but stomped the brake, and looked straight at her.

"Whatta ya mean you never heard anything?"

"In his letters... Me an' Paddy wrote back an' forth for a while after he went to the Army. We kep' it up even after he went overseas, but the letters stopped comin' after a while. Didn't you know that?"

"Hell no, I didn't know it. An' I don't think anybody else knows it neither... Did ya write him back?"

"Well, yeah."

"Damn Amy. You know he went to the Army to keep from goin' to jail, don't cha?"

"I know Cubby. But Paddy ain't really bad. He just had it rough growin' up. It's not like he killed anybody... least-ways not while he was here. He needed a friend, an' I guess I got elected."

Main Street cleared, and I pulled out, feeling a little protective again, wondering if Paddy was back or if I just imagined it.

On the way to her house Amy fiddled with the radio and didn't mention Paddy any more. Neil Diamond was singing *Sweet Caroline* as we pulled back in her drive way, and we both sat and listened to the song, before I shut off the engine.

She started to reach for the door handle, but turned and grabbed my arm, then leaned over and kissed me on the cheek.

"What the hell was that for?"

"Cubby, I'm sorry I didn't watch out for ya any better. I just got all caught up in me an' Randy. I'm sure ever'thing's gonna be alright for ya. An' besides, I wanted to tell ya thanks."

She saw the puzzled look on my face.

"If it waddn't for you, Randy might not-a seen the light, an' we wouldn't be back together."

I leaned back against the car door, again with a curious look.

"Why's that?"

"He asked me one night about me an' you goin' to the prom. Tell the truth, I think he was jealous of ya."

That was a new one on me, and I couldn't help but grin.

Amy said thanks again, got out of the car and went in the house. I looked at my watch, and saw it was only 7:30, so I drove around for a while to see if Danny or Will was out and about, but never found either one of 'em.

And I looked again for the tan Pontiac we'd seen. If it really was Paddy Leary that was driving through town, I wanted to talk to him. We hadn't seen ole Paddy since they sent him off to the Army almost three years ago.

TWENTY

I got up early the next morning so I could finish up the mowing I'd promised, then sprayed off the Corvair before I got cleaned up.

At 6:00 on the button, I picked up Angel and we drove up to Townsend, stopping at a store on the way to get some Vienna sausages, pork n' beans and some drinks. Angel had brought a can opener, some plastic forks and a pack of soda crackers with her, and we drove up in the mountains till we came to a picnic area on the side of the road where nobody else was around.

On the drive up, she told me all about her trip to Washington, and for the most part, it was the same thing Amy had told me the night before, but with a few more details. I listened close, but Angel never mentioned any of the other kids on the trip.

So far, so good.

But while she was spreading out a table cloth and unpacking the cans out of the grocery poke, she glanced up at me, and softly said, "I got to meet your Carrie Ann on the trip."

Whatever it was that I'd been thinking was hanging over my head, collapsed all over me, and for a second I felt like I couldn't get my breath. I looked directly in her eyes before I spoke.

"Angel… she ain't my Carrie Ann. So you need to get that outta your head."

Angel looked up at me with troubled eyes.

"Are ya sure?"

I held out my arms to her and she set down the Coca-Cola can she was holding, came and sat in front of me on the picnic table bench I was straddling. She leaned her back against my chest and laid the side of her head against my cheek and I wrapped my arms around her and held her close. She was warm and soft, and holding her was the only thing I wanted to do right then.

"Angel... Right now it's me an' you. There ain't nobody else in my life... an' I ain't lookin' for nobody else."

She scooted back, snuggled in closer against my chest, and wrapped her arms around mine. For the next few minutes, we sat there hugging one another, watching the sun spots that peeked through the leaves, as they danced around on the table cloth, to the tune of a mountain breeze blowing through the trees.

After a while, we ate our picnic, and talked some more about her trip, and our senior year in school that was coming up, and about the upcoming football seasons at our schools. Just before the sun started setting, we cleaned up the picnic scraps and started back down the mountain so we could get through the worst of the curvy roads before it got pitch dark. By 9:00, just as the last of the sunset faded, we were snuggled up on her front porch swing, and that's where we stayed till I left.

She never mentioned Carrie Ann again, but I knew very well that green-eyed blond was still somewhere in the back of her mind—and truth be told, she was probably tucked back somewhere in mine too.

We went out again on Friday and Saturday nights for the next two weekends, and each time I was with her, I fell further and further under her spell. And I liked it.

So much for "slow and easy."

On the last day of July, Danny called asking if I'd heard about the body they'd found off the trail that went up to the Winter

Cave. He said some hiker stumbled across a dead girl, and all the Sheriff's boys and the state boys were working on it.

He came by and picked me up, and we rode to the jail to see if we could find out anything, but everybody was running around busy, so we didn't hear much. Only that it was a teenage girl, and given the condition of the body, she'd probably been there for a week or so.

They didn't have any idea who she was. There wasn't any identification on her. The only thing she had in her pocket was a poster about some kind of music concert up in New York and they were thinking she might be one of the hippies that hitch-hiked up and down the highways every now and then. They were sending the body to Knoxville to see if they could find out how she died, but because of the shape she was in, they weren't real hopeful of finding out much.

Me and Danny allowed that if we were wanting to hide something, the old logging trail up to Winter Cave would be a dang good place to hide it. The area was rough, about half way up the mountain off the road to Flat Ridge.

There was a great lookout half-way to the cave, where you could see the mountains. It was a little off the beaten track, and you had to be going to it to get there. But on clear days you could see dang near to the Cumberland Plateau, and even when it wasn't clear, the view would take your breath away.

It was probably a great place to hide something—like a body—since practically nobody in their right mind went on up to the cave. Because it was half collapsed right past the entrance, everybody from these parts knew it was dangerous.

We didn't hang around the jail too long, since there really wasn't a lot of information to get, and we headed home after about an hour.

Last year's football season had been pretty good, ending up with seven wins, two losses and one tie. But we thought we could do better, so long as Coach Little didn't sabotage us with his crazy ideas. Over the summer, most of the varsity guys had been going to the weight room, and doing some running so we'd be ready. But our biggest worry was the changes that Coach had made in the spring.

Me and Will and a couple of the other seniors tracked down Coach Little and tried to explain that we were much better suited to play power football, like what we'd been doing under Coach Quarters. But it looked like Coach Little had his own ideas. He told us he was making a few changes to what we'd done in the spring, but he wouldn't tell us exactly what. I figured we'd be finding out when two-a-days started.

Everybody that was going out for the team, showed up to draw equipment at the dressing room the second Friday in August. Lettermen from last year had dibs on the new pads and helmets, and the rest of the guys got the leftovers that were stored in the equipment room. Once everybody got outfitted, we all went out and sat on the bleachers for the first team meeting.

While the stapled pages of plays we were going to be working on got handed out, Coach Little told us again how we were going to outsmart the teams on our schedule. He said he knew some of us thought we ought to be playing the same as we did before, and if we kept that attitude, he'd find somebody else to play his kind of game. When he said it, he looked right at me and Will and the other guys that had talked to him earlier.

When he looked at us, I elbowed Will and we both sat up a little straighter. I think if anybody else had said something like that to us, we might have worried about it. But coming from a squirt with a squeaky voice, that I really thought I could break in half if I had a mind to—it didn't bother me even a little bit.

When he finished his speech, we filed out of the bleachers, onto the field, and started running. Before we could go home, the whole team had to do a fifty yard touch-and-go. Eleven of us at a time would start at the goal line, run to the ten yard line, touch it and then run back to the goal, touch it and run back to the twenty, then back to the goal, and so forth, touching the yard line on the field every ten yards, till we ran the full fifty, up and back.

After the whole damn team finished puking, we staggered into the dressing room, showered and went home.

Will dropped me off at my house and I barely made it to the couch in the den, my legs were so wobbly. I'd no more than got sat down when Mom hollered from the kitchen that I'd got a phone call while I was at practice. When I asked who it was, she walked to the door with a grin on her face that went ear to ear.

"It was Carrie Ann. I thought you might want to return that one."

"Reckon what she's wantin'?"

Mom gave me the evil eye, and said, "Ask again Cubby."

She was a stickler about proper speaking, and I was so tired I just fell back into 'mountain speak' without thinking. With a tinge of sarcasm, I repeated my question.

"I wonder what Carrie Ann is wanting, Mother?"

"That's better. I don't know, but she seemed anxious to talk with you. And given your history, I thought you might want to call her."

"Hmmm... I will, just not right now. The only thing I wanta do is get somethin' to eat an' go to bed."

By 8:30 I was out like a light, and slept through the night, till about 6:00 the next morning when I woke up with a cramp in my calf muscle. I walked it off, got a glass of orange juice, peed, and got right back in bed.

When I finally got up, I thought about looking for Danny, to see if he had any idea what Carrie Ann might be wanting, but he was nowhere to be found. The weather girl out of Knoxville said we might have rain moving in later on in the evening, so I didn't bother washing the car. Mom and Dad were gone out, so I fixed a sandwich and watched TV to kill time before my date with Angel.

Somewhere around 3:00, I heard car doors slam in the driveway. As he came in the door, Dad stopped and pulled my set of keys for the Corvair off the hook and tossed 'em to me.

"It's all yours now Cubby. I just finalized the deal with Candy Roberts for a pick-up truck. Since it's your senior year, an' it looks like you're gonna be drivin' back an' forth to Walland to see that girl, I figured we needed another vehicle."

I got the standard lecture again about being careful, and not getting too speedy and all. But it was worth it. The Corvair was mine, and I didn't have to ask permission to use it any more. Things were beginning to look up for me.

I picked up Angel at 6:00 and we drove to Maryville and split a pizza, talked about football and drove back to her front porch swing for a little snuggling time. I was still pretty tired though, so I was headed back home by 10:30.

The predicted rain set in early Sunday morning, and me and Danny sat in the balcony and played tic-tac-toe on the back of the church bulletin during the sermon. I told him about getting the car and we whispered back and forth some about football practice.

He told me he was going that afternoon to Walland to see Lisa. But as soon as he said it, lightning flashed and a big clap of thunder rolled past that shook the whole church. I wasn't sure if it was an omen or not, but I believe if I'd have been him, I'd have thought twice before I went to Walland.

I'd just finished helping clean up the dishes after Sunday lunch and was getting ready to settle in for rainy afternoon nap when the phone rung and I picked it up.

"Cubby, this is Carrie Ann."

When I heard her voice, all of a sudden I could practically feel her body up against mine, and I could smell the honeysuckle and baby powder, and the old feelings from before kind of flooded back.

"Oh… Hi… Mom told me you called, but I been sorta busy. What's goin' on?"

"Well… I kinda wanted to talk to ya. Uh… I know from before, how important this football season is to you an' Will, an' I wanted to tell ya somethin' I heard."

"OK…" She paused for a few seconds, like she was reconsidering whether to continue or not. But then went on.

"You know Dad played on the Lincoln team right after the war, an' he keeps up with what's goin' on. He rarely misses a game. I heard him talkin' to Mom the other night.

"Uh… How much do you'all know about the coach?"

"Just that he's a scrawny little snot that wants to do things his way without takin' into consideration what we're actually good at doin'… Why?"

"Well, apparently Dad an' some of the other guys that used to play, are thinkin' the same thing, an' they did some checkin' on him. Did you know Coach Little never played a single play of football in his life?

"He was a manager at the high school where he went, an' apparently he was a manager where he went to college. His degree is in phys-ed an' health, an' word is he took a bunch of classes in football coachin', but that's the extent of what he knows."

"Oh hell… That explains a lot of things…" I let my voice trail off and just sat there while it all soaked in.

"Are you still there?"

"Yeah… I'm sorry. I was thinkin'."

"Dad thinks that you'all should have a pretty good team with the guys that are returnin' this year. But he said all the old players are afraid Coach Little is gonna screw it all up."

"I'm thinkin' he might be right. Coach changed ever'thing we'd been doin' on offense an' we got our butt's whupped bad in the spring scrimmage game with Seymour. Me an' Will an' some of the other guys tried to talk to him over the summer, to get him to change things, but he kinda let us know last Friday when we drew equipment, that he was the one callin' the plays. I don't know how much we can do about it now, if we can do anything at all."

"Well… I just wanted to talk to ya, an' let ya know. The dances after the home games aren't too much fun when you'all have a bad game."

She paused, and the memories of holding her while we danced, brought a smile to my face. Then I got a panicky feeling that she was finished and about to hang up… and I didn't want her to.

But then, after a few seconds she went on.

"Other than what's goin' on with football, how's ever'thing goin' for ya?"

"Not too bad. I stayed pretty busy over the summer…"

"Yeah… Me too…" Another pause, and I was hoping she was searching for words like I was, so we could keep on talking.

"Well… Uh… I guess I'll see ya at school."

"Yeah… I'll, uh… I'll see ya at school. An' really… thanks again for callin'."

I wanted to keep talking to her. Actually, I wanted to get in the car and drive straight over to her house and put my arms around her. But instead, I just hung up the phone… and sat there thinking about her.

After a few minutes, I pulled myself together, and called Will, telling him everything Carrie Ann had told me. He agreed it explained a lot, but neither one of us could come up with anything we could do about it. We said we'd both think on it, and maybe we could figure out something.

On the national news that night, Huntly and Brinkley reported that the movie star Sharon Tate, coffee heiress Abigail Folger and several other rich and famous folks had been murdered at a house just outside of Los Angeles. The details were pretty sketchy, but the worst part of it was that Sharon Tate was pregnant, and the report said the scene looked like a slaughter house.

What the hell was the world coming to?

TWENTY-ONE

Monday morning we started two-a day practices for the next two weeks, getting ready for the Jamboree that was scheduled for August 22nd—which was also the first day of our senior year.

We were on the field at 8:00 and after exercises we split into two groups: backs and receivers with Coach Little, and the line with Coach Thompson, who was the basketball coach, doing double duty. I never knew what all the backs and receivers did, but the linemen started with conditioning drills: monkey-rolls, weaving around dummy pads set out, practice blocking and crap like that.

After about 45 minutes, we got a 10 minute water break and then they brought us all together in one group. We ran a few plays and half-speed scrimmaged with a defense in front of us for about an hour, then did a fifty-yard touch-and-go, and hit the showers. That went on morning and afternoon for eight days.

The news over the next weekend gave us reports about the thousands of hippies that had piled in on a farm for the Woodstock Rock Concert, up in New York somewhere. They showed pictures of kids everywhere, grooving to music done by all the rock groups we were hearing on the radio. Lots of people, lots of drugs, and lots of rock-'n-roll.

On Wednesday afternoon and Thursday morning of the second week, we ran through our plays in shorts and on Thursday afternoon they handed out the new game uniforms. They were beautiful.

We had white pants with a red and blue stripe up the side, red jerseys with blue and white UCLA stripes at the shoulders, and our name across the back in white letters and big white numbers. Right after practice Wednesday morning they took all our helmets to the body shop that did all of Candy Roberts' work, and had 'em painted midnight blue with a red stripe in between white stripes across the top. The combination was about the best looking football uniform I'd ever seen.

During two-a-days, we found out Coach Little might have listened to some of what we were trying to tell him. The line splits got narrowed down just a bit, from three to about two feet. And he changed to a two back set, instead of just keeping one half-back in the backfield. He also put in a couple of quick dive running plays. The passes were still all long routes though—none of the quick-ins across the middle and short throws in the flats that we were more suited for.

Walking through 'em, the plays appeared to be pretty simple. But then it would be another thing when an actual defense was coming full steam, trying to beat us to death.

August 22nd was the first day of our last year at Lincoln High School. I think we were all looking forward to getting on with it, but with a little bit of dread for what was on the other side.

At 8:30 the late bell rang, but nobody was in the halls to hear it. The whole student body was in the gym, juniors and seniors in the folding chairs set up on the floor, and sophomores and freshmen in the bleacher seats on the side. Principal Webster gave a big speech about us seniors being the last ones of the decade, and how we were expected to go out in the world when we graduated, and make everybody in Lincoln proud. It was all the standard horse shit they always said.

After Mr. Webster and the teachers finally quit talking, we filed out in the hall—seniors first—where home rooms were posted on sheets of paper, locked behind the glass that covered the bulletin boards. In home room, which was our first period class, the teacher took roll and gave out a list of classes. There were several subjects that the seniors were required to take, but depending on how many credits we'd built up over the last three years, we could choose a few elective courses.

Several of us already had thirteen course credits toward the sixteen we needed to graduate, so we just had three that we had to take. My required classes were World History, Geometry, and Senior English, and Will, Mary Beth, Danny and Amy all had the same kind of schedule. So, it looked like we were going to finish school together, the same way we started out.

Since me, Will and Danny were jocks, we only got to pick two electives, since we were pretty much required to keep athletic study hall in the sixth period slot.

The only reason we were there that Friday was to pick up our schedule of the required courses and get a list of elective classes that we'd have to turn in on Monday. When the bell rang at 11:00, we took all the papers we had to fill out and high-tailed it out of there.

It was a short day, and we were grateful for it. We had to get ready for the Jamboree.

Apparently Walland did such a bang-up job the year before, all the coaches decided to have the Jamboree there again. We drew the second quarter against Happy Valley, a team we'd whipped pretty bad in the '68 season, so we weren't too awful worried about beating 'em again.

Like before, the team gathered at the dressing room about 3:00 to get everything ready, had a pre-game snack around 5:00, got part-ways suited up and we were on the bus by quarter past 6:00. The thirty-minute ride was quiet, and we unloaded at the Walland High field just as Townsend and Tallassee were starting the first quarter.

By the time we got our shoulder pads on and did our warm up exercises, it was time for us to take the field for the second quarter.

We were the home team for our quarter, and our kick was received by Happy Valley's deep back on their twenty. He made a good fake left, then reversed field and ran up the right side line to the fifty, so we started the night giving em' really good field position.

On the first play from scrimmage, Happy Valley got set in a power-I formation and ran it right up the middle. Our defense was in a 5-2 set with a roving monster-back, but their guards went straight out to cut off the linebackers, and their entire backfield led the tailback through the hole, cleaning poor ole Charlie Nunn's clock.

Charlie was a 5 foot-8, 180 pound junior, getting his first start at nose-man, head-up on the center. Happy Valley's center hit him first pushing off his right shoulder, then the full back hit him with the power back following right behind. It sprung their running back for a twenty-three yard gain, and left poor Charlie laying in a heap on our forty-five—out colder'n a mackerel.

It took a few minutes for the trainers and coaches to make sure he wasn't dead, and carry him off the field. While they were taking care of Charlie, Coach Little paced up and down the sideline, talking to himself. About the time they got Charlie almost to our bench, I heard my name being called.

"Cubby!! Go in at nose-man!"

I was back behind the bench doing practice snaps with Kenny when I heard it, and I raised up and hollered, "What?"

The damn fool repeated it, telling me to go in on defense to take Charlie's place—at a position I'd never even practiced for.

With my helmet in my hand, I trotted up and told Coach just that. He looked like he was fixing to have a stroke, all red-faced and bulging eyes, and he grabbed my shoulder pad and shoved me onto the field screaming.

"We gotta get some beef in the middle, an' right now, you're it!! Get in there!!"

As I trotted out, I thought to myself that I really couldn't argue with his assessment. I was 6 foot-nothing and somewhere around 240 pounds... at least he had the part right about beefing up the middle.

So on the second play from scrimmage, Happy Valley had a first-and-ten on our twenty-seven, and their fans were going crazy. I don't think they did it to avoid me in the middle of the line, but the next play was a power sweep left, and then the same play to the right, but on both plays our defensive ends and outside linebackers stopped 'em. On third down, they threw an incomplete pass, and then tried a field goal kick that wasn't near long enough. We took over the ball on our twenty, got one first down, and then stalled out on our own forty and punted it back.

The rest of the quarter, both teams ran, passed and kicked to one another, and we ended our twelve minutes on the field with no score for either team. It was a total embarrassment.

We'd beat Happy Valley 28-0 last season, and there was no way they could have gotten that much better since then. And surely we hadn't got that much worse.

As we left the field, I saw Angel just outside the fence with the Walland team, watching us play. She was still the trainer for Walland, and was standing next to Coach Renfro. She looked right at me and smiled, and I nodded back to her. But there wasn't anything for me to be smiling about.

Like he did after the spring scrimmage with Seymour, Coach Little lit into the whole bus on the way home. Me and Will were sitting together, and I reckon both of us must have realized right then, it was going to be a long season.

TWENTY-TWO

_____

I was still in bed when Will called the next morning and laid out what he said he'd been up half the night thinking about.

Up front, I thought it was a cock-a-mamie idea, but he really thought we had to get several of the guys together and figure out what to do about the football team, or we'd regret it the rest of our lives. I pretty much agreed we needed to do something, but I had no idea what to do, or how to go about it.

After going through the spring and fall workouts with Coach Little, we were pretty dang sure that he didn't have a clue what actually playing football was all about. Sure, he might have some book knowledge, but there wasn't anything practical in it. And what Carrie Ann had told me just confirmed what we were thinking.

We set about calling a few of the starters, and told them to call some others and we'd meet that afternoon to try to figure it out. When we got to Wilson's Restaurant, we found out the whole dang team was apparently thinking the same way we were. The phone lines must have gotten pretty hot, because by 3:00 word spread, and the back room of the restaurant was completely full.

Since he'd been elected Team Captain, Will took over like he was Chairman of the Board. He laid out our situation, and asked if anybody disagreed. Nobody spoke up, except to tell him they thought he was on the right track.

Will said if we didn't make our own changes, he couldn't see where we'd win a single game, and that wasn't the way he wanted his senior season to go. A lot of heads nodded in agreement.

Will told the team he'd been looking over the play sheets we'd been given, and the way he had it figured, we could most likely keep the formations Coach Little had us running on offense, change up the blocking scheme a little, cut down on the splits in the line, and add a few wrinkles of our own. Since we didn't think Coach Little really knew all that much about football to start with, we might be able to pull it off, and he'd be none the wiser. And again, I saw heads nod.

We split up—backs on one side of the room, and line on the other side, with the defense guys helping point out where they thought the weak spots were. After going over the plays for a while, we realized we were going to have to actually do a walk through to work out the details, so we agreed to meet at Will's house the next afternoon. But before the meeting broke up, we all swore to keep what we were about to do, secret.

As me and Will walked to our cars, I asked him if he was sure we were doing the right thing. For all intents and purposes, we were essentially hi-jacking the team. He leaned up against the tailgate of his truck, crossed his arms and looked me in the eye.

"You ain't gettin' cold feet about this, are ya?"

"No. I reckon I'm with ya on this all the way. But if that little fart they hired for a coach figures it out, he might just throw us off the team. An' even if he don't figure out what we're doin', there's a good chance Coach Thompson might."

"Yeah… I thought about that… Might be we'll hafta have a little talk with him later on if we think he's gettin' wise."

I wasn't real sure what "havin' a little talk with him" might involve, but whatever it was, I figured we'd do it together. After thinking on it a few seconds, we left—him to get ready to go see Mary Beth, and me to see an Angel.

I'd made it a rule, not to talk too much football with Angel. Not that I didn't trust her, but I didn't want to put her in a position where she might know something about our team, or what we were doing, that could help out her own team. There just wasn't any need to put her in the middle like that. But, as soon as I picked her up, football—or at least the way the Lincoln team looked to be playing it—was the first thing out of her mouth.

"What's up with you guys? I'm no football genius or nothin', but I've been around Coach Renfro long enough to pick up a few things, an' Lincoln's just not doin' somethin' right."

I hated to think it was that obvious. I didn't tell her what we were planning to do to fix things, but I did say that several of us recognized there was a problem, and we were working on it. She nodded, to let me know she understood I wasn't going to talk about it, and that was the last said about football.

We both had a few other things on our minds.

We drove up in the mountains again, going this time back towards Lincoln. She held onto my hand when I wasn't shifting gears, and every now and then, she'd rub her thumb along the side of my hand, or I'd feel a slight squeeze. We sang along to the music on the radio, throwing in some harmony when we could.

Half-way up the mountain, I pulled into an over-look that opened up to let us see the blue-grey ridges that stretched to the south-west. We got out and sat on the front of the car, with our arms around one another, and watched the sun as it hid behind clouds that dotted the sky. A few cars passed while we sat there, but none of 'em stopped. It was like we were the only two people in the world.

When the top of the sun finally dipped below the ridge, the horizon took on an orange glow just before the dark crowded out the last of the light.

I slid off of the car and turned to face her, leaned in close, and we kissed. It was a slow, long kiss, and by the time it was over, she'd slid off the hood of the car too, and we were standing with our arms around one another. I could feel the shape of her body pressed up against mine. She was soft and warm, and the feeling was something I couldn't describe.

I wanted her, and I think she felt the same way, because once our lips parted, she took a step away from me, looked down at her feet, and in her soft Angel voice, told me she thought we needed to head back to the swing on her front porch.

That wasn't exactly what I had in mind, and I mentioned that there sure weren't too many cars coming by… and we had a whole car all to ourselves…

I think she actually thought about it for a second, but when she shook her head, I knew it still wasn't the right time.

Damn slow and easy…

I called Angel after church the next afternoon, and we talked in low, soft voices to one another, till it was time for me to go to Will's and meet with the other guys to run through the plays we'd talked about. Driving out there, my mind sure wasn't on football.

Will had the mimeographed copy of our plays, with marks penciled in where we'd figured we needed to make changes, and he walked us through all the position sets, blocks, and runs. We had most of the starters on both offense and defense, and in the run-throughs when we saw something that didn't work, we all threw in our suggestions to try and fix it.

Single blocks turned into double-teams that could spring a run, and on long passes, he had the tight end release ten yards into the middle or out in the flats as a safety valve while the other receivers ran long. Splits between linemen got cheated in so we could help one another on blocking, and backs got blocking assignments instead of running off trying to fake out the defense.

The formations looked dang near the same, and every play we changed started out looking the same as what Coach Little's play sheets showed. We just did things a little different than what he'd told us, and we put a little more power in it.

By the time we were finished, we thought we might at least have a fighting chance.

Monday morning, I met up with Danny, Will, Amy, and Mary Beth in homeroom to start off the first full day of classes. We all had the same schedule for the first two classes of the day, then started splitting up. But when me and Will looked at our papers, we both had a gap for third period, right before lunch that we needed to fill with one of the elective classes. Problem was, there didn't appear to be anything offered that we could take.

The only classes we had to choose from were freshman Geography and Library Science—and we didn't even know what Library Science was.

But then we saw there was a Home-Economics class that period. Apparently the idea must have hit us both about the same time, and I reckon his grin was as big as mine.

The way we had it figured, they got to cook in Home-Ec, and we were both big on eating. And the class was full of girls that could give us a little help through the sewing parts, and stuff. And then, did I mention the class was full of girls? Sounded like it might just be a pretty good fit for us.

So, come third period we showed up at the door of the Home-Ec room. Only problem was, Mrs. Peeler, the Home-Ec teacher, wouldn't have it. First she asked what we thought we were doing there, then she pitched a duck-fit, telling us we couldn't take Home-Ec because we were boys. She said it just wasn't done.

When we told her there was nothing else on the schedule we could take, and it was our intention to stay, she took both of us by the arm, marched us out the door and took us straight to Principal Webster's office. She was still preaching at the top of her lungs to us when we got to the front of the office. Mr. Webster walked out of his door to see what all the commotion was about, and Mrs. Peeler started in saying she wasn't going to have boys in her class, and he was going to have to do something about it.

Me and Will stepped back some, watching the show and grinning, waiting to see who was going to win, and Mr. Webster was looking up at the ceiling—I think he was praying—while Mrs. Peeler gave him her sermon.

She was about to the invitation hymn part when we saw somebody in the Principal's office walk up to the door, and lean up against the door frame. He crossed one leg over the other and had his hands stuck in the pockets of his jeans. His dark hair was short, and he'd put on a little weight, but the grin was unmistakable.

Lo and behold, it was Paddy Leary, in the flesh.

TWENTY-THREE

We hadn't seen Paddy since our sophomore year, when they'd hauled him off to the jail in handcuffs. We knew he'd gone off to the Army, and he'd written Amy that they were sending his battalion to Viet Nam, but from there, we hadn't heard anything else. So me and Will scooted over to Paddy to shake hands and welcome him home.

"I see you two ain't changed none. Still doin' just enough to piss somebody off."

While Mr. Webster looked over our schedules, and Mrs. Peeler got to her benediction, we started firing off questions to Paddy so fast, the two of us sounded like Amy talking.

"How are ya?... When'd ya get back?... What 'cha doin' here?..."

But before he could answer, Mr. Webster came over, took us by the arms again, and started with us out the door. We looked over our shoulders, and Paddy waved us on, saying he'd catch up with us later.

Principal Webster escorted us down the hall, giving us his version of a sermon this time, saying he wasn't going to put up with our shenanigans this year. We tried protesting that we were only wanting to learn to cook, but he came right back at us, saying we weren't fooling him a bit, and he knew very well what we were doing. He marched us straight to the library, and had Mrs. Holiday sign us up for Library Science—whatever that was.

As it turned out, Library Science was learning about books, how to index 'em, and how to find stuff by looking in the card catalog and things like that. And as a bonus, there were several girls working in the library, so except for the lack of food, it looked like we were going to get what we wanted anyway.

Will wasn't real happy about it, since Mary Beth happened to be in the third period Home-Ec class. And I was disappointed that we weren't going to get to eat all the stuff that we'd learn to cook. But that's just the way it had to be.

We listened to Mrs. Holiday lecture all of us on how great a thing libraries were till third period let out. As soon as the bell rang, we put our notepapers and books in our lockers, walked to the lunchroom, and got in line to load our trays. I saw Danny, Amy and Mary Beth were already at a table close to the door, so after loading up with food, me and Will joined 'em.

I'd just started to dig into the country fried steak and gravy, when Paddy Leary got in the lunch line with his tray. I was still curious about what he was doing at school, and waved at him, but he apparently didn't see me. Paddy looked over the food on the serving line, shook his head and set his tray back in the stack. The last we saw of him, he was headed toward the door that went out to the smoker's corner.

Amy started off our lunch conversation that day asking why Mrs. Peeler wouldn't let me and Will be in the Home-Ec class. She thought it was downright sexist that boys weren't allowed, and said we needed to do a protest about it. I noticed Will didn't say a whole lot about it, and I kept my mouth shut and listened to Amy complain and try to rile everybody else up.

The bottom line was that we didn't really give a rat's ass about learning how to cook, or sew, or anything else—or at least I didn't. My motivation was being in a class full of girls, and I think that was Will's reasoning too, although I guess Mary Beth being in the class was part of it for him.

We let Amy wear herself out on the subject, basically ignoring everything she said and things got quiet for a few minutes, till Danny wondered out loud, more or less asking himself why Paddy was here at school.

Mary Beth commented that she wasn't real interested in getting all that friendly with him since it was her book that got set on fire and got him sent off before. But as was her way, Amy jumped in and took control.

"We ought not get so high an' mighty 'bout Paddy. He's had a rough life, an' can't be blamed entirely for what all he's got into. An' I'd like to hear what happened to him. I figured he'd write an' tell me if he was comin' home. But I hadn't heard nothin' from him for a while."

When she said that, everybody dropped their forks and turned to look at her. I just sat there and kept my mouth shut, since Amy had already told me.

"Whadda ya mean, you hadn't heard nothin'?"

Amy's cheeks turned a little redder, and I guess she realized she'd said something she didn't intend to.

"Well... You'all know Paddy wrote to me when he first got sent off to the Army. An' I told ever'body he'd got orders to go to Viet Nam.

"Well, we kept up writin', till about three months after he got over there, an' then the letters stopped comin'. I didn't know what happened to him, but I never saw anything in the papers 'bout him gettin' shot or nothin'. After a while, things got kinda busy, an'..."

Her voice kind of faded out for a second while we all looked at her.

"I just figured he didn't have anybody else to write to."

With that, Amy put a fork-full of mashed potatoes in her mouth and looked down at her plate.

I had Geometry fourth period with Coach Thompson as the teacher. Since math of any kind wasn't my strong suit, I was hoping for a little extra help from Coach to get through it. What I wasn't expecting was to have to think through my "Carrie Ann problem" again.

I spotted the back of her blond head as soon as I walked in the classroom, so being of good Baptist up-bringing, I purposely selected a desk in the back, close to the door. But Coach saw me slip in just as the bell rang, and made me move to a desk up front. And the only one with nobody in it was right in front of Carrie Ann.

She looked up at me and I nodded to her as I slid into the seat. But I caught the scent of honeysuckle and baby powder right off, and my mind started to wander a bit. I managed to get myself adjusted in the seat, opened up my notebook and did my best to keep my eyes to the front. But I don't rightly remember anything Coach said that day. The memories were too loud.

My fifth period class was typing, another elective for me. I figured I probably needed to learn how to do more than hunt and peck, and to tell the truth, once I saw who all was in the class, it was just what I needed to get my mind off of Carrie Ann.

Typing class was another one that was full of girls, and some of 'em were real lookers. I wasn't sure how much typing I was going to learn, but the possibility of that being my favorite class went to the top of my list.

After getting assigned a typewriter to share with a few of the girls in the class, and getting the workbook that told me where I was supposed to be keeping my fingers, the dang bell rang again, and I headed out to the last class of the day, athletic study hall. I can testify that seeing all the guys in there was a real let-down after the scenery I'd just left.

Coach Little was his usual ass-hole self, walking around, making sure we all had our nose in a book. I spent most of the period looking through my history book, and watching the clock, trying to will it to move faster. As soon as the bell rang, the school started emptying and me, Will and the rest of the team headed to the dressing room to suit up and get on the football field.

First up on our schedule, on the last Friday in August, was Eagleton, away. Lincoln had played Eagleton in years past, but the two teams hadn't played one another for a while, so we didn't know a whole lot about 'em. And after the poor showing at the Jamboree, I don't think folks in town had their expectations up too high. It looked like we were going into this one as the underdog.

Coach Little ragged on us all week in practice, and for the most part, we did what he told us. But we'd set up signals where Will or Kenny could holler out a color just before we got set in our stance, and we'd make adjustments to run the variations on the plays we'd made changes to. We had to really keep our minds on what we were doing, but we'd actually done it a couple of times in practice, and we were pretty sure Coach hadn't caught on to it.

On the bus ride down the mountain that Friday we were all a bundle of nerves, but looking forward to seeing if our plans were going to work. We won the coin toss and deferred, so on the first series, we played defense, and didn't do too bad. Eagleton took the kick-off and brought it back to their forty, then got a first down after running a sweep. After that, we got settled down and stopped 'em when they went for it on forth and a foot, and our offense took over on our thirty-one yard line.

Coach called a long pass for our first play, that dang near got intercepted, but their safety just knocked it away at the last second.

Our next play was supposed to be a draw up the middle, and the way Coach Little had it designed, it was supposed to look like another pass, with the backs running downfield to draw off the defense.

As we came to the line, I saw that Eagleton had gone into a 4-4 defense, and with the proper blocking scheme, it was set up perfect for us to make some good yardage up the middle. I heard Will holler, "Go Blue!" and just like we'd done in secret practice, as we went into our stance, the linemen cheated in on their splits.

On the second "Hut," I centered the ball to Kenny and our guards and tackles double-teamed the man in front of 'em, I moved out to block the left middle linebacker and Will came through the hole and hit the right linebacker. Kenny dropped back like he was going to pass, and then stuffed the ball in Johnny Holt's gut. With the blocking changes, Johnny sprung it for a twenty yard gain.

When the play was over, one of their defense backs was on the ground holding his ankle, so with an injury time-out called, Coach called us over to the sideline to get instructions for the next play. But as me and Will trotted over, I saw Coach Thompson grab Will by the face-mask and get up in his face.

"What the hell was that?"

Will's eyes cut over to me, standing next to him and I saw his face set. He looked at Coach Thompson with the meanest look I've ever seen, and spoke in a low voice that only Coach could hear.

"Just go with it right now. We'll talk when this is over."

Coach gave Will's face-mask a little shake before he let go, and stared back at him for a split second before replying.

"You're damn right we'll talk."

Coach apparently kept his mouth shut about it. For the rest of the game, every time we caught Eagleton set in a defensive alignment we could run against, Will would holler, "Go Blue!" and we'd run one of our modified plays.

Going into the fourth quarter, we had 'em tied 14-14, and we'd played to a standstill with two minutes left in the game.

Our offense drove down to Eagleton's fifteen, but couldn't push it any further and Coach called for Kenny to try for a field-goal to put us ahead. When the ball was snapped, their end came fast from the outside and made a dive for the ball just as Kenny's foot hit it. The kick was low, but luck was with us, and the ball hit the top of the cross-bar on the goal post and bounced over to give us a three point lead.

With a minute and ten seconds left, we kicked to them, gave 'em one first down, and then our defense held. We stopped their drive on our thirty-seven yard line and held on to get the win, 17-14.

Coach Little went crazy, and on the bus ride home, took all the credit, telling us it was proof his system worked, and the win was the evidence of it.

TWENTY-FOUR

_____

The bus ride was fairly quiet coming back, except for Coach Little breaking out with a war-whoop every now and then, celebrating his first win as a coach. We had to grin at it, since we thought the changes we'd snuck in were what carried us through. But we kept our mouths shut.

Me and Will looked for Coach Thompson in the dressing room, figuring he'd be wanting to have that talk with us, but didn't see him anywhere. So as soon as we got dressed, me, him and Kenny walked up to the parking lot together to head home. And there's where we found Coach Thompson, leaning up against the front of Will's truck with his arms crossed.

"Alright boys. I want to know what's goin' on?"

The three of us stood, side by side, like gunfighters ready for a shoot-out, looking at Coach, trying to size him up. Will decided to draw first.

"Coach, the way we see it, if you want to coach here or anywhere else, your future kinda depends on our success. Wins an' losses are what you're gonna be judged on. An' there's a few of us on this team that wanta go on to play on a college team, an' maybe get some scholarship help to pay for our education."

We saw Coach nod his head as he thought about it, so Will went on.

"After gettin' our ass handed to us at the scrimmage in the spring, we come to the conclusion that Coach Little's offense waddn't workin'. So we got together an' made a few minor changes to make it work."

"An' you didn't tell Coach Little?"

"We tried talkin' to him, but he just dug his heels in an' wouldn't even consider any changes. So the whole team got together an' worked out what we thought we needed to do—an' we done it. An' from what happened tonight, it looks like we mighta been right on the money."

Coach Thompson pushed off of the fender he'd been leaning against and took a threatening step towards us.

"Don't you guys know that Coach Little has political pull, an' if he figures out you've shanghaied his team, he could end whatever future plans any of you have for playin' college ball?"

"Yeah, we talked about that. But to tell the truth, we don't think he actually knows enough about football to recognize the changes. We thought you might figure it out, but we think there's somethin' in doin' this for all of us. That's why we're comin' clean with you now."

"Dad-gum it guys, you're playin' with fire here." He shook his head an' looked up at the light in the parkin' lot. "You're right about him not listenin' to anybody. I tried talkin' to him about makin' changes to better fit the personnel early on, but I didn't get anywhere either."

He leaned back up against the fender of the truck and thought about it for a few seconds more, then looked back at us.

"OK boys. I'm still not totally convinced, an' before I take a step that could end my career, I wanta know more. I've got a plannin' period the last hour of school, an' I want you three to come an' help me on Monday, an' maybe for a few days after that. An' you're gonna tell me ever'thing you're doin'. OK?"

He looked each of us in the eyes till he got a nod from us.

"And one more thing... What makes you think you can pull this off?"

Now it was my turn.

"Look around you Coach. The world's changin' ever'where. Young people are doin' whatever it takes to fix whatever's wrong. President Kennedy said it when he got swore in. The torch is passin' to a new generation."

Coach Thompson just looked at me like I'd shot his dog. After a few seconds he shook his head and muttered something about all of us fixing to get our nuts chopped off, and then told us to go home.

Figuring we'd dodged a bullet, we got in our cars and left.

I talked to Will and Kenny Saturday afternoon for a while and we agreed to get together at Will's again on Sunday to figure out what we'd be telling Coach Thompson.

Then I went to pick up Angel for our date.

We talked about the Lincoln-Eagleton game a little and she told me about how Walland whipped up on Seymour, and then we turned our attention to one another. It felt good to be with her, and I really didn't want to leave at 11:00 after the goodnight kiss she gave me.

I talked to Danny at Church the next day, filled him in on our meeting with Coach Thompson, and got his opinion on how to handle him. Then before going out to Will's, I called Angel, and re-lived the feeling of being with her, all over again.

For the most part, Monday went pretty good. I tried sizing up the girls that were in the library science class, listened to Amy yak about something or other while I ate a good lunch, then did my best to avoid Carrie Ann in geometry, before checking out the girls again in the typing class. Sixth period came fast, and it was time to meet Will and Kenny at Coach Thompson's room for our talk.

We tag-teamed the changes to the plays we'd come up with, explained how we'd got together at Will's to walk through everything, and how we were getting the signals to the rest of the team. By the time we got finished, Coach Thompson was throwing in suggestions to improve on our ideas.

We found out that Coach actually played football at the same school in North Carolina where Brad Main, Rocky's Chief Deputy, had played. But he liked basketball more, so that's what he got the coaching job for.

By the time the bell rang, signaling the end of the day, we had him hooked, and agreed that he might be needing our help with his "planning period" for a few more days.

Practice that Monday, and for the rest of the week went a lot smoother, with Coach Thompson giving instructions that fell right in with some of our changes, and we got a chance to actually practice at full speed, right under Coach Little's nose. I really don't think the little shrimp ever did figure out what we were doing.

Getting through football season wasn't going to be easy, but now that we had a co-conspirator in a high place, we had the feeling we might just make it.

What I was going to need help with though, was the geometry problem. At least that's what I called it. The problem wasn't with the class—it was a certain person in the class.

TWENTY-FIVE

Since the first day, when Coach made me move up and sit in front of Carrie Ann, I'd done my best to keep my wits about me. But the scent of honeysuckle and baby powder that drifted up from behind me, brought back some outstanding memories, and my resistance was beginning to fail me.

Before the first week was out, we'd started talking to one another, and by the second week, I was walking with her to the lockers, before heading to our next classes. Like it was the plague, we avoided talking about anything that had to do with our earlier relationship. She knew full well I was going out with Angel, and mentioned to me about meeting her on the church trip. She even told me to tell her 'hi' when I talked to her.

Now I might not be the sharpest pencil in the pack, and last year, the school guidance counselor had all but called me stupid. But knowing the wide streak of jealousy that ran through Angel, even I knew better than to mention Carrie Ann's name to her.

Things between me and Angel were going pretty good and I liked it that way. But I kept having green-eyed memories that kept interrupting things.

On the way home after a short pre-game practice on Thursday, WNOX radio news reported that Ho Chi Minh, the President of North Viet Nam, had died. 'Uncle Ho' had been steering the communist's boat throughout the war, and we thought there might be a possibility things would change without his leadership. But the Chinese were promising to keep supporting the North in the fight, and that probably made it more likely any kind of settlement on the war would keep being just out of reach.

That night, the Vonore Blue Devils came to Lincoln. The year before, we'd played 'em to a hard fought tie, and we knew we were in for a fight. But we had a good week of practice, and felt like we were ready for their kind of smash-mouth, power football.

Even though the calendar said September, summer was still hanging on, and at game-time the temperature was still in the high 80s. But there was a light breeze out of the north that held out some hope for fall. The stands on both sides were full and we could feel the tension surrounding our first home game.

We had a scouting report on Vonore and Coach Thompson had worked with the defense all week to get ready. From the first kick-off, the game was a pure defensive battle. Both sides ran their best plays, and would get a couple of first downs, but then the defenses would dig in and the drive would stall out. Even the plays we'd made changes to weren't working. For the most part, the whole game was played in the middle of the field.

With a little under four minutes to go in the fourth quarter, Vonore started a drive, pounding out yardage to our nine yard line. On first and goal, they threw an incomplete pass, and we stopped a sweep at the line of scrimmage on their second try. On third and goal at the nine, they ran a fade pass to their tight end, who was drifting to the corner of the end zone, but the throw was a little high and the receiver tipped the ball right into our cornerback's hands— and he dropped it.

Having gotten the closest they'd been all night to the goal line, Vonore wasn't going to go away without getting points on the board, and sent out their kicker to try a field goal. Coach Little called a time-out to try to freeze him, but when the kick was made, we could tell from the roar that came from the visitor's side, that it split the uprights.

We got the ball back with a little less than two minutes on the clock, and no time-outs. We did our best to move the ball down field, but we never got past the fifty when time ran out on us and we got handed our first defeat that year, 3-0.

In the dressing room, Coach Little gave us a royal ass chewing. We sat quiet, let him get it out of his system, and then headed for the showers.

Like they'd done over the past several years, the Letterman's Club sponsored an after-game dance in the school gym. I really wasn't in a mood to go, but Will insisted, so as soon as we got dressed, we walked up the hill to the main building.

The 'Jim-Tones,' a pretty decent band made up of local guys, were playing again this year, and we could hear the heavy bass beat of rock-'n-roll before we got to the door of the gym. It was dark inside and the only illumination was the flickering strobe and multi-color lights of the band.

We could barely make out who was who, but somehow Will was able to find Mary Beth, standing at the back of the crowd that surrounded the dance floor, and when she saw him, she threw her arms around his neck and gave him a big kiss. I didn't think that was much of a consolation for losing the game, but then, I wasn't the one getting kissed.

I stood at the edge of the dance floor while Will and Mary Beth were all snuggled up with one another, and saw Danny dancing with Jenny Wilton, still dressed in her cheer leading outfit. About the time I got my hand raised up to wave at him, I felt a tap on my shoulder, and turned around to look directly into the granny glasses perched on Amy Higgins' nose.

"You guys got shit stomped, huh…"

"Kiss my ass, Amy."

"Bare it."

"Ya know, you're gonna be real damn embarrassed some of these days if I do…"

"Cubby… You know as well as I do, you ain't never gonna do it… Besides, you had your chance to get in my pants, an' ya missed it… 'cause you're too sweet."

She knew damn well I hated being called 'sweet,' and she did it on purpose to get me riled up. But I wasn't in any mood to fight with her, and I turned back around to face the dance floor, waiting for the next song to start.

"Well hell… If you won't argue with me, dance with me." She took me by the hand and pulled me into the middle of the dance floor as the 'Jim-Tones' played the first notes of the Beatles ballad, "*That Boy*."

TWENTY-SIX

———————

Amy put her arms around my neck, I put my hands on each side of her waist, and we started to move in rhythm to the music. As usual, I wanted to sing along—but typical Amy, she wanted to talk.

"I thought maybe you'd figure out how to get Angel here?"

"Naw. Walland was playin' somebody way off, an' there waddn't no way."

"Uh-huh... So you thought you'd come an' check out some of the local talent?"

I leaned back and looked down at her.

"Again Amy... Kiss my ass."

She seemed to think about it for a few seconds while we moved around the floor, but then continued on.

"You know, there's somebody here that's been lookin' for you all night..."

"Yeah... Danny."

"Hell no. Not Danny... Carrie Ann's been watchin' the door for somebody ever' since we got here. An' when you walked in, she brightened up, so I figure you're the one she was lookin' for. Ya probably oughta go ask her to dance."

I thought about it for a second.

No—that's not exactly right. Being truthful, the thought had actually come to mind several times since I'd seen Carrie Ann at school, and she'd wished me good luck in the ballgame and said she'd see me at the dance afterward.

As the song ended, I looked down into Amy's glasses, and as casually as I could, said, "I'll think about it."

I looked around and saw Carrie Ann walk off the dance floor and sit with a bunch of other girls in the bleacher seats closest to the side door that went into the school. So I went in the other direction to the concession stand, and since I was parched, guzzled down a couple of Cokes.

I did my best to stay clear of her most of the night, waiting till she was dancing with somebody, before crossing over the floor to go into the school where the bathroom was. On one of my trips, I ran into Danny heading the same way.

Standing at the urinals, we talked a little about the ballgame and stuff. When he finished his business, he walked over to the window, zipping up his pants, and stood there, sniffing.

"What 'cha lookin' for?"

"Nothin' I guess. Just checkin' to see if the smell's stronger outside. Smells like somebody's burnin' leaves or somethin'... but sweeter."

I'd caught a whiff of something too, but it wasn't anything I could identify, and we couldn't see any smoke or anything burning through the slit of the windows that were slightly cracked. So we went back to the gym.

The 'Jim-Tones' were coming back up on stage after taking their last break, and were tuning their guitars to start the last set as I came through the door. I paused before going on into the gym and noticed that Carrie Ann wasn't sitting in her usual seat, then started across the floor to the other side of the gym. But I only got half way before I ran smack into her.

"Have you been avoidin' me?"

"Uh...Not on purpose..."

I lied. And I could tell by the look in her gorgeous green eyes, she knew I was lying.

"Looked like a really tough ballgame…"

"Yeah… Vonore's got a good team. We just couldn't get any offense goin'."

We stood there in front of the stage while Jimmy Dawkins, the band's lead singer, announced that this was going to be their last set, and they were going to slow it up some. The first chords of the Bee-Gee's song, "*To Love Somebody*," came through the speaker, and I held out my arms and asked if she wanted to dance.

She didn't say anything, but I got my reply when she took a step forward and put her arms around my shoulders. I put my arms around her and held her close.

Nothing much had changed. Our bodies fit together like pieces of a puzzle, and her form against mine was warm and soft. The fragrance of honeysuckle with a hint of baby powder made my head swirl, and I could hear my heart beating in my ears.

When the song ended, I stepped back, told her thanks, and walked back to where I'd been sitting. But the words kept ringing in my mind:

> *You don't know what it's like,*
> *Baby, you don't know what it's like…*
> *To love somebody,*
> *To love somebody…*
> *The way I love you.*

By the time I got to the other side of the gym, I felt like I couldn't breathe if I stayed there. I turned and walked out the door, got in my car—and left.

I drove around till almost midnight. I tried turning up the volume on the radio, but after a while I turned it off and listened to the whine of the engine, and the hum of the tires on the asphalt.

The words of the song kept playing in my head:

> *To love somebody,*

To love somebody,
The way I love you.

What the hell was wrong with me!

If I tried real hard, I could see Angel's dark, smoldering eyes, and hear the soft, slightly nasal sound of her Angel voice. I could feel her hand in mine, and the touch of her lips when we kissed. I loved the way she looked at me... like there wasn't anybody else in the world but the two of us.

But all it took was one dance... to hold Carrie Ann in my arms for only a few minutes... to feel the tickle of her hair as it brushed against my cheek... to look into her eyes and see the hint of freckles that ran across her nose and onto her cheeks... to smell the honeysuckle and baby powder...

All it took was one touch, and everything I'd felt before, I felt again. And feeling that way tore my heart in half.

TWENTY-SEVEN

———————

Sometime during the night, a front moved through and dropped enough rain to paint wet shadows around the cracks and make little puddles in all the low spots on the road. The front must have come out of the north-west, because the temperature dropped about ten degrees from what it was the day before, and 70 degree weather was a welcome relief.

At 6:00 sharp, Angel was waiting for me at the door, ran out and got in the car before I even had a chance to turn off the motor. As soon as she got the door closed, she leaned across the seat and gave me a quick kiss on the cheek.

"What was that for?"

Her eyes looked up toward the headliner and she reached for my hand.

"Just somethin' I've been thinkin' about all day," she said, grinning.

I pointed the Corvair toward Maryville and we sang along with the radio as the sun lowered in front of us. It didn't take long before we pulled in the stall at the Hum-Dinger Drive-In restaurant and put our order in. We ate and talked till it got dark, and then started back-tracking the way we got there.

I was happy, and Angel was happy. When I was with her, there was no yesterday.

By the time we pulled back into her driveway, to spend a little 'quality' time on the porch swing, it was on the dark side of dusk. Angel stepped in the front door to tell her folks we were back. She looked at me with a grin, and quickly reached inside and clicked off the porch light to give us a little privacy. Then she came running back to the swing.

The breeze was just cool enough to give us another reason to snuggle up close to one another. But it didn't take long before she steered the conversation to what she wanted to know.

"What'd ya do after the game?"

I couldn't lie to her, so I told her I walked up to the dance with Will.

"Did ya dance with anybody?"

"Yeah, a couple-a times. Amy grabbed me as soon as I walked in the door an' gave me a hard time over the game."

I'd discovered a while back that mentioning Amy didn't tip the balance on her jealousy scale. I'd told her too many times about what a dumb-ass Amy was. And besides, Angel knew her from before and had spent a few days with her on the church trip, getting to experience first-hand what a ding-dong she was.

I thought I'd dodged a bullet... but I apparently thought wrong.

"Did you dance with Carrie Ann?"

Awww, shit!! If I lied and Angel found out later, there'd be hell to pay. And if I told the truth, I knew I was fixing to fall off a steep cliff. But relationships couldn't be built on lies.

"One time... An' then I left."

In the blink of an eye, everything changed and I could feel the cold winds blowing through the canyons of hell. I felt her body shift slightly away from me, and a second later, Angel coughed into her hand.

"Cubby, I'm not feelin' too good an' I don't want to make you sick if I'm comin' down with somethin'... so you probably oughta go."

She stood up, and started for the front door, and I started to follow.

"No… You need to go… Really…"

Things that night had started out so good. And when she'd switched off the porch lights, the look on her face showed a whole lot of promise for things to come. And I had to go and screw it all up…

There was nothing else to do, but watch the screen door slam behind her. I turned and walked to my car, slowly backed out of the driveway and headed toward Lincoln.

I really thought I'd done the right thing—telling her the truth, that is. And despite all the thoughts I'd had about Carrie Ann since last night, after all was said and done, I kind of thought I was dang near a hero for having the will power to leave the dance when I did.

I figured I'd give Angel a little time to stew on it, and maybe even get Amy to call and talk to her.

I'd just started up the mountain heading home when my Corvair bucked and coughed the first time, but it smoothed out and ran another three or four hundred yards before the front-end started to nose dive and finally chugged to a stop. Luckily, there wasn't anybody behind me, so I pushed the shifter into neutral and let it roll back down hill, till I got to a wide spot on the shoulder and pulled completely off the road.

I tried the starter a couple of times, but it was no use. I definitely wasn't a mechanic, but I looked at the gauges on the dash anyway, to see if any of 'em were lit up. It was then, I noticed the needle on the gas gauge was below the empty mark.

I'd never run out of gas before. I slapped at the steering wheel, wondering what else could go wrong tonight.

I sat with my forehead between my hands on the steering wheel for a few minutes, trying to figure out what to do, and finally came to the understanding it wasn't anybody's fault but my own. And it was my place to get myself out of it.

I either had to walk to the closest house to find a phone, or try to hitch a ride on into Lincoln. Whichever, I figured I could call Danny, and we could get some gas and go back for my Corvair.

I'd just locked it up, and walked to the front of the car when I heard the deep throaty sound of a big engine, and saw the glow of headlights starting up the mountain. If I could flag down whoever it was, I might be able to catch a ride into town and find Danny.

As the headlights got closer and the engine got louder, I stepped over to the edge of the road and got ready to stick out my thumb, hoping I could get whoever it was to stop. But they roared on by.

Then I saw brake lights came on, the car skidded to a stop, and began backing up. As it got closer, I saw it was a light colored Pontiac, and I started walking to close the distance a little.

When the passenger door got even with me, I looked in the window to see who my chauffeur was. The one and only Paddy Leary grinned at me from behind the wheel.

TWENTY-EIGHT

"Cubby—what the hell are ya doin' out here?"

"Damn Paddy, am I glad to see you. I run outta gas. Can you give me a lift back to Lincoln? I'll find Danny an' get him to bring me back with a gas can."

"No problem. Get in."

The passenger door squeaked with metal on metal when I opened it, and as soon as I slammed it shut, Paddy shoved the T-handle Hurst shifter into first, popped the clutch, and squealed tires for about twenty yards to get us moving. It didn't take long till the wind was rushing through the open windows, and when I looked over at the speedometer, I saw we were already doing sixty-five on the narrow curvy road.

One of the switch-back curves going up the mountain was coming up and on instinct, I braced my feet against the floorboard and reached out for the dash.

"Damn Cubby, you're as skiddish as that hippy girl I picked up comin' outta Nashville was. You need to chill out."

Paddy chuckled to himself and down-shifted, nosing the big Pontiac into the inside of the curve, sliding through it with ease and then steering us back onto the right side of the road.

"Where'd you learn to drive like that?"

"Hell, I've been drivin' since I was fourteen. Back then, I run a few loads of 'shine down to Knoxville for a couple of the boys that hung around Ridgetop where Daddy worked. I had to know how to drive to get the load delivered, an' I made some good money for it."

It was pretty obvious he knew what he was doing, because he slid through the next switch-back curve the same way. I figured he'd made it this long, so I was probably safe and I relaxed a little—but it was a precious little.

Over the roar of the engine, I asked, "Who was the girl?"

"I never got her name. Said she was tryin' to get to some concert in New York, an' then she went to sleep on me this side-a Lebanon. Bitch woke up just before we got to Knoxville an' started askin' questions about my hair. That 'uz back a few months ago, right after I got discharged, when it was still pretty short.

"When she found out I'd just got back from 'Nam, she called me a baby killer an' spit on me... Can you believe that? I give her a ride all that way, an' the little bitch spit on me."

"What'd ya do?"

He hesitated for a second and glanced over at me before looking back to the road.

"Hell... I... uh... I set her ass out somewhere around malfunction junction, told her to have a nice concert, an' drove off. Damn hippies ain't got no idea what's goin' on over there."

"Whatta ya mean?"

We'd got to a fairly straight part of the road, and Paddy looked over at me again, as if to decide whether to answer or not.

"The Army taught me two things, Cubby. How to peel potatoes an' how to kill Charlie. Problem was, a lotta the time ya couldn't tell who was Charlie, an' who waddn't."

Paddy hesitated again for a few seconds, and then decided to keep on talking.

"We'd get a report about a village bein' controlled by VC, an' they'd send us in to clean 'em out. Most of the time the only thing there was broke down old men an' women an' kids, an' we'd figure all the actives had skipped out an' we'd start to relax. Then outta nowhere, the shit 'ud hit the fan. By the end of our tour, it got to the point where we didn't trust none of 'em."

After a second, I asked, "Reckon that's why they keep talking about civilian casualties?"

"That'd be my guess. We was sent over there to help 'em. But we didn't hafta be in-country long to find out we waddn't welcome. A lot of the natives wanted us outta there... in the worst way.

"Problem was, after a few times seein' guys gettin' tore up or killed, steppin' on mines or fallin' in holes full-a bungi stakes, ya start gettin' used to it, an' killin' don't mean nothin' no more. They shoot us, an' we shoot them. Simple as that."

Paddy's voice kind of trailed off, like he was talking to the air. He seemed to be wanting to talk, so I sat quiet and waited for him to go on.

"My bunk mate from Basic, all the way through AIT, was a black guy from Colorado named Lester Gold... just a year older 'n me. We landed at Tan Son Nhat together, were in the same infantry company, everything. About four months in-country, they dropped us in a hot LZ on a search an' destroy mission, just outside of a village that was supposed to be full of Charlie. But like usual, we didn't find nothin'.

"Intel took all the old men back behind a row of huts an' was talkin' to 'em, tryin' to find out where the bad guys went, an' we started givin' chocolate an' chewin' gum to some of the kids, tryin' to make friends. Lester was down on his knees, handin' out the shit, when another kid, not more'n ten year old come runnin' up. We all thought he was wantin' to get in on the giveaway.

"But he run up in front of Lester, reached behind his back an' come out with some kinda old revolver, an' put a bullet right under Lester's eye."

He paused for a second and lit another cigarette.

"Blew the whole back of his head off."

"Damn… What 'd ya do?"

"I didn't do nothin'—I froze—but the other guys in the squad that was standin' there, cut the kid in half with M-16's on full auto. I just stood there an' watched. All the kids scattered an' just left us standin' there."

Paddy's voice trailed off, and I could tell he was seeing it all over again in his head. As we passed the Lincoln City Limits sign, he cleared his throat, and came back to the here and now.

"Cubby… it ain't like nothin' you can imagine. When ya see shit like that over an' over, some guys just snap… an' shit happens. I ain't sayin' what happens is right. But I can understand it—if that makes any sense."

As we passed the Courthouse, I looked down the street and saw Danny's Chevy parked in front of his Daddy's Shell Station. Apparently Paddy saw it too, and he pulled in beside the Nova. Danny had an old towel out and was wiping the beads of water left over from the car wash, off of the hood of his car.

I leaned out the window, told Danny I needed him to take me and some gas back to my car, and turned to thank Paddy for the ride. As I started to open the door, Paddy reached out and grabbed my arm just above my wrist.

"Cubby… I probably said more'n I should have to somebody that's straight as you are. But you was always nice to me—never looked down on me like I 'uz trash, like some others done… I'd appreciate it if you didn't say nothin' 'bout what I said."

"Not a problem Paddy. It's all between you an' me." I got out, and then stuck my head back in the window before he could pull out. "If you ever want to talk, let me know. I'll listen, an' it'll be just between us."

He nodded an' I thanked him again for the ride. Then he pulled the Pontiac back out onto Main Street, and drove off.

"What was that all about?" Danny asked, taking a last swipe at the water.

"Nothin'. Paddy was just jawin'. Where's a gas can? I want to get my car before some ass-hole runs over it in the dark."

TWENTY-NINE

On the way back down the mountain with the gas, I told Danny what happened with Angel when I admitted to her I'd danced with Carrie Ann. He just shook his head and told me that apparently I really was as dumb as I looked, because telling her was one of the stupidest things he'd ever heard. We went through all the possible plans to try and fix things, but never came up with any way that we could figure.

Danny said I really shouldn't fret over it, because from what he could see, it looked to him like Carrie Ann might be trying to make a move to get back together with me anyway. But that brought up a whole new set of problems to think on, so we talked that out too.

Being the worldly kind of person he was, Danny was full of all kinds of advice—not that any of it was any good. But he was full of it.

Danny never asked, and I never mentioned to him anything more about Paddy.

The next two games on the football schedule were Townsend away, and then Greenback at home. Since the first one was away, there wouldn't be a dance that week. But there was always the week after that we could look forward to.

When I got home from church the next day, I called to talk to Angel but her Mama said she was sick. I tried again later on that evening, but got the same answer, so I gave it up for the night.

When I walked into geometry class, Carrie Ann asked if everything was alright. She said I'd disappeared in a hurry the other night and wanted to be sure it wasn't anything she'd done. I told her it wasn't, that I was just tired from the ballgame. But for the rest of that week, I tried to keep my distance from her.

I finally got to talk to Angel on Wednesday, and I played it like she'd really been sick, and not just pissed off at me. She seemed a little stand-offish, but I called every night and things warmed up as the week went on.

Since she'd be traveling with Walland to their game, and we were playing at Townsend, we weren't going to see each other on Friday, and I started feeling better about things when she agreed to a date on Saturday.

We'd been able to handle Townsend pretty easy the year before, but with all the changes and since we'd be playing on their turf, we figured we'd be in for a battle. Friday came soon enough, and our bus pulled up to the field in a misty rain.

The game turned out to be mostly a defensive battle again. Both teams scored twice, but our advantage turned out to be Kenny's foot that night. He made both our point-after kicks, and they missed both of theirs, making the score at the end of regulation, 14-12. It was a messy win on a wet field, but a win was a win.

Saturday, I picked up Angel and we drove to Maryville, shared a pepperoni pizza and talked. The subject of Carrie Ann never came up, and by the time we got back to her house, I felt like things were almost back to normal. Once we got in the front porch swing, she made me forget all about Carrie Ann… and everything else for that matter.

The lead story on the national news on Tuesday was the announcement from the White House that they were bringing 35,000 troops home from the war. It looked like President Nixon's Vietnamization policy just might be working—either that or he was starting to buckle under the pressure of all the protests and draft card burnings and such.

That Friday, we had Greenback at home, and after the game, a Letterman's Club dance. It so happened that Walland had an open date, so Angel worked it out to catch a ride with some of the kids from Walland that were coming to watch our game, then stay for the dance, and I'd take her home. I knew Greenback was going to be a tough game, but I was really looking forward to the dance and being with Angel.

Practice that week was a bitch. Same as last year, Greenback was a power football team that flat-out ran over folks. Coach Thompson worked on our defense all week, shifting guys around on the line, and putting in all kinds of stunts and twists. Anything that might confuse their blocking and give us an edge. And for this game, we had to have more size in the defensive line so again, I got called to supply it.

Trying to plug up the middle, we ran a 5-2-Monster, and Coach stuck me in at the nose-man position, right over the center. And when we went to a 4-4 alignment, I moved to middle linebacker, but I pulled up tight to the line. In both formations, it was my job to stack up the middle and let the linebackers clean up anything that came in that direction. In practice, it seemed simple enough, but at game time, it might be another matter.

That Friday, the temperature was in the mid-70s and kept falling all night. The stands were full on both sides, and everybody was expecting a barn burner of a game. Greenback came into town undefeated with a 3-0 record, and we were 2 and 1. Even though they were favored by two touchdowns, we thought we were a pretty close match.

Greenback took the opening kick and in six plays—all runs—got two first downs, to our thirty-five. On second and four, Bobby Lloyd, our outside linebacker, caught their quarterback as he came around the end on a sweep, put his helmet on the ball and popped it loose. Josh Kent, our half-back on that side, picked it up on the bounce, and seeing nobody in front of him, ran like the hounds of hell were behind him, sixty-five yards for the first score. Kenny's kick for the point after was good and we went ahead 7-0.

On offense, either Kenny or Will was hollering "Go Blue!" about half the time as we came to the line, and when we ran those plays, we generally gained yardage. But when we stayed with Coach Little's scheme, Kenny and the rest of the backs took a beating. No matter what we did, it seemed like Greenback had a dad-gum wall of guys there waiting on us.

The defensive movement and stunts we'd put in just for this game must have confused their offense, because they played off balance the whole night. At the beginning of the fourth quarter, we were still up on 'em, 7-0. We just had to hold on for another twelve minutes to get the upset.

We beat each other half to death for the next eight minutes, with neither team making a first down. We'd run three plays, kick for field position, and they'd do the same thing.

Then with four minutes to go, our punter shanked the kick off toward the visitor's side. It bounced once on Greenback's thirty, their receiver picked the ball out of the air and tight-roped the sideline all the way in to score. But instead of kicking the point after, their Coach decided to go for two and the win.

With three minutes and change on the clock, we had to make our goal-line stand to stay on top. Coach Thompson signaled us to go into the 5-2, and I took my position at first on the center's nose, but as soon as he reached for the ball, I shifted to his left shoulder, and Charlie Nunn, who was playing the roving monster linebacker got in position right behind me. I watched the ball and the center's hands like a hawk, and when the muscles in his arms stiffened, I moved out of my stance at the same time the ball moved, and hit the center's left arm and shoulder. I think it was the fastest I'd ever moved.

My helmet and shoulder hit the center's arm about the same time he put the ball in the quarterback's hands—or at least he tried to put it in his hands. The timing was perfect to mess up the exchange, and the ball hit the ground the same time Charlie came over the top and plastered their quarterback, who was looking around trying to find the pigskin. Greenback's halfback jumped on the loose ball, but half a-dozen red jerseys piled on him, and their attempt to go ahead was stopped.

With the momentum going our way, we took their kick-off and in spite of everything they tried, they couldn't get the ball back. We made two first downs, stringing out the plays for as long as we could, and ran the clock out to hold on for the win, 7-6.

We'd pulled off the biggest upset of the season, but we were beat up and totally tuckered out.

And we still had a dance to go to…

THIRTY

In the dressing room, Coach Little strutted around like a banty rooster, again taking all the credit for the win. I saw Coach Thompson, leaned over against the wall, taking it all in, with his arms crossed and a sneer of a grin on his face. He knew very well that without the changes we'd made, we probably would have wound up with negative yardage. And to be truthful, I thought the win was pure luck. Both teams scored on fluke plays, ours on a fumble and their's because of a missed assignment on punt coverage.

We all just kept quiet, let Coach Little think what he wanted, got our showers and got dressed. We had other things on our minds. As tired and as bruised as we were, me and Will were kind of anxious to get to the dance.

By the time we got to the gym, they'd already been going for about forty-five minutes, and we could hear the music as we walked up the hill from the dressing room. We stood for a few seconds inside the doors to let our eyes adjust to the dark, and looked for Mary Beth and Angel, finally spotting 'em sitting in the bleacher seats on the right side of the gym floor. They were sitting with Amy of all people, who looked to be holding court.

Figuring we needed to rescue the girls from whatever Amy was lecturing about, we started toward where they were sitting. But didn't get far before Angel and Mary Beth saw us coming, and both ran over to meet us, leaving Amy sitting all by herself.

Angel flung her arms around me, giving me a big hug, and I've got to say, it was the best tackle I got all night. She asked me if I was alright, and said the game was one of the most exciting she'd ever seen. Being with her kind of perked me up, and gave me a warm feeling.

We walked back over to where Amy was, and sat down to talk. After playing the whole game, the simple act of sitting for a spell felt pretty good, but then talking was another matter. The music was so loud, we had to put our heads close so we could hear one another. At some point, Angel slipped her hand into mine. It was just the natural thing to do.

We didn't dance to too many of the faster songs that the 'Jim-Tones' played that night, but when the slow songs started, it was a grand opportunity to snuggle up close, and we took advantage of it. Angel would lay her head on my shoulder and put her arms around my neck, and together, we'd move in sync with the music.

I enjoyed watching everybody else to see who was dancing with who, and who they weren't dancing with. I figured it was a good thing to know. But as the night wore on, I caught myself looking a little too often to the other side of the gym, where Carrie Ann generally sat.

I don't think I was looking for her in particular, but I realized I was looking in that direction more than anywhere else. And once, I caught Carrie Ann looking back at me. She did a little half wave and I nodded to her, and then looked away. There was no way I could do more with Angel sitting right next to me.

I was certain that being with Angel that night was where I wanted to be. To hold her and feel her close to me was important, and was what should be. It bothered me that Carrie Ann continued to slip into my thoughts. I didn't understand why, but she did, and for some reason I couldn't help it.

Right after 11:00, Jimmy Dawkins announced that their next song would be the last one for the night, and they were going to do a new song they'd been working on by the Association, *Never My Love*. Angel held me close and I softly sang as we danced.

> *You ask me if there'll come a time*
> *When I'll grow tired of you...*
> *Never My Love...*
> *Never My Love.*

When it was over, we walked out of the gym, arm in arm to my car and drove back to Walland. On the way, she scooted over to the middle of the seat, and put her head on my shoulder. We held each other again for a few minutes at her door, and then Angel placed her hands on my cheeks, stood on her tip-toes and we kissed... a long, passionate kiss. Then, as our lips parted, she pulled my head slightly down, flicked out her tongue and licked the tip of my nose.

She grinned, said a quick good-night and slipped into the front door of her house, leaving me with a lot to think about on the drive up the mountain.

As I went through town on the way home, I saw Danny's car parked at the Jail, close to several County Cruisers and a couple of flat-bed trucks, stacked high with what at first glance, looked like brush. It was just a little after midnight, and I was tired, but my curiosity got the best of me, so I pulled in behind the Chevy and got out to see what was going on.

Danny was standing in front of the Jail with Mack Stephens and a couple of the other Deputies, but came over when he saw me.

"Whatta ya think of this?" he asked, pointing to the truck bed.

"Think of what?"

"While we was at the ballgame an' the dance tonight, Rocky's boys was out harvestin' a marijuana field. This is a bunch of drugs that'll never make it on the streets."

Danny was always proud of his big brother, but that night he was beaming. And I reckon, rightly so.

He told me somebody had called in a tip about a patch of dope still in the field about a mile off the Oak Creek Road. Once they found it, they staked it out to see who came around, hoping to catch whoever was tending it. But nobody ever showed up, so that night they went out and cut it down.

Some of the stalks that were stacked on the trucks were five or six feet long with a bunch of leaves on 'em, and me and Danny figured it was probably a whopping load of weed. Whoever had lost their crop, was for sure going to be pissed.

I didn't stay much longer after that. We agreed to talk again the next day, and I headed home to the bed.

The morning headlines on the Knoxville Journal said 'Nixon Cancels Draft.' But when we read on down in the story, it was just the draft calls for November and December. Two months' worth was a little encouraging, but the way our luck was going, they'd be sure to pick it back up after the first of the year.

Angel was going somewhere with her mother on a family thing that night, so I didn't have a date, and come to find out, Danny was at loose ends too. So we decided to run around and do some catching up, starting with supper at Wilson's Restaurant. We talked about him and Jenny, me and Angel, Will and Mary Beth, and even Amy and Randy, before we turned to other things.

When the subject of the confiscated marijuana came up, Danny leaned over the table to me and asked if I ever heard anybody say anything about who might have spiked the brownies at last year's Prom. We'd gone several months without talking about it, and with everything else going on, I'd shoved the whole thing to the back burner. But now that he brought it up, I thought it was kind of unusual for something like that to be kept so quiet.

With nothing else to do after we finished eating, we decided to go hang out at the Jail for a while. Happy Sims was working the Dispatch, and since it was fairly slow for a Saturday, he had some time to talk. They were all pretty excited about their haul the night before, and Happy mentioned that they weren't too awful worried about the good ole boys running moonshine any more—marijuana was the cash crop now.

Apparently the dirt and the temperatures here in the mountains were a pretty good match for growing the stuff, and all the lawmen had been put on alert to watch for growing fields in the hills. According to the state boys, some of it was still being brought in from outside, but more and more of the home-grown variety was showing up in the cities, particularly in college towns.

Happy said the state boys wanted all the locals to be looking for fields where the weed might be growing, and after harvesting season, to be watching for it to be transported. He mentioned again that dope was taking the place of moonshine, and probably some of the old 'shine runners were hauling marijuana now.

Something clicked in my head when he said that—but all the dots weren't hardly connecting at the time.

THIRTY-ONE

News about the Sheriff's Office cleaning out a field full of marijuana plants was all over the school on Monday, and it seemed like everybody had an opinion. Some said the weed was the first step to other drugs and had to be stomped out. Some said smoking dope wasn't any worse than drinking beer. I didn't know whether anybody was talking from experience, or just talking to sound cool. Whichever it was, it looked like we'd found one more thing to divide up over.

In geometry class, I spoke to Carrie Ann as I passed her on the way to my seat, and we talked for a couple of minutes before the bell rang. She asked how Angel was, and said she started to come over and speak to her, but then thought better of it. I was about to tell her I was glad she didn't, but Coach Thompson closed the door to start the class, so we had to get quiet.

Once Geometry was over, I started gathering up my papers and books, and when I turned around, Carrie Ann was standing in the aisle in front of me. The rest of the class was already at the back of the room going out the door, absorbed in their own lives, and weren't paying any attention to us. But Carrie Ann just stood there. When she cocked her head over and looked directly at me, her bangs fell over her forehead and brushed her eye lashes.

"Cubby… are ya happy?"

The question kind of caught me off-guard, and I didn't know what to say.

Just exactly what was she getting at? Was she wanting to know about football—or school—or life in general?

Or was she wanting to know about me and Angel?

And why the hell should she care? She certainly hadn't given a damn about how I'd felt before?

I had to go to the other side of the school to get to typing class, so I muttered a quick "I reckon." But she continued to stand in the aisle looking at me. As I stepped around her to get to the door, our bodies brushed against one another, and I could feel the tingle in my chest, and a lump in my throat.

On Wednesday, the national news was all about the opening day of trial for the "Chicago Seven." That's what they were calling the ringleaders that got all the protesters stirred up and got the riots started in Chicago at the Democratic Convention the year before.

I'd read the articles in the papers and magazines about it, and really couldn't figure out what it was they thought they were trying to accomplish, since there wasn't any way they could change what was happening at the convention. Even on the national stage, it was most likely already a done deal for Humphrey to get the nomination—same as it was when Candy Roberts ran the Republican nominating meetings right here at home.

Seemed to me the only thing they did was to tear up Chicago and give the rest of the country a reason to vote for Nixon.

The next two weeks of football should have been easy for us. On the last Friday in September, we'd be going to Lanier, and the next week, Happy Valley was coming to our house. If we could get by those two without anybody getting hurt or anything serious happening, we had an open date that would give us two weeks to rest up.

We'd beat Lanier last year by one touchdown at home, and figured they'd be laying for us when we got to their field. For the first quarter, we squared off pretty even, with neither team having any success. But halfway through the second period, their halfback broke through the line off tackle and ran forty yards for the first score of the game. They tacked on another touchdown in the third on a pass across the middle, and for the rest of the game we just pushed each other around.

The game ended with a loss for us, 14-0, and the evening ended with another ass chewing from Coach Little, this time pointing a finger at the guys he thought sucked—including me. I thought seriously about waiting on the little fart in the parking lot, and "discussing" my shortcomings with him. But after I cooled down some, I figured I didn't really want to spend time with the guys at the Jail.

But I tucked it back in my memory for later.

I looked forward to seeing Angel on Saturday, hoping she could sooth some of the hurt, both physical and emotional. But for some reason, when the night was over, I drove back home not feeling much of a change. Angel was sympathetic and all, but I didn't get the total support and TLC I was looking for. Maybe it was just me... but I left feeling cheated.

On Monday, as soon as we got on the practice field, Coach Little called me off to the side. I saw him swallow hard before he started talking, and look over to where Coach Thompson was standing, making sure he knew where his reinforcements were, in case he needed 'em. I outweighed Coach by a good 75 pounds and stood almost a head taller, and I glared down at him when he started talking.

"Cubby, I'm movin' you off the center position to play tackle on offense. I know that ain't what you wanna do, but I think we've got to get somebody else ready for next year… An' besides that, you need to learn you can't always get what you want…

"Best I can tell, you guys are doin' somethin' funny. I ain't figured out exactly what it is yet, but the team gathers around you. So I figure you're one of the ringleaders.

"Now, go report to Coach Thompson."

I made a feeble attempt to protest, reminding him the exchange between center and quarterback was something that had to be developed and practiced, and changing in the middle of the year purely was a stupid idea. In fact, I came right out and told him it was the most dumb-ass thing I'd ever heard of. And as for the team gathering around me to get instruction—I was the center, and the team huddle formed around the center! Where the hell did he think they were going to gather!!

I'd always been taught to have respect for authority, but this guy was a totally incompetent idiot. He was screwing up what should have been a good football team, and in the process, was screwing up our future.

There wasn't anybody else around—it was just me and him, standing on the side of the practice field, and I guess I just lost my head. When I told him he was a moron, he just glared at me.

"If ya don't like it, quit."

I stood there for a second, trying to keep my Irish under control.

"Coach, if you knew anything for sure, you'd kick me off the team. But ya can't do that, 'cause there ain't nothin' there. You're just tryin' to blame somebody else for your own shortcomin's, an' that somebody happens to be me.

"I ain't quittin' an' there ain't no way you can run me off. I'm gonna stay right here… an' I'm gonna be watchin' an' takin' notes on ever'thing you do. An' when the time comes, me an' you are gonna settle up."

Then I turned and trotted over to where the rest of the linemen were going through their drills.

Coach Thompson looked at me when I got to him.

"He thought you'd quit the team... Are ya?"

"Hell no."

"You know we've got to play this the way he wants. If he gets any proof of what you guys are doin'—an' what I've been doin' to help—we'll all be in trouble."

"Yep... I figured that one out... So I guess you need to show me what the difference is in a center an' a tackle, besides not centerin' the ball."

I was so pissed, I was shaking as I settled the helmet on my head and snapped the chin strap.

The rest of the week, I worked on learning the blocks and techniques at the tackle position. It was a little change from what I'd been doing for the last three years, but not all that much. I did find out Coach Little didn't have the guts to take me off of playing defense. At least Coach Thompson was able to salvage that for me.

Me, Will and Kenny got our heads together and talked over the whole mess, coming to the conclusion that we had to play it out for now. And later when I talked to Danny, he said the same thing.

I wasn't all that happy about it, but I couldn't do anything to change it.

Early Friday evening Happy Valley brought their team to Lincoln. We'd beat the crap out of 'em last year, but in the Jamboree at the first of this season, they played us to a 0-0 draw. Now that we had part of the season behind us, and we were gonna get four quarters against 'em, we thought surely we could find their weak spots, get some points on the board and outlast 'em.

Coach Little designed our practice all week around film from last year's game. We ran plays to beat last year's team—not the team we played in the Jamboree, even though we kept telling him they were doing different things this year.

When we got on the field on Friday night, in spite of everything we tried, nothing worked. Coach had moved up a sophomore, Lynn Polk, to take over at center, and he and Kenny had problems with the exchange all night. When they did get it right, we either screwed up something else, or Happy Valley's defense stood their ground and stopped us.

In the second quarter, we managed one score on a "Go Blue" call when Kenny dumped a quick pass over the middle to our tight end. He caught it right behind the linebackers and managed to run over their safety for a fifteen yard score. But that was all we could muster for the night, and when the last whistle blew, we were on the losing end one more time, 21-7.

Of course we got the usual reaming out in the dressing room. Coach Little called us everything but a football team, and I could see that more guys than me were getting pretty sick of being told what a bunch of losers we were.

Team morale was sagging to the lowest point I'd ever seen, but there wasn't anything we could do about it, unless we were willing to stage an open revolt. Of course, the way things were beginning to stack up, the possibility of that happening was growing. But it wasn't time yet.

When the little fart finally wore himself out, we got cleaned up and gladly left the depressing air that filled the dressing room.

I really wasn't in any mood to go to the Letterman's Club dance that night, but there was something I had to find out.

THIRTY-TWO

───────────

After Coach Little made the position changes—and we'd had our little 'discussion' at Monday's practice—my disposition was pretty rotten, and Carrie Ann must have picked up on it. All week, it seemed like dang near every time I turned around, she was standing there, and she made a point of trying to say the right things to make me feel better.

On Thursday, she told me she was planning to go to the dance after the game, and said she hoped I would be there. I told her I'd probably come by for a little while, but a lot depended on how the game went. Then on Friday, she managed to mention the dance several times, saying that I really needed to come up after the game. She said getting my mind off of what was going on would be good for me.

I'd called and talked to Angel that week, and told her a little about the changes Coach was making, and how I thought it was going to work against us, but she was no help at all. She'd listen for a while, but then change the subject to talk about how good a season they were having at Walland, and how great their team was, and how a couple of their seniors had already gotten letters from colleges about playing for 'em, and such. By the end of the week, I was sick of hearing it.

The dance had been going on for almost an hour by the time me, Will and Kenny walked in the back of the gym. The 'Jim-

Tones' had just finished up their cover of the Buckingham's song, *Don't You Care*, and the dance area was starting to clear while everybody waited to see what the next song was going to be.

Danny was leaned up against the wall at the back of the gym with his hands in his pockets, and when he saw us come in, pushed himself off the wall and started over. But on his first step, he got the heel of his penny-loafer caught in the slack of rolled up volleyball net that was laying in the floor, and almost fell on his face. He hopped twice on his right foot, shaking the net loose from his left shoe, and then did a complete 360 spin, catching his balance at the last minute. After everything else that'd gone to shit that night, his acrobatic stunt was welcome comic relief.

"Smooth move, Danny. That was pure grace." I told him when he got over to us.

"You guys took your damn sweet time gettin' here. I've had to dance 'bout ever' dance to keep all the girls busy while they was waitin' on ya. I finally had to hide back here in the back to get a little rest."

I glanced over at Will to make sure he wasn't wondering about whether Danny'd been dancing with Mary Beth or not. I don't think he was paying any attention at all. He was already on the hunt to find Mary Beth, finally sighting in on her sitting with Amy over on the right side of the gym, not far from the concession stand. Once he saw where she was, he headed her way, and I followed, thinking a cold Coke and some place to sit a spell might be just the thing I needed.

When she saw us coming toward 'em, Amy got up and intercepted me, pushing me onto the dance floor as the band started their version of Clarence Carter's *Slip Away*. And typical Amy, she talked through the whole thing.

"Come on... Will an' Mary Beth probably want some time, an' I wanta dance... So you're elected...

"Now, tell me what the hell is goin' on with the football team? You guys don't look like you could chew gum an' walk at the same time. Happy Valley whupped the hell out of ya."

I was about to spill the whole story to her, when out of the corner of my eye, I saw somebody moving down the bleachers really fast. I turned my head just in time to see Paddy Leary's fist bury itself in Wally Lawson's belly, bending him over and forcing him back into the doorway that went into the school. One quick punch was apparently all it took with Wally, since it was one quick punch from Danny at the Prom last year that did the trick. And it happened so fast, there weren't many people aware of anything going on.

But me and Amy saw it, and headed that way as quick as we could without attracting too much attention. I got in between Paddy and Wally, and kind of walked Paddy back a few steps while a couple of others hustled Wally out into the hall.

"What the hell's goin' on Paddy?"

"That Wally guy's pretty much a ass-hole," he said as he looked past my shoulder, watching as they escorted Wally out the door.

"He was pickin' on Short Stack, an' I didn't think it was a fair match... So I evened up the odds some."

I glanced over to my right and saw Arch Kanally all red faced, standing with his fists bunched up, looking toward the door. He had the same 'go-to-hell' look on his face that Paddy did. And I knew Arch well enough to know that he wasn't about to take any crap.

Arch was one of the guys on the football team, although most wouldn't have thought it to look at him. He was just about five-foot five, and if you put a couple of ten pound weights in his pockets, he might go the 150 pounds the football program said he weighed. But his looks hid a little package of dynamite. He was tough as a pine knot, quick as a cat and strong as a little bull. I'd seen him side-step guys twice his size and jump right back to make a play on defense. And he had a mind that was sharp as a steel trap—especially when it came to football.

Problem was, because he was so small, the coaches overlooked him, and even though he was a junior and been on the team for three years, he only got called to go in for a couple of plays a game, and only then when we were way ahead or way behind. Coach Quarters never could remember his name, so he took to calling him 'Short Stack,' and it kind of stuck.

I glanced back to the table at the back door where the teachers and chaperones were sitting to see if any of 'em were headed our way, but they were still talking amongst themselves. Most likely, everything happened so fast, none of 'em even noticed, so I turned back to Paddy, thinking I might have to do some talking to cool things down some. But when I looked at him, I saw there was nothing I needed to do.

He ducked his head, stuck his hands in the pockets of his jeans, and then looked up at me with a grin on his face.

"Think you can take it from here, Cubby? I can't afford to get in no more trouble, so I think I'm gonna hit the road."

"Yeah... We're cool, Paddy?"

Arch stepped up beside me and stuck out his hand to Paddy.

"I appreciate your help, but I think I coulda taken him."

Paddy shook Arch's hand, and said, "Yeah, I'm sure ya coulda. But I don't like bullies pickin' on my friends...

"Well... I'm outta here. I'll catch you guys on the flip side."

With no more said about what had happened, Paddy turned and walked to the back of the gym past the table full of adults that were supposed to be watching us. Arch just shook his head and walked back to where he was sitting, leaving me wondering what just happened.

Either I said it out loud, or Carrie Ann was a dang mind reader, because when I turned back around, she was standing in front of me. She cocked her head over to the side, and matter-of-factly told me she'd seen the whole thing.

The front strands of her blond hair curled around her face and the way her bangs fell across her forehead and brushed the top of her eyelashes made my heart skip a beat, and for some reason I got an overpowering urge to touch her. She smiled, and in the dim light, I could make out faint traces of the freckles that ran across her nose and dotted her cheeks.

Without a shot fired, I was completely captured by her emerald green eyes. All of a sudden, the most important thing in the world to me, was to hold her.

I didn't know where the hell Amy was, and to tell the truth I really didn't care. The 'Jim-Tones' strummed the first chords of their version of *Walk Away Renee,* and I heard myself ask Carrie Ann to tell me all about what she'd seen—while we danced.

Between the volume of the music, the caress of her arms around my shoulders, the smell of honeysuckle and baby powder, her lips close to my ear, and her soft voice telling me what she'd seen, what I learned was mostly what I felt, not what I heard.

Seems to me I recollect something about Paddy sitting on the top row of the bleachers watching everybody... and something about Wally picking, and picking at Short Stack, till she reckoned, he'd taken about all he could take... and she saw Short Stack square off in front of Wally... and next thing anybody knew, Paddy came out of nowhere, punched Wally in the belly... and it was all over...

At least I think that's what she said.

To be honest, my thoughts weren't actually on Paddy, or Wally, or Short Stack, or anybody else... but her.

THIRTY-THREE

———————

My head was spinning with all kinds of thoughts. When the last notes of the song bounced off the ceiling of the gym, I took my arms from around her waist, thanked her, and stumbled back over to where Danny, Will and Mary Beth were. Apparently while I was dancing with Carrie Ann, Amy made her way back and was sitting next to Mary Beth, leaning forward with her chin cupped in her hand, and her elbow resting on her knee.

She held her tongue as I got closer, watching me all the way in, and finally spoke when I sat down next to her.

"Ya know Cubby… you're 'bout the biggest dumb-ass I've ever seen."

Danny was sitting in the row just in front of us, and when he heard Amy's comment, turned half way around, grinned at me, and added his two-cents.

"I told him the same thing. I reckon he's the only person in the whole damn school that don't know how bad eat up with the dumb-ass he is over that girl."

Mary Beth was nodding too, and when I looked at Will, he just shrugged his shoulders and gave me a pity look.

The band started playing *Kind of a Drag* by the Buckinghams, and I stood up, pulled Amy's hand out from under her chin, and drug her out on the dance floor.

And as I did it, I told all of 'em to kiss my ass.

I tried telling Amy all I was doing was getting information on what happened, that I was going out with Angel and doing just fine with things the way they were, and that me and Carrie Ann were just friends. But from the way she looked at me when I said it, I could tell she didn't believe me.

And honestly, I was having a hard time believing it myself. But I tried to keep that thought in my head anyway.

That night, I danced with Amy a couple more times, and even got Mary Beth out on the floor for a fast dance once. But the scent of honeysuckle lured me back to the other side of the gym a couple of times.

Along about 11:30, I was worn out—both from the ballgame and from dancing—and had already decided to sit out the last song. But as the band started the intro to *Don't Let the Sun Catch You Cryin'*, I saw Carrie Ann walking toward me.

She stopped at the bottom row of the bleachers, and motioned to me to come and dance. As if I was in a trance, I obediently stepped down to the gym floor, took her hand and walked with her to the edge of the dance area.

As we put our arms around each other, she laid her head over on my shoulder and again, our bodies came together perfectly. We moved slowly, our hips swaying in sync with the beat of the music. Holding… touching… Experiencing Carrie Ann for the brief time the music was playing was wonderous.

So why did I feel like such a piece of crap?

When the song was over I told her thanks, turned and made a bee-line out of the gym with everybody else. I didn't talk to anybody, and when I got to the car, I sat in the parking lot for a good fifteen minutes, till most everybody else had left, trying to figure out what was happening to me.

Then I drove home.

I picked up Angel the next afternoon, and we drove up in the mountains to look at the trees. As October began, oaks, maples and other hardwoods on the upper slopes of the ridges started turning all shades of yellow, red and orange, mixing with the dying green of summer. After sun set, we drove back to her house and spent a few hours in the dark, sitting on the porch swing.

We talked a little about football and the games our schools played the night before. When she asked if I went to the dance, I told her I went by for a few minutes and talked to Danny, but left pretty quick.

Flat out, I lied to her.

That night, I held Angel close, and I really tried—but something about it was different. I figured it was me feeling guilty about dancing with Carrie Ann and having to fib about it. I was sure that had to be it.

We talked about going out the next weekend, and Angel said Saturday would probably work, but she'd have to make sure about it. She'd be at the Walland game with the team on Friday night, but we had an open date, so I was free as a bird.

Danny picked me up the next morning for church, and he lectured me the whole time about following my heart. He told me I was going to have to be really careful to keep my head on straight if I was going to go out with two girls. I tried to tell him I had no intention of doing that because I was dating Angel, and me and Carrie Ann were just friends. I tried to explain that I might dance with other girls on occasion, but there wasn't anything to it.

He nodded, muttered, "Uh-huh," and looked at me like I was an idiot. It was the same look I'd gotten from Amy when I'd told her that Carrie Ann was just a friend.

The football team was tired, beat up and our morale was at rock bottom. By the second week in October, we sorely needed the open date, and hoped a week off would do some good to improve things for us. We had two weeks before we had to go up against Walland, and if we couldn't get some changes made, we all knew it was going to be a disaster. Coach Little reluctantly let us off from practice on Monday, and then ran us till our tongues hung out the rest of the week.

But truth be told, at that point in time, football was beginning to take a back seat to other things happening around me.

None of what we'd been taught as children was now just accepted as truth. Everything was being examined again to see what we believed and what we didn't.

The world around us was going to hell in a handbasket. Our country was fighting in the jungles of Viet Nam, trying to help folks that didn't appear to want our help. And we were fighting right here at home over whether we ought to be fighting over there. Men who were supposed to be our leaders, representing the will of the people, were telling us one thing, but the news reports were telling us the exact opposite.

Nothing we knew or were told could be accepted at face value.

If we were morally obligated to defend the freedom of people half-way around the world, what about our moral obligation to defend the freedom of people right here at home? What about the God given rights of black folks and the poor? Didn't they have a right to the same chances and opportunities that everybody else had?

Just because things had always been one way or another, didn't make it right. We could see the wrong in the world, and trying to make it right was tearing us apart.

It looked to me like all anybody wanted was the chance to be happy. Leastways, that's what I was looking for. And the battle going on inside my head was growing to a fever pitch.

Angel was precious to me. With her, there were times I felt a passion I'd never experienced before, and it was something I wanted to last. But there were other times when I felt a distance and a separation I couldn't explain.

And then, thoughts of Carrie Ann kept sneaking into my head—usually when I least expected 'em. I did my best to deny the way I felt and I tried to hide it all away. But I had to admit she had a grip on my heart I couldn't explain.

One thing was for sure—something was going to have to give.

I talked to Angel a few times during the week and we set a date to get pizza on Saturday. But since we had the open date, I was kind of at loose ends for Friday, because Angel would be traveling with the Walland team to Loudon, leaving me to my own devices.

I checked with Danny and Will to see if we could get up a poker game on Friday, but both of 'em already had dates planned. And I thought about making the trip to Loudon to watch the battle between two of the best coaches in East Tennessee. Coach Renfro and Coach Ratledge were both high school football legends, and seeing 'em square off against one another promised to be something to see. But I really didn't want to drive all that way by myself.

I'd just about decided I'd hang out at the Jail for a while, and then read or watch TV, but when I got to sixth-period study hall, Danny informed me his date got called off. When I asked about me and him driving over to watch the Walland-Loudon game, he jumped on it, and said he'd pick me up at 5:30.

THIRTY-FOUR

As expected, the game was a dang chess match, with the coaches directing their men this way and that, power driving one place and faking someplace else. I saw Angel on the sideline, taping ankles, patching up cuts and scrapes, and generally tending to the players, but the game was so close, I really didn't pay a lot of attention to what she was doing.

Walland and Loudon waged war against one another all night. Two minutes into the third quarter, Loudon went up by three after kicking a twenty yard field goal. Then in the fourth, both teams swapped touchdowns, but when the horn sounded at the end of regulation, the field goal turned out to be the winning difference and Loudon came out on top by three points.

Me and Danny mixed in with all the other fans and walked to the parking lot with the rest of the exhausted crowd to head home. Then as we were crossing the bridge just north of town, an idea came to me, and I told Danny I wanted to stop by Walland to see if Angel wanted a ride home.

He wasn't real thrilled about it, not liking the idea of being the third wheel that generally had been my position. But I shamed him into it, reminding him of all the times I'd gone with him. He kept protesting, saying he didn't think it was such a good idea to just show up without Angel knowing about it. But I'd already decided it was what I wanted to do, thinking she'd really appreciate the fact that I was thinking about her.

We took the long way home, and diddled around awhile, stopping at a market to get some donuts, allowing the Walland team bus plenty of time to get ahead of us. When we got to the school, the bus was there and we pulled into a back space in the parking lot where we could see people leaving the dressing room.

In groups of two or three, the team members came out, got in their cars and left while we were waiting. Then after about thirty minutes, we spotted Angel walk out, supporting a player on crutches, nursing a heavily wrapped ankle. She was carrying his gym bag, and I was thinking it was awful nice of her to be so helpful.

I started to reach for the door handle to get out of the car, but Danny must have seen something I didn't, because he grabbed my arm, and told me to sit real still. I'd heard that tone of voice from him before, and I'd long ago learned that when I heard it, it was time to listen to him. So we sat quiet, in the shadows at the back of the lot, and watched.

Angel walked with the guy to a new looking black Mustang, and opened the passenger door while he propped his backside up against the side of the car. Then, after she'd stuck the gym bag in the back seat, she stepped in front of him, and both of 'em looked toward the dressing room, to be sure nobody was watching.

When they decided the coast was clear... she stepped closer and wrapped her arms around his waist...

And they kissed...

Then she helped him settle into the car seat, bent and gently lifted his leg into the car.

Angel, tucked the crutches in next to him, closed the passenger side door, and never even looked around the parking lot. She got in the driver's side behind the wheel of the Mustang, adjusted the seat so her short legs could reach the pedals, started the car and drove off.

Me and Danny sat there in total silence. The only sound was the buzzing of the lights in the parking lot. He waited a few minutes, to be sure they were far enough ahead of us, then started up the Chevy, pulled on the headlights, and steered us toward Lincoln.

I reckon I was too shocked by what we'd just witnessed to be pissed off, and Danny knew better than to say anything. I listened to the roar of the Cherry Bomb muffler till we got to the turn-off onto the road up the mountain, before I finally broke the silence.

"Well... Shit..."

Danny looked over at me, I reckon to be sure I wasn't intending to open the door and jump out of the car. He waited a few seconds, and cleared his throat before saying anything.

"Cubby... Did you an' Angel have any kind of exclusive arrangement or anything?"

"Nope..."

"Well... Did ya have any idea she might be seein' anybody else?"

"Nope..."

"Hmmm... Kinda caught ya blindside, huh?"

"Yep..."

Seconds passed while he thought about the whole situation. "This pretty much makes ever'thing OK then."

I'd been watching the road ahead of us, but when he said that, I looked over at him.

"Whadda ya talkin' about?"

"Don't cha see, dumb-ass...? This makes it OK for you to make a play for Carrie Ann... An' now, ya don't have to sneak an' do it."

He stopped talking for a few seconds, concentrating on his driving skills as he down shifted and steered us into one of the switch-back curves.

"An' if you're intendin' to date both of 'em, now you've got the chance of havin' the best of both worlds... You are gonna keep seein' both of 'em, ain't cha?"

In all honesty, I hadn't been thinking about Carrie Ann. But now that he'd brought it up—after all we'd just seen—I figured it might be something I ought to consider.

"Well hell... I've already got a date set up with Angel tomorrow night. I don't know whether to call it off or what..."

Danny thought about it for only a few seconds.

"Cubby, looks to me like you've got a golden opportunity that's fell in your lap. An' besides... it ain't like you're in this situation with clean hands. I mean, after all, you're the one that's still got a thing for Carrie Ann..."

I started to protest again, but he cut me off.

"Now, you can keep on claimin' that shit about just bein' friends all ya want, but you're just foolin' yourself on that one. If ya really believe it, you're the only one that does, 'cause ever'body 'cept you, knows it. It's plain as the nose on your face."

As we drove up the mountain toward home, I sat and halfway listened to him jabber on while I thought about what we'd seen. I didn't hear all of what he said, but what I did hear, sort of made sense—in a Danny kind of way—although I should have known better than to listen to him since his track record wasn't anything to write home about. Just before I got out of the car at my house, he did say something I thought was pretty good advice.

"Cubby, I know you've gotta be pretty hurt over what happened tonight. An' after ya have time to think about it, you're gonna be really pissed. But ya need to listen to me on this... Don't do nothin' stupid. Ya need to go on your date with Angel tomorrow night like you don't know nothin's happened. See what she says an' how she acts... You'll know what to do."

I'd got Danny to promise not to say anything to anybody about what we'd seen. And I especially made him swear he wouldn't talk to Amy. She thought she knew how I ought to be living my life anyway, and I really didn't want to be giving her any gas to throw on the fire.

I couldn't sleep that night, and I did a lot of thinking. Danny was right about one thing—the more I thought about it, the madder I got. It took me most all the next day to get my Irish under control.

That evening, at the appointed time, I pulled into Angel's driveway. When she got in the car, she leaned over and gave me a quick peck on the cheek. Then she adjusted her fanny to get comfortable, turned the radio up, and asked about going to the Italian place in Maryville, saying she was hungry for spaghetti.

On the road, even though I was looking for some sign, I didn't see anything different from the way she'd always acted when we were together. It made me kind of wonder if she'd been seeing other guys all along, and I just hadn't realized it.

But now I did know.

I did my best to act like usual, but I reckon I maybe wasn't as talkative as I normally was. As we passed the Parkway Drive-in, coming into Maryville, Angel reached out, turned down the volume on the radio, and asked if anything was wrong.

"Nope… Just thinkin', I guess."

"You're sure?"

"Yep… Is there anything wrong with you?"

"No…"

"OK then. I reckon we're both good then, huh…"

Angel turned back around and sat quiet for a few seconds, looking out at the road in front of us. Then she shrugged her shoulders and turned the radio back up.

That was as close as we got to saying anything about what me and Danny had seen, or what was going on between the two of us, or what was going on between her and anybody else. The rest of the night wasn't really any different from any other date we'd ever had, and I left about 11:00, more mixed up than I was before.

THIRTY-FIVE

The next Friday night, Walland was coming to Lincoln and we started the week's practice reviewing films of their games with other opponents and then hit the field. We worked all week on how to defend against their offense, and how to beat some of the holes we thought we saw in their defense. It was a tough week.

Between the long workouts on the football field, then going home to finish up on any studying that wasn't finished in study hall, and with the days getting shorter all along, there just wasn't a lot of time for doing much else. I called and talked to Angel for a few minutes a couple of times, but what we had to say to one another was less and less every time.

I thought a lot about Angel, and what me and Danny had seen. And while I was at it, I came to realize that Carrie Ann was hovering in the recesses of those thoughts. While Danny probably had a point—that I wasn't coming into the situation with clean hands—at least I hadn't acted on what I might have been thinking. Hell, if we could be convicted on what we were thinking, the jails would be full and running over.

On top of everything else that was going on, that week started the two weeks of preparation for Homecoming, the week after our game with Walland. At Homecoming, seniors on the team traditionally escorted a candidate for Queen at halftime—and I definitely wasn't looking forward to it.

On Wednesday, we had to turn in the name of whatever girl it was we were going to escort. My problem was, I'd had my mind other places, and I hadn't given the whole thing a thought.

Will would escort Mary Beth of course. And the other seniors on the team had already asked several of the other girls to be their Queen candidate.

I was running out of time and I knew it. So I fell back on my old standard—the girl in our class I'd always more or less depended on—good ole Amy.

Tuesday night after practice, I called her up and asked if it was OK to turn her name in for me to escort for Homecoming Queen. I reckon I expected her to say OK, and she'd be thrilled about it. But I guess I just assumed too much, and when I asked, I pretty much got my title read clear.

"What the hell do you mean callin' me an' askin' somethin' like that at the last minute? You really do just take me for granted, don't-cha Cubby? You think I'll just drop ever'thing an' come runnin'? An' for what? A popularity contest? You don't give me a lick of respect!!"

In my mind's eye, I could see her pulling on her collar, like Rodney Dangerfield when he'd do his routine on Johnny Carson's show. Somewhere in the middle of her tirade, I tried to get in a word to defend myself, but she went right on like I wasn't even a part of the conversation.

Then all of a sudden, she stopped and asked what I was doing right then. I told her I'd just got home from practice.

"Well... I'll tell ya what. You go pile your ass in that little green car of yours, an' you drive it right over here to my house, an' you can ask me like a gentleman, an' then I'll consider it...

"An' besides that, I'm thinkin' you need a good talkin' to anyway. I'll be waitin' for ya on the carport, so get a move on. I'll see ya in a few minutes."

The phone clicked in my ear signaling that our conversation was over—for a little while. I knew, in my best interest, the only thing I could do was what she said to do. So I got my keys, and like a whipped pup, got in the Corvair and drove to her house.

When I pulled in her driveway, she was leaned up against the back end of her Momma's big Chrysler, with her arms crossed and a look on her face that told me I was fixing to get what for. I no more than got the car stopped, when she marched over, got in the passenger seat, and told me to start driving.

I could tell Amy was mad enough to spit nails, and I held my tongue, waiting for her to take the lead—which she was apt to do anyway. It took a few seconds for her to calm down enough to talk, and once she did, the flood gates opened.

"Lemme get this outta the way first.

"I wanna know what the hell you mean, suckin' back up to that little girl in Walland, after she stabbed ya in the back, bein' with somebody else?

"I mean… You saw her with your own eyes, an' ya still went right back an' took her out on a date? Damn Cubby… Where's your self-respect?"

I looked over at her and pulled the gear-shift down from third to fourth gear as we drove out the road towards Oak Creek.

"How the hell do you know about that?"

"Aw, shit… You know Danny MacMahan can't keep his mouth shut. An' besides, he's worried about ya. An' he knows full well I'm probably the only one that can help get ya straightened out."

I actually figured Danny would say something, and I figured he'd probably tell Amy at some point. But I was hoping he could hold out for at least a few more days before he set her loose on me.

"Damnation Amy. Danny's the ass-hole that told me I ought to keep goin' out with Angel. He said I needed to date her an' go out with other girls at the same time..."

"Do you not know better than to listen to him by now? Hell Cubby... Look at his track record. I'd take advice from a jack-ass before I'd take Danny's advice!!"

Looking at it that way, I had to admit she made a lot of sense. Of course, it really didn't occur to me at the time to question what her qualifications were to be giving advice. But then, that never stopped her before, and it didn't look like it was going to stop her now.

"You gotta cut your ties with that little girl. I don't care what it is she's doin' for ya... Ain't nobody worth losin' your self-respect over."

She stopped for a second, I reckon to finally get a breath, so I thought I'd get in something to defend myself.

"That'll leave me with nobody again—'cept you. An' no offense, 'cause you know I love ya dearly, but me an' you are more likely to kill one another. Besides, you've got Randy still on the hook, don't cha?"

Amy sighed big, and it was real obvious she was dang near disgusted with me.

"Cubby... I told ya the other night at the dance, that you were the biggest dumb-ass I'd ever seen. A blind man can see that you've still got feelin's for Carrie Ann. An' it's pretty damn obvious to me, that she's got feelin's for you. We hadn't figured out why exactly, but me an' Danny both think the two of ya deserve each other.

"Now... Do what I'm tellin' ya. Give it a chance with Carrie Ann. Stop bein' Angel's plaything. Open your eyes an' do it. You deserve to be happy."

By that time, I'd turned around in the Ridge Top parking lot and was fixing to pull out on the road and head back toward Lincoln. I told her I'd think about it, and thinking it might stop her from lecturing me some more, reached out to turn up the volume on the radio. It must have been off station, because all I heard was the crackle of static, so I turned it down and listened to the hum of the motor and the whine of the tires on the road.

As we passed the city limits sign, I heard Amy clear her throat, and thought she was going to launch in on me again. But instead, her voice was soft and meek.

"Now... What was it you wanted to ask me about?"

For the life of me, I couldn't think what it was, my head was swimming so.

"Uh... I don't remember..."

"Homecomin', you dumb-ass!!"

"Oh, yeah...

"Uh... Amy, will you do me the honor of allowin' me to escort ya as candidate for Homecomin' Queen?"

She shook her head like she was even more disgusted with me, but I could see the grin on her face out of the corner of my eye.

"Dear Lord... I don't know what you'd do without me. Yeah, I guess I'll do it."

Now it was my turn to twist the knife a little.

"You know if you win, you'll have to kiss me, right in front of ever'body sittin' in the stands..."

"Shit... Havin' to hold onto your arm an' walk out on the field's gonna be bad enough... Well, I don't reckon it'll make any difference. Just bein' your friend has already ruined my reputation. One kiss ain't gonna matter."

Wednesday turned out to be a big day that week. I turned in Amy's name at school and made it official that I'd be escorting her at Homecoming.

That night on the national news, Huntley and Brinkley reported that millions of students had walked out of classes at colleges all across the country to protest the war. They were calling it Viet Nam Moratorium Day.

THIRTY-SIX

In spite of everything we tried at the ballgame that Friday, Walland was up on us by ten points at half-time.

In the dressing room, we took our traditional ass chewing from Coach Little, and went back out to try to execute his game plan in the second half. But we got the same results as we had in the first half. When it was mercifully over, they'd whipped up on us by seventeen points, 27-10, and to tell the truth, I thought we were lucky to get out of it that easy.

I saw Angel over on the opposite sideline, but there wasn't any chance to speak to her, or even wave. We already had a date set for the next night, and for once, it was a date I really was not looking forward to. Even after hearing Amy's sermon, I still hadn't decided what I was going to do, or how I was going to go about it. But I knew I had to do something, and most likely it wasn't going to be pretty.

At the Letterman's Dance after the game, I danced with Amy a few times, and with a couple of other girls. And I danced with Carrie Ann a bunch, making sure I was close enough to get to her first when the 'Jim-Tones' played a slow number. Despite having lost the game, it was a fairly enjoyable night, and once we got to the dance, it went way too fast.

As they played the last notes of the last song of the night, I was pleasantly surprised when Carrie Ann raised her head off my shoulder, turned to look up at me, and asked if I could give her a ride home.

I could feel my insides shudder, and it took all the willpower I had to keep my imagination in check. I told her I'd be happy to oblige, to get her coat and I'd meet her at the door. I walked to the bleachers where I'd left my letter jacket, but Amy had already beat me to it, and was holding it out for me to put on. She never said a word, but there was no way to miss the grin on her face.

When we got to the parking lot, I unlocked and opened the door for Carrie Ann. She told me she thought my car was cute, and I realized that was the first time she'd been in it. I remembered thinking about going by to take her for a ride the night I got my driver's license, but at the time, we were on the outs, and the opportunity hadn't presented itself since.

It didn't take but a few minutes to drive the few blocks from school to her house, and I walked her to the front porch, where we'd stood so many times before. At the door, she turned to face me and thanked me for the ride.

Looking at her, in the shadows of the porch, I felt my insides melt. Instinctively, I reached up and brushed her hair off of her cheek. When I did, she took hold of my hand... and we stood there for a few seconds, looking into one another's eyes. Then I pulled her close, leaned down and kissed her... softly and passionately.

When our lips parted, she muttered something about seeing me at school, but I barely heard her.

I must have driven home on automatic pilot, because I don't remember stopping for any of the stop signs, or any of the cross streets or anything.

As I opened the car door to go in the house, a set of headlights pulled in the driveway behind me. Since it was almost midnight, I wondered who was calling at that time of night, and walked back as Danny rolled his window down.

"Where the hell've you been? We've been waitin' for dang near thirty minutes on ya."

I bent down to window level and saw Amy riding shotgun with him, and both of 'em had the damnedest 'told-ya-so' grins I'd ever seen.

"How 'bout both of ya kissin' my ass..."

I walked toward the house, trying to ignore 'em, but they were laughing so loud I could hear it over the roar of Danny's Cherry Bomb muffler as he backed out.

But it really didn't bother me—so long as they couldn't see the grin on my face.

Around 3:00 the next day, Angel called to tell me she had to go in to the training room to do a few things, and would be running late for our date. I started to say something to her right then, but instead told her I'd just pick her up at the school. She hesitated a few seconds, saying she didn't want me to go to any trouble. But I kind of insisted and told her it wouldn't be a problem, and I'd be at the school at 6:30—then hung up before she could object.

A little before 6:00, I backed my car into a spot next to the playground that was on the hill above the parking lot at Walland High School. I wasn't exactly trying to hide, but in the fading light, you had to really look hard past the big metal playground slide to see the car. I couldn't see the dressing room from where I was, but I could see any cars coming in or going out of the lot.

The more I'd thought about what Amy told me I needed to do, the more I thought I needed to bring this thing to a head. Part of me really didn't want to do it. Even knowing that she was carrying on behind my back, I still had special feelings for Angel. I don't know why, but there was a spot in my heart where I'd always hold memories of her.

But what Amy said about self-respect kept sticking in my throat. And I figured the time had come to clear it.

I didn't have to wait long before my suspicions were confirmed, and I watched as the black Mustang me and Danny had seen before, pulled up the hill from the direction of the football field, heading for the exit road. I glanced at the time and saw I had about fifteen minutes to wait. At twenty-five after, I turned the key on the Corvair, pushed the shifter into first, and drove down the hill to the dressing room.

I didn't have to wait long before Angel walked around the corner of the building. She waved and started toward the car, but as she did, I saw her eyes scanning the lot to be sure there weren't any other cars there.

As she shut the car door and I turned to back out of the parking space, I realized the time was right.

"What was it that was so important you had to do it tonight?"

"I had to re-tape one of the guys that got hurt last week at the Loudon game. He had a pretty bad ankle sprain. He's been keepin' it iced, an' last week Coach started him on some exercises to get it back up to strength. But we've got to keep it taped for the support, so he doesn't re-injure it."

"Is that the guy that drives the black Mustang?"

I saw her stiffened slightly, and knew I'd hit pay dirt.

"An' I guess you been helpin' him with his breathin' treatments too, huh… though I've never seen anybody doin' mouth-to-mouth standin' up."

"What're you talkin' about?"

"Me an' Danny went to the Loudon game. On our way back, I made him stop by here to see if we could give ya a ride home, an' both of us saw you walk the guy on crutches to his car. An' we saw ever'thing else too. I was just kinda wonderin' when you were gonna tell me about it?"

I heard Angel exhale and give a slight moan as she dropped her head and looked at her hands in her lap. I'd got to the exit road out of the lot by then, but instead of pulling out, I stopped, put the gear in neutral, and reached for the parking brake. I turned toward her in the seat… but she wouldn't look at me.

To her credit, she didn't deny it.

"Cubby… I don't know what to say to ya, 'cept… I'm sorry… It's just somethin' that happened."

There really wasn't anything she could say. I released the brake, engaged the gear and pulled out on the highway.

"Ain't much to say, darlin'… I'll take ya home."

Those five miles between the school and Angel's house were about the quietest five miles I believe I ever traveled. I think I heard her sniff a few times. But I don't know for sure, because I couldn't look over at her.

When I pulled in her driveway, she hesitated for a few seconds, then told me again she was sorry before she got out. I watched her long dark hair sway from side to side, as she ran to the porch.

I put the car in reverse, backed out on the road and turned toward the security of my mountains.

Even though I had what I thought was good reason this time to break it off with Angel, I didn't feel any better about it than when I'd done it before. I didn't want to see or talk to anybody right then, so after stopping at the Quick-Mart for a pack of cigarettes and a Coca-Cola, I continued on through Lincoln, took a right off the Oak Creek Road and drove up the mountain to the little church at Flat Ridge where Old Man Sharp was buried.

I sat in the parking lot next to the Church, wishing I'd had the foresight to score a couple of beers, and smoked dang near a whole pack of Lucky Strikes. The radio signals must have been bouncing off the atmosphere just right that night, because WLS-Clear Channel out of Chicago came in like I was sitting next door to the station. I stayed till about 10:30, thinking about everything that had happened between me and Angel—and what might have been.

And I thought about what all had happened between me and Carrie Ann, and wondered what the future might be.

And I listened to the disk-jockey, play rock-'n-roll from the big city that was far away from the mountain top where I was.

THIRTY-SEVEN

We only had three more games left in the 1969 football season. Since this was our last shot at it, a few of us were still hoping things might change so it could be a stepping stone to play in college. But that dream was drifting away like the smoke that rose off of the hills that surrounded us.

I don't think I ever will figure out what happened. We had some good, skilled guys on the team, and really, our schedule wasn't all that hard. We should have had a good year. Even with the changes Coach Little had made, we should have done better.

Coach's constant harping on us, telling us how bad we were, had us walking around hang-dog. But that was no excuse. With three wins and four losses so far, team morale was about as low as it could get, and for the most part, I could see that the guys just wanted to get through what was left and be done with it.

Of course, with all the troubles that were going on at colleges across the country, with the protesting, and marching, and all, finding a school to go on to after graduation wasn't looking too easy either. After Tricky Dick got elected promising he'd get us out of the war "with honor," we thought things might improve. But then he upped the ante by bombing the shit out of Cambodia.

He was starting to pull out a few of our boys and bring 'em home. But it appeared the troops that were still there were being left short-handed and vulnerable. There just wasn't a good answer. He was damned if he did, and damned if he didn't.

And it looked like I was in about as big a mess as the country was.

After Danny arranged for me to get back with Angel, I got to thinking things just might work out. And for a while, we had a good run. But now, that bridge appeared to be pretty much burned forever.

I had a feeling there might be a glimmer of maybe getting something going with Carrie Ann again. But then, that might just be my imagination. Carrie Ann had always been a mystery to me. I never did have any idea what was going on behind her green eyes. Was she just wanting to be good friends—or did she have something more in mind?

As far as I knew, nobody'd issued a set of instructions on how we were supposed to get through these times. I wished somebody would just tell me what to do. But then it came to me that maybe that was what friends were for. Danny and Amy were famous for telling me what I ought to do, and what I ought not do. Could be they were God's idea of an instruction book...

Naw... There wasn't any way God would allow things to be that screwed up.

Homecoming, I reckon, was some kind of big deal. Always before, at half-time of the Homecoming game, I'd been in the dressing room, chomping at the bit to get back on the field, trying to figure out what was taking so long. I'd tagged along for the festivities in the week before, and always had a good time at the bonfire and the pep rally and such. But all the whoop-la over crowning the Queen, really never registered with me.

On Monday before the game, the cheerleaders started posting signs and banners all over the halls, and they had a bonfire and pep rally planned for the Thursday night before the game. And this year, they were going to recognize some of the old players from past Lincoln football teams.

Danny's big brother Rocky, who was the High Sheriff of Andrew County, and his Chief Deputy Brad Main were two of the former players to be recognized. And I saw that Butch Mallory, Carrie Ann's Daddy, was also on the list. He'd played back in the late 40's, when they were still running the single-wing, and word was he was one hell of a football player back then.

But the Homecoming Queen announcement was the thing that got everybody fired up. I thought it was purely a popularity contest, and most bets were on Mary Beth Rivers getting the nod. But there was talk that since Will had sort of taken her out of circulation, she might not get it.

On Friday morning, the day of the game, the entire school voted in homeroom for Queen, and it was pretty much kept a secret till the announcement at half-time. I guess the whole process was fun for some of the girls, especially the ones that were friendly and outgoing. They gave away Halloween candy, flirted with all the guys, and had a good time with the whole thing.

But now, Amy was independent as a hog on ice about it. She declared it didn't make a bit of difference to her who got picked, and said she only agreed to do it to help me out. I thought the whole thing was a pain, but it was a tradition we were expected to do.

When she found out I was going to be escorting Amy, Carrie Ann made a point to find out if the two of us might be dating again. I thought it was pretty neat that nobody had still figured out the act that me and Amy had put on for the Prom the year before. But when I mentioned it to Amy, she wasn't too impressed that folks were still associating her with me. Carrie Ann seemed to be kind of relieved when I assured her me and Amy weren't dating, and I'd put her name up for Queen just because we were good friends.

I hemmed and hawed all week, trying to get up the courage to ask Carrie Ann to meet me after the game for the Homecoming Dance. I'd about run out of time when I spotted her at the bonfire on Thursday, and as casual as I could, asked if she had a date for the dance. I felt like I was standing in front of a firing squad, waiting for her answer.

When she said she didn't have a date, but was planning on being there, I stammered a little and asked if she'd wait for me at the dance. I explained I had to escort Amy in at the beginning, since I was escorting her for Queen, but after that, I'd really like to spend the evening with her. She grinned, looked down at the ground, then looked back up at me, and nodded her head.

I asked if I could give her a ride home after the bonfire that night, but she'd told her Daddy she was going to be with a bunch of other girls in her class, and if she showed up later on with me, she'd probably get in trouble.

I was a little disappointed, but as we stood there, listening to the cheerleaders trying to rouse everybody up, she reached her arm around my back, and I put my arm around her shoulders. We stood off to the side of the bonfire, holding one another, and watched the cinders climb toward the clouds.

Standing there arm in arm, the heat from the bonfire didn't hold a candle to the heat I felt inside.

Our opponent for Homecoming that year was Tallassee—a bunch we'd beat handily the year before. But the way our season was going, we couldn't take anything for granted.

At game time, the temperature was in the upper 50s with a cool, brisk breeze coming out of the north. It hadn't rained since we couldn't remember, and what grass was left on the field, crunched under our feet every time we took a step.

The Homecoming signs that had plastered the school halls were now tied up on the fence that ran all around the field, and the stands on our side were full of folks all decked out in the school colors of red, white and blue. Even though our season hadn't been anything to write home about, everybody stood up and gave us a rousing welcome when we came out on the field.

We returned the opening kick-off to the thirty yard line and on the first play, Will took a pitch around the right side for twenty yards to start a new set of downs at the fifty. The next two plays were runs through the line that gained us seven yards, leaving us with third and three to get a first.

Our running game was going good and we felt like we could punch out short yardage for a first down, but instead, Coach Little called a long pass to Marty Palmer, our wide receiver. That particular play hadn't worked all year, and none of us were expecting it to work this time. And we didn't have a 'Go Blue' play that was similar enough to run, so we were stuck with it.

When the ball was hiked, Kenny stepped up in the pocket, threw as far as he could, and lo and behold, ole Marty ran under the ball like he'd been doing it all along, and took it across the goal line for our first score of the night. We were all so shocked, it took us a few seconds to realize we had to run to that end of the field so Kenny could kick the extra point.

The rest of the first half went the same way. Our offense positively clicked and we scored two more times in the second quarter. Defensively, we held the Tallassee eleven to one touchdown. So we closed out the first half with a fourteen point lead.

As the rest of the team went to the dressing room, the senior players lined up on the sideline, to escort the Queen candidates. We had to wait while they recognized the old players, telling a little about each one, their position, and how their team did back in the old days, but it didn't take all that long.

Then, it was time to present the Homecoming Queen candidates. As each girl's name and her escort was announced over the loudspeaker, we walked arm-in-arm, onto the field and turned to face the stands. Amy whined because I was dirty and sweaty, but I have to admit she looked right good with her hair put up on top of her head, wearing a long navy blue dress, and holding the long stemmed rose that they gave to each one of the girls.

I'd actually voted for Amy, but she swore to me she'd voted for Mary Beth, so she wasn't too surprised when the drum roll ended and Mary Beth's name was called as the winner. They draped a Queen sash around her shoulder, and Will helped put the crown on her head before planting a big kiss on her mouth that brought all the fans to their feet, hollering and clapping.

I told Amy I was sorry she didn't get it, and she smacked me on the shoulder pads, told me we had one more official chore, and to get back to the ballgame.

We kicked off to start the second half, and the Tallassee receiver must have lost the ball in the lights, because he fumbled the reception, and a host of red jerseys jumped on it. Two plays later, on a "Go Blue" call, Will took the handoff on a dive off tackle for another score.

The rest of the game went the same way, and we got every break, finishing up with 28 points to Tallassee's 14 at the end of regulation. Of course, Coach Little took credit for the win. But we didn't have time to dawdle.

We cleaned up and dressed as quick as we could, heading for the gym and the Homecoming Dance. The Queen candidates were all waiting on their escorts, so they could be introduced and get the Homecoming Court's Dance out of the way, and get on with the night.

When they announced Amy's name, we walked to the dance floor, and I scanned the bleachers looking for Carrie Ann. It took a few seconds, but I spotted her sitting next to the door to the hall, where she usually sat, and nodded to her when she gave me a little wave and a smile.

As usual, there wasn't anything Amy didn't see—and when she caught me nodding to Carrie Ann, she slapped my arm, told me to pay attention, and then motioned over next to the refreshment room, where I spotted poor ole Randy Taylor, with a dumb-ass grin on his face.

When the music started, me and Amy put our arms around one another, and danced to the 'Jim-Tones' rendition of the Four Season's hit, *Can't Take My Eyes Off You.* But with every turn, both of us actually had our eyes on somebody else.

THIRTY-EIGHT

When the song ended, I bowed slightly and in an overly formal way, thanked Amy—then made a bee-line to where Carrie Ann was sitting, and I reckon Amy went straight to where Randy was. I never actually looked for her and Randy, and now that I think about it, I didn't see hide nor hair of either of 'em for the rest of the night. To tell the truth, I really don't remember seeing much of anybody else that night. Apparently, I must have been pretty focused elsewhere.

Carrie Ann was an absolute knock-out, and I couldn't keep my eyes off of her. She was wearing a red sweater over a white blouse and she fit really well in a pair of bell-bottom jeans. Her short blond hair seemed to glisten in the dimly lit gym, and the way her bangs hung, brushing the lashes of her beautiful green eyes, was downright alluring.

That night we talked and laughed in between dances. When the band played a slow number, and we got the chance to hold one another and snuggle up close, we made it a point to be one of the first couples on the gym floor. Each time I put my arms around her, I inhaled her scent of honeysuckle and baby powder like it was a drug. There was no doubt in my mind that I was hooked.

I knew very well we had a history that wasn't all that good. But that night, whatever was in the past between the two of us, and anything that might have happened with anybody else, didn't matter. Carrie Ann was the only girl I had eyes for, and the way things seemed to be going, I kind of thought she might be feeling the same way about me.

Somewhere around 11:30, the '*Jim-Tones*' announced the last dance of the night, and I heard the first notes of the 'Casinos' "*Then You Can Tell Me Goodbye*", a song we'd danced to the year before. The words captured my thoughts perfectly.

> "*Kiss me each morning, for a million years,*
> *Hold me each evening, at your side,*
> *Tell me you'll love me, for a million years,*
> *Then if it don't work out,*
> *Then if it don't work out,*
> *Then you can tell me, goodbye.*"

Like I said, me and Carrie Ann had some history, and I knew full well there was a chance it could all go up in flames again. But I was willing to take that chance just to get to hold her... and look into her eyes... and touch her face... and kiss her lips... just for a little while.

When we left the dance that night with all the others, we found each other's hands, and I thought to myself that I had to be one of the luckiest guys on earth.

As we pulled out of the parking lot, everything seemed to be right with the world. But then, Carrie Ann reached up and turned the radio off, looked over at me and in her soft, little girl voice, asked me about Angel.

"What about her?"

"Well... I know you an' her have been datin' for a while...

"Cubby... I don't have any interest in bein' the 'other girl.' An' the way things went tonight, I'm kinda gettin' the feelin' that you'd like for me an' you to be a little more than just friends... Or am I mis-readin' ever'thing?"

I had to take a deep breath to assure myself that what was happening, was what was happening.

"I'd say you're readin' it 'bout right...

"Carrie Ann... Things didn't work out with Angel, an' I won't be seein' her any more... An' yeah... If you want to... I'd really like to give me an' you another try."

Everything got quiet in the car as we pulled to the curb in front of her house and I heard the crunch of the leaves under the tires as the car rolled to a stop. I turned off the engine, and turned to look at her... hoping to get an answer.

She sat for a few seconds, looking out the window. I could feel my heart beating in my chest as I sat, waiting for some sign from her. Then she turned back to face me, reached and put her hand on the back of my neck, and pulled me to her.

As I recall, it took about thirty minutes for us to 'work things out' there in the front seat, before I walked her to the door where we again took a little while to say goodnight. All in all, it was a pretty good night.

The rest of the weekend was pretty good too. We had supper at Wilson's the next night, and talked for a long time. I would have preferred a little private time—just me and her. But honestly, I was happy just to talk.

Of course, I was a lot happier when we got back to her house, and we took a little of that private time saying goodnight.

With only two more games left to go in what was to that point, a tied-up, win-loss football season, I reckon it was just time for the wheels to come completely off the wagon. After Coach fussed at us all week in practice, on Halloween night we went to Wildwood and played 'em to a 7-7 tie for three quarters.

Two minutes into the fourth, on a play that had us spread all over the field, they blitzed what looked to be their entire team, and poor Kenny wound up on the bottom of a huge pile. He laid on the ground for a good five minutes with the coaches, trainers, and anybody that knew anything about injuries hovering over him, before anybody would even attempt to move him in order to figure out what part of him wasn't hurt. I'd played football for four years, and it was the first time I'd ever seen anybody hauled off in an ambulance.

After that we really fell apart. Joe Drake, who was the back-up quarterback, never got in a rhythm and he fumbled the exchange from center several times. Handoffs were completely haphazard, and we never completed another pass. Wildwood scored two more times, and we took another loss back home with us on the bus, and of course, we got another ass chewing.

We were all worried about Kenny, and I was in no mood to be told how bad at playing football I was. Will could tell my Irish was getting up, and got between me and Coach Little, shaking his head to tell me killing him wasn't the best idea I'd ever had. Since Will was one of the few people I actually listened to, I calmed down some, and we got cleaned up and drove to the hospital in Maryville.

The Doctors had already checked him over and said Kenny had a couple of cracked ribs and a separated shoulder, so they were going to keep him overnight and send him home the next day.

He was all wrapped and bandaged up, and they'd apparently already told him his season was over. When I heard it, I was actually a little jealous that he wouldn't have to listen to any more of the crap Coach Little kept handing out, and I think Will was probably thinking the same thing.

Me and Carrie Ann drove into Maryville to the walk-in theatre the next night to see Robert Redford and Paul Newman's new movie, *Butch Cassidy and the Sundance Kid*. The movie was pretty good, and having the chance to put my arm around her and snuggle close while we shared the popcorn made it even better.

The next morning I met Danny at church and we sat in our usual spot in the balcony. I have no recollection of what the sermon was about, because my mind was filled with the memory of the night before. For some reason, I kept thinking I needed to get forgiveness for some of the things I was thinking.

Later that afternoon, I talked to Carrie Ann on the phone, and then right after super, I called and checked on Kenny again. He said he was sore all over and he'd have to keep his throwing arm in a sling for a couple of weeks. They'd given him some pills to take the edge off, and he was supposed to stay in for a couple of days. But the Doctors thought he'd make a full recovery, and he should be back to school before the week was out.

In Geometry class on Monday, Coach Thompson told me to report to him during study hall, and he'd square it with Coach Little. To tell the truth, I had my attention focused on Carrie Ann's legs, so it was a wonder I remembered it.

Coach was sitting at his desk grading papers when I got there at the beginning of sixth period, but he looked up and set his red marking pen down when I walked in the door.

"Cubby, are you datin' Carrie Ann Mallory?"

I reckon just the thought of Carrie Ann put a smile on my face, and my grin answered his question.

"Well, that might explain why Coach Little's been comin' down so hard on you. Word is the School Board's been puttin' the screws to him over the way the season's been goin'. Apparently, the Board's gettin' pressure from a bunch of the alumni. An' from what I'm hearin', Butch Mallory is one of the ring leaders that's screamin' for Coach's head.

"We've only got one more game in the season, so for the rest of this week, you need to try to lay low an' stay out of his sights. An' you need to tell Carrie Ann to steer clear too.

"I've got a feelin' that Coach's job is hangin' by a thread right now. An' if we don't beat Oak Creek this Friday, there's a good possibility he won't be around very long. Bein' a football coach is Coach Little's dream. That kind of pressure can make people do stupid things.

"Just thought you needed to know."

I told Coach Thompson I appreciated the head's up, and I toted some boxes, and delivered some papers to the office for him before the last bell rang, and I had to start my last week of practice.

I did my best to stay out of the way that day, and for the rest of the week. It didn't keep me from catching hell whenever Coach Little decided to take the opportunity to blame me and some of the other guys for things. I didn't like it, but I held my tongue. There wasn't any sense in poking a stick at the bear.

As soon as I got home from practice, I called Carrie Ann and told her what Coach Thompson said about avoiding Coach Little. She confirmed that her Daddy had been talking to a lot of the old players, and with anybody else he could find that would listen. I really couldn't believe Coach Little would stoop so low as to take it out on her, but I warned her off anyway. Like Coach Thompson said, it was something she needed to know.

That night, President Nixon made a national address, asking for the country to get behind his efforts to end the war in Viet Nam with honor. He said we'd committed to help defend the government in the south, and we'd continue to do just that till the communists agreed to a "fair and honorable peace"—or until the South Vietnamese could defend themselves on their own. Tricky Dick asked the "great silent majority" to hang in there, and let him continue to work for "peace with honor."

It looked to me like he was trying to do the right thing. But the problem was, doing it was killing our boys. It didn't look like there was any end to it, and it wouldn't be too long before it would be our turn.

THIRTY-NINE

_____

Our last high school football game was with Oak Creek, and usually for both teams, it was the biggest game of the season. The rivalry between the two towns went back to the time when the county was first formed and the Union loyalists settled in Lincoln, and folks supporting the Confederacy all moved across the ridge and settled on the banks of the creek.

Even I had to admit the actual town of Oak Creek was really a pretty place. They'd made the waterway the centerpiece of the town and the land on each side of the creek had been preserved as a park. Everything was kept neat and clean, and the folks that lived there were really proud of the place.

But old feelings die hard, and the fact was, we plain ole didn't like one another.

We'd won the game easily last year, and neither team had lost many players to graduation, so we were pretty confident we'd be putting one more "W" on the tally to finish out the season. And it sure would be nice to go to the last home game dance with a win under our belt.

We had two good days of practice that week, in spite of all the screaming Coach Little did. Then the rain set in, and we got a steady, cold drizzle that kept up for the next two days and we had to practice in the gym. On Friday morning, the skies cleared, the sun came out, temperatures dropped into the 40's and a gorgeous late fall day hit us right in the face.

Sixth period, the whole school filed into the gym for a rally and a pep talk from Coach Little. He squeaked out a short speech about how the team had struggled this year, and how important it was for us to beat Oak Creek that night, and horseshit like that. Then the cheerleaders did their best to rouse up the student body.

Danny was sitting on the bottom row of the bleacher seats making semi-obscene gestures at Jenny Wilton while she was trying to lead the cheers. Coach made the football team all sit together, and when I spotted Carrie Ann, I waved to her and saw her grin back at me before she leaned over and whispered something to Mary Beth, sitting beside her.

From there, the team all went to the dressing room to get everything squared away. Several of the guys laid on the benches or huddled together talking while we waited to take our last walk up to the cafeteria for the pre-game meal.

Me and Will decided to go walk over the field, while the managers put the final touches on the yard lines and the cheerleaders were putting up signs on the fences. After two days of rain, the ground was a little mushy, and what grass was left on the field after a season of games, was trimmed up and neat.

By the time we got back to the dressing room from the cafeteria, a few of the early birds had already started staking out their spot in the stands. We got dressed out, making sure all the laces and straps on our pads were tight. Then after a final, threatening, 'crap talk' from Coach, we headed out the door and onto the field.

Even though it was a cold night, the stands were full on both sides, and the fences around the field were lined with guys standing and hollering at us. This game was one we played every year for the title of 'County Champ,' and you could feel the excitement in the air.

Both sides were standing and the noise was deafening as we kicked off to start the contest. The ball sailed low and long, and on the first bounce, Oak Creek's half back took it on their ten yard line, running right up the middle to the thirty.

On the first play from scrimmage, from my defensive tackle position, I came hard and fast across the line, split the two linemen in front of me and turned inside four yards deep. I lucked out and timed it just right. The Oak Creek wing-back with the ball ran straight at me on a reverse. There was nobody but me and him, and I popped him for a four yard loss. But on the next play, they gained it back plus some, and the rest of the half went back and forth, with neither of us getting past the other's twenty yard line.

At half time, Coach Little screamed at us so hard his voice gave out, and he had to turn it over to Coach Thompson to try to give us some direction that might break the standoff when we got back on the field. He made a few changes on our defense to stop Oak Creek from getting outside on the sweeps they were running, but never said anything about any adjustments on offense, until we started out the door.

Coach Thompson grabbed Will by the arm, looked directly in his face, and told him we were going to have to really "Go Blue" if we were going to pull this one out. Will caught his meaning right off, nodded to coach and led the team out on the field.

We took the kick to start the second half and ran it back to the forty yard line. Coach called two pass plays that were both incomplete, and we were faced with third and ten with a power sweep around the right side called in the huddle. As we came to the line, Will hollered out 'Go Blue' and like it was a magic elixir, the whole team seemed to perk up a bit.

Joe Drake, who was quarterbacking in Kenny's place, took the snap under center, reversed out and followed the entire backfield around the right end. The line all blocked down and the first back through kicked out on the defensive end, allowing Joe to cut up field for a forty-five yard gain. It was the longest run we'd had all night.

We ran 'Go Blue' plays several more times in the third quarter, with practically the same results, and at the start of the fourth, the scoreboard showed our side ahead, 13 to 0. So far, it had been a really tough game. It wasn't supposed to be, and we'd had to make our own breaks, but at least we were winning.

Three minutes into the last quarter, Oak Creek had moved the ball to our thirty-five, but they stalled out on the first two plays and were faced with third down and five yards to get a first. Once they got set, I recognized the same formation they'd run the reverse out of on the first play of the game, and knew for sure I had 'em pegged again.

When the ball moved, I charged across the line hard, again splitting the guard and tackle, and stopped four yards inside the Oak Creek backfield. But just as I started to turn, ready to drop the halfback for another loss, I felt the impact, and whoever it was that hit me, raked his helmet up, catching my facemask with his, pushing it up and exposing my face. I think I heard my nose snap about the same time I caught the flash of white visitor's jersey whip past me—then everything went black.

Kenny, who was standing on the sideline in his street clothes, told me later it was the first time all season Oak Creek had run a trap play, and they'd picked the perfect time to do it. The play powered through with pin-point down field blocks, scoring to bring 'em to only six points down.

I got my senses back in just a few seconds, but Coach Thompson made me sit out a few plays. I reckon with all the blood that gushed out of my nose and split lip, and the fact that I'd blacked out for a few seconds, he was worried I'd got my brains scrambled. I tried to tell him I was OK and ready to go back in, but he wouldn't hear it. I had to stand on the sideline with Kenny—ready to go, but not getting the call.

With five minutes showing on the clock, the laces broke on Keith Lynn's shoe, and I heard Coach Little's hoarse voice holler for Short Stack to go in at the halfback spot for him. As Arch started out on the field, coach grabbed him and sent in the play, '44 Reach.' On that play, the left halfback, took the hand-off and followed Will through the 4 hole, between our guard and tackle, on the right side of the line.

I thought at the time that maybe Coach wasn't really aware of what he'd done, since the position Arch was substituting for was the number "4" back. Ole Short Stack relayed the play to Joe, who broke the huddle, and everybody started to take their positions.

Just before Joe started calling the snap count, I heard Will holler, "Go Blue!" then the linemen got down in their stance. When the ball was hiked, Short Stack snatched the hand-off, got on Will's heels, and followed him through the line like his tail was on fire, running for a fifteen yard gain before they hauled him down from behind on the twenty.

Keith Lynn went back in the next play and Short Stack came off the field. All of us standing on the sideline went up to him to slap him on the back for making such a good run. Then I heard Coach Little's raspy voice.

"Damn, Short Stack. Why hadn't we been lettin' you run the ball all season?"

Short Stack took his helmet off, tucked it under his arm, and glared straight back at Coach Little.

"Probably 'cause you're a total dumb-ass." Then he turned and walked over to the water cooler to get a drink.

I looked over at Kenny, and apparently he'd heard Short Stack's comment too, because both of us busted out with huge grins, and walked over to where Arch was standing to congratulate him again on his run—and his comment.

We stalled out after that and turned the ball over, and after three tries, they punted it right back to us. We ran for a couple of firsts and got it back to the fifty, but then stalled out again, and gave 'em the ball back with a little under two minutes showing on the clock.

I tried one more time to get back in the game, but finally Coach Thompson told me to go sit on the bench and stop bothering him. At that point, I realized my high school football career was over. From then on, I became just another fan.

As both teams came to the line, Oak Creek's fans came alive, and apparently they must have had some influence on their team, because they started grinding out yardage and running time off the clock. When they got the ball to our five yard line, we had to put on a goal line stand. Oak Creek only needed two yards to get a first, but time was running out on 'em.

With ten seconds left in the game, the teams came to the line on third and two, and Oak Creek set up with a full backfield. When the ball was centered, their quarterback turned twice, handing the ball off to what looked like, both the right side and the left—and stepped back to look toward all the bodies that were piling up in the middle. Then he brought his hands around from behind his back, tucked the ball in the crook of his arm and trotted around the left end, into the end zone, untouched, to tie the score, 13-13.

It was the absolute best fake and bootleg run I'd ever seen in my life.

The Oak Creek side of the field erupted in screams, as the rest of us looked at the clock to see that regulation time had expired. And Oak Creek still had a shot at the win if they could kick for the extra point.

After a second of watching their whole sideline hop up and down in celebration, their coach shoved the kicker out on the field, and both teams took up positions. The ball was snapped, the holder put it on the ground and everybody in the stands held their breath— as we all watched the kick split the uprights.

The noise, with the Oak Creek side screaming at the top of their lungs, jumping up and down and clapping one another on the back, rivaled anything ever heard out of Neyland Stadium.

On the Lincoln side, you could have heard a pin drop. It was like somebody'd let all the air out of an inner tube.

Not a word was said in the dressing room as we took off our pads for the last time. We'd finished out the season with four wins and six losses—the first losing season for Lincoln High football for as long as anybody could remember. I could feel the chances of getting to play any college ball, evaporating. And with it, any prospect of getting any help paying for school.

I was seriously bummed out, and I know Will felt the same way.

We got showered, and dressed, and I cleaned up my nose and lip as best I could. Doc Cane stopped in to check on everybody, and straightened my nose so it was more or less in the middle between my eyes. He put a strip of tape across my face to hold it in place, and told me to get some ice on it as soon as I could.

But there were a few other things on our minds right then. Will helped me fix up a plastic bag with ice, and we walked up the hill to the gym, where we hoped Mary Beth and Carrie Ann would be looking for us.

FORTY

———

Carrie Ann had a way of knowing when something important was in the wind, and I guess she realized that night was a big turning point for me. She did her best to ooh-and-aah over me, asking if I was hurt anywhere else, other than my taped up nose. Even with the ice bag, it was already starting to swell and I could feel my face getting puffy around my eyes. Any other time, I'd have begged to get that much attention from her.

I had a hollow feeling in my gut, sort of like somebody had closed down the world, and left me outside the door.

Football had been my identity. In my mind, it was a big part of who I was. It was what people connected me with. It was something I could do, and do half way right.

But now it was over.

About the time the 'Jim-Tones' took their second break, Carrie Ann went to the little girls room, and I spotted Danny headed out the door of the gym. I needed a little air, so I grabbed my jacket and caught up with him just outside.

"Tough game tonight, huh…"

"Yeah. It's hard tryin' to figure out which way to go from a disaster like tonight—an' a disaster like this whole season's been."

He reached in his coat pocket, and pulled out a pack of Marlboro's, shaking one out for himself, and then handed the pack to me. I pulled out a cigarette, stuck it between my lips, and leaned over to the flame of the match he'd struck to light his. When I saw the orange glow, I inhaled the smoke deep into my lungs. The effect was almost immediate and my head started to swirl, and sounds around me moved away a distance.

We stood there, in the quiet cool of the night for a few seconds, then I heard Jenny calling Danny from behind me. He looked at his just lit cigarette, handed it to me, said something about talking later, and went back inside. I didn't need two smokes at the same time, so I flicked the fire off of his, twisted the burnt end so the tobacco wouldn't leak out, and stuck it in my pocket for later.

The concrete steps outside the gym door were cold, but I sat down anyway, holding my head in my hands. I had the cigarette between my fingers, thinking about how my face was starting to throb, when I felt the cigarette being pulled out of my hand.

"What the hell are you doin' out here in the cold?" Amy asked as she took a drag off the smoke, and handed it back to me.

"Tryin' to figure out what's next, I guess. We screwed up the football season pretty good, an' embarrassed the whole school in the process. So there's probably no chance of any of us gettin' to play college ball. An' to tell ya the truth, I was kinda hopin' that would be my ticket to goin' on to school."

I handed the cigarette back to her, then propped my elbows on my knees, and looked down at the ground. I was fixing to spit, when I felt a slap on the back of my head, and pain shot through the front of my face that felt like fireworks going off.

"Cubby James... that's about the stupidest thing I've ever heard you say."

She sat down on the cold concrete step next to me, took a draw off the cigarette, saw that it was burnt almost to the filter, and handed it back to me before continuing, her voice softer now.

"I know your spirit's gotta be pretty low right now over losin' the game... an' I'm sure your nose is hurtin'... Hell, you look like you oughta be in the hospital—your face is a mess!!"

"Thanks. I think you're cute too." I said in the most sarcastic tone I could muster.

"Don't get smart...

"Now, I want you to get your head outta your ass on this. You didn't screw anything up. Shit just happens.

"An' you don't hafta depend on football to go on to college. I know you 'bout better than anybody. You can be a real ass-hole sometimes, but you're capable of doin' anything you put your mind to. You're smart, an' you're half-way good lookin'... even with your nose mashed up.

"There's a lot of us that depend on you. An' there ain't no way I'm gonna let you wallow in a pity puddle, an' think this is the end of the world."

I lit the butt I'd put in my pocket off of the burning cigarette in my hand, flipped the first one out in the road, and we both watched what was left of the burning tobacco scatter like shrapnel.

Then her voice got even softer.

"Cubby... you told me one time that God had a plan an' a purpose for all of us. We've all got something we're meant to do that'll make things better. It's our job to find it, an' do what we're intended to do.

"I'm pretty sure God didn't send you here to play football. If He did, He wouldn't't've put you on such a shitty team. So I'm bettin' there's somethin' else out there for ya... I don't know what it is, but it's your job to find it.

"Now... get up off your ass. Carrie Ann's lookin' for you, an' she needs somebody to hold her close tonight."

Amy pulled my arm and we stood up and started back in the gym.

"Oh... an' one more thing. If you ever tell anybody about me bein' this nice to you, or anything of what I said, I'll never speak to you again."

I thought for a second, it might be worth it to print it all in the paper, if it might slow down her talking some. But then I also thought that I cared more for her right then than I ever had before.

My nose was hurting so bad, me and Carrie Ann left not long after that. When she kissed me goodnight, she made me promise to go straight home, and put ice on my face. I followed her orders and did just that.

The next morning, Carrie Ann called to check on me, and said to come to her house about 6:00. She said she was going to fix spaghetti and after supper, we could watch TV in the den. Amy called right after that to make sure I was OK, and I talked to Danny and Will that afternoon too.

We ate supper with Carrie Ann's Mom, Dad and her little sister, and I had to be careful when I took a bite, not to split open my lip and start it bleeding again. While we ate, Mr. Mallory quizzed me about the football season, and the changes Coach Little had made. He also asked if the rumors of how Coach talked to us were true. I didn't want it to sound like sour grapes, but I answered him as honest as I could, and told him everything.

After I helped Carrie Ann clean up the dishes, we caught the last part of *Jackie Gleason*, switched to *Adam-12*, and then watched *Green Acres* on the TV in the den. I don't know where the rest of her family went to, but they made themselves scarce, and I didn't see any of 'em the rest of the night.

Carrie Ann and I actually did watch TV, but we spent a little time holding one another too. It was really hard to leave her, when 10:30 rolled around.

FORTY-ONE

I went to school the next week with two black eyes, but by Tuesday the worst of the swelling had gone down, and the edges of the bruises were starting to turn green. I checked back with Doc Cane, and he told me I'd probably have to see a nose specialist later on, but for now, as long as I could breathe through it, I ought to be OK.

I actually was expecting to hear some snide comments from some of the kids at school, but nobody said anything to any of us about the football season. Or at least, if they did, I didn't hear it. The sun came up every morning, we went to school, and life went right on.

The next night, Walter Cronkite told the nation a story published that morning in the big city papers about a massacre of Vietnamese civilians that happened back in March of '68. He said the Army had been investigating reports that our guys had shot somewhere between 200 and 500 old men, women and children at a village called My Lai. He said the Army had charged Lieutenant William Calley, and the men in his company that supposedly did the deed. And the way it was reported implied that the Army was trying to cover up the whole thing.

For the protesters and all the folks in the anti-war movement, the news just confirmed everything they'd been saying was wrong with the war. But it was a hard pill to swallow for some that were brought up to respect and honor service in the military—and I was one of 'em.

This sure wasn't the way I understood what America was trying to do. A thing like this, if what they said was right, was the exact opposite of trying to do the right thing and help people that didn't want to live under the boot of communism.

But if they had enough evidence to bring charges against our own troops, it was a damn good bet this might just be true. Again, we didn't know what to believe anymore.

With football over, I discovered I had a lot of time on my hands, and it didn't take me long to figure out that my bank account needed feeding. So, I went looking for an after-school job that hopefully wouldn't involve working on weekends, since I was wanting to keep that time free for other things... particularly spending time with Carrie Ann.

I checked at the hardware store again, but they still weren't hiring. I also talked to Mr. Parker at the Five & Dime. He asked me about playing Santa Claus again in December, and I agreed to do that, but he didn't have any work to do until the Christmas season started. I couldn't even get anything worked out to bag groceries part-time at the Piggly-Wiggly.

I was about to give up, when Danny mentioned Rocky was looking for somebody to do office work at the Jail. He said he hadn't really thought to tell me about it. He was such a damned sexist, he thought it was something a girl had to do. But then he reckoned I could put on a dress and go do the filing and report typing they needed done. Ole Danny could be such an ass-hole at times.

I went straight-ways to the Jail and talked to Brad Main, Rocky's Chief Deputy, and from what he told me, the job looked to be exactly what I was wanting. They only needed somebody part-time, organizing and filing paperwork, and typing a few reports.

There weren't any certain hours for the work, as long as it got done, and I figured I could come in after school and take care of most of it in a couple of hours. And having to type the reports would give me a chance to practice the typing stuff I was learning in school, without having the distraction of all the girls that were in the class.

I asked if we could work it out so I could still be Santa Claus at the Dime store in December, and Brad didn't see any problem, telling me I could come and do their filing and stuff any time, since the Jail was open 24/7.

I didn't even have to think about it, and as soon as he finished telling what all it involved, I asked for the job.

On Thursday that week, 45,000 protesters marched through the streets in Washington for what they called the 'March Against Death.' The next day, President Nixon watched as Apollo 12 blasted off on another mission to the moon. And then on Saturday, the news reported that over half-a-million protesters across the country, demonstrated in the second 'Moratorium Against the War.'

With the news about everything going down the dumper in Viet Nam, and the number of protesters that were coming out to demonstrate against what was going on, it's no wonder the President sneaked down to Cape Kennedy to watch the rocket launch. Things just didn't appear to be going too good for him that week.

And as a reminder that we could very easily blow one another to smithereens, U.S. and Russian diplomats started meetings the next Monday in Finland, to try to work out the details on a Strategic Arms Limitation Treaty. The SALT talks were supposed to try to reduce the number of nukes on both sides that we could use on each other.

And we heard follow-up stories about the massacre at My Lai. The report said our boys were searching for enemy soldiers in the village, and started shooting the civilians as they ran from their huts. Then they rounded up the rest of the villagers, herded 'em into a ditch and shot the ones that were left.

And to convince the skeptics, a newspaper in Ohio printed what they called proof positive. The pictures of the dead sure didn't look to be soldiers—they were pictures of old men and women and children.

To hear it made us sick. This was what the Nazi's and Japs did in World War II. It was the kind of thing Americans were willing to go to war to put a stop to. This purely wasn't what the U.S. military forces and America were all about.

Something was bad rotten and had to be stopped.

The next Monday, the Army Board of Inquiry announced that Lieutenant Calley and his troops would stand Court's Marshall for the My Lai Massacre. As if in response, Viet Cong and North Vietnamese Regular troops launched attacks the next day on our guys at outposts that were located up and down the border with Cambodia.

The tar baby that was Viet Nam, all of a sudden got stickier, and we watched as the casualty list got longer, and the body count went higher… and more and more red, white and blue draped boxes started to make their final trip home.

FORTY-TWO

For the rest of that year, we kind of settled into a regular routine. After school, I went by the Jail and filed reports that the deputies had written out in long hand, and typed a few that had to be sent off to the state or the feds. And Brad put me to work listing the different offense classes so they could tell the total number of each type of call they were getting.

Looking at the charts, it didn't take long to see that what they classed as 'Substance Abuse' was going off the page. Alcohol was still by far the winner, but reports and arrests for marijuana, and pills were catching up fast.

Since me and the guys had taken a few trips up in the mountains and drunk a few beers, we had a little bit of experience with alcohol. And then there was the spiked brownies that magically appeared at the prom. But other than that, as far as I knew, none of us had experienced anybody really getting messed up on serious drugs.

But then, I'd had my mind on football most of the time, and since Danny was my best friend, and Danny's brother was the High Sheriff, I guess we really weren't in a position where we would see anything.

Me and Carrie Ann started going out, more or less on a regular basis, meeting at the basketball games on weeknights and to restaurants and movies on the weekends. It didn't leave a lot of time for the guys, but then, Will and Mary Beth were most always together, and it appeared that Danny and Jenny had decided to overlook each other's faults for a while, and had entered into some fairly involved peace negotiations. And best we knew, poor ole Randy hadn't yet caught on to the honey trap Amy'd laid for him.

Thanksgiving that year worked out real nice. I got to eat with my family, then help Danny with some of his family's left-overs and even do a little clean-up on the pies at Carrie Ann's house.

The second week in December, Nixon announced that the War in Viet Nam was winding down and he expected everything to be over pretty soon. The way he was seeing it, his 'Vietnamization Policy' was working, and he thought it wouldn't be long before we could turn the whole shebang over to the South Vietnamese to run their own show.

I really couldn't figure how he got to that conclusion, since nothing we'd seen of what anybody had been doing, looked to be working. But right then, I was willing to give him the benefit of the doubt, hoping he knew something the rest of us didn't.

The next night, David Brinkley announced on NBC News that a group of hippies in Los Angeles had been arrested for the murders of Sharon Tate and all the others at her house back in August. And they'd added the murders the next night of a grocery store owner and his wife to the indictment. The hippies were some kind of family headed by a guy named Manson, and the more we heard about it, the crazier the whole story was.

None of it made any sense.

The same week Tricky Dick decided the war was about to be over, I started work as Santa Claus again for Mr. Parker at the Dime Store. Mostly I talked to little kids, but at the end of the first week, I got a visit from some bigger kids.

Whispering and giggling, Amy, Mary Beth and Carrie Ann came and stood in line to see Santa. Mary Beth just told me what Will was wanting, and all Amy wanted to do was bounce up and down on my leg and pull on my beard. But Carrie Ann made my day when she sat on my knee, put her arms around my neck and whispered that she was looking for a big hug and a kiss from Santa.

Thankfully, Santa got to take a break after that.

Christmas was supposed to be a happy time of year—but for me, it was one of the saddest times.

Moms and Dads would bring in little kids with bright eyes, and big expectations, reciting lists of toys, and dolls, and sleds, and all manner of things. Some of 'em, I was certain, would wake up Christmas morning to find a pile of gifts under the tree. But some of 'em I knew, wouldn't get much if anything of what they were wishing for. It wasn't for lack of their folks wanting to do it, but the reality was that a lot of families purely couldn't.

For too many, times were still hard in the mountains. In a land of plenty, there were a lot of folks that couldn't even get the basics. It simply wasn't right.

It started raining Friday morning, the eve of my birthday, followed by a cold front that left about an inch of snow on top of a sheet of ice. My car slid in a few places when I drove to work Saturday morning, but by noon, the roads were pretty much melted off.

Since the roads looked to be clear, as soon as the Dime Store closed for the day, I hustled home, cleaned up, and headed right back out for Carrie Ann's and the promised birthday supper. What I didn't figure on was whatever water that was left on the roads from the melting snow and ice during the day, froze solid as soon as the sun went down.

I made the mistake of taking the back street to get to Carrie Ann's house, instead of getting on Main Street. As I topped the hill, about half-way there, I put my foot on the brake to stop for a Stop sign, and felt the front of the car start to slide. I took my foot off the gas, and geared down, but nothing I did would slow it, and I slid through the intersection sideways. Barely moving, the front-end of my Corvair nosed into the light pole on the corner, busting the right front headlight and bending the bumper back into the front tire so I couldn't move it.

I had to walk a couple of blocks up to Wilson's Restaurant and call Dad to come and get me—and while I waited, I called Carrie Ann to tell her I most likely wasn't going to be able to make it that night. I think she was disappointed, but she sounded like she was glad I wasn't hurt.

So much for my 17th birthday.

The next week brought news of more troop withdrawals.

Could it be that Nixon actually knew what he was talking about, and the War really was starting to wind down? The closer we got to having to register for the draft, the better news like that was sounding.

I didn't get my car back from Candy Robert's Body Shop till two days before Christmas, so while it was being fixed, I had to either borrow Dad's pick-up or depend on Danny for transportation. I'd managed to make a few shopping trips early on, and already had presents bought for my family... and a few special things for Carrie Ann. So we got through Christmas without too much problem.

On Saturday before Christmas, me and Carrie Ann double dated with Will and Mary Beth and went to the dance. The Letterman Dances at the school had been such a hit with all the kids, the 'Jim-Tones' decided to rent out the community room in the basement of the Masonic Lodge once a month and have a dance. They made a few bucks and it gave everybody something to do.

Amy, Mary Beth and Carrie Ann got together and had a New Year's Eve party in Amy's basement. They had a bunch of snacks, and we played games and had a good time. For me, the high point of the night was getting to hug Carrie Ann, and get the first kiss of the New Year, right after watching the ball drop on TV.

It was finally 1970. I couldn't help but wish that maybe the world would come to its senses and things would get better.

We could only hope.

FORTY-THREE

———————

On New Year's Day, the guys got together again for our annual poker game at Will's house, and watched Ole Miss beat Alabama in the Sugar Bowl. With everything going on, we hadn't had a chance to play much poker, but it didn't take me long to figure out Danny hadn't learned anything over the past year. He still couldn't remember the rank of hands, and he continued to bet out of turn. I hated to do it, but I pocketed most of his Christmas money again.

School started back on the 5th, and after getting to sleep-in the last few days, we all came in bleary eyed that morning. All that is, but Carrie Ann. When I saw her in the hall before Home Room, she was bright eyed and excited to get on with the year. I was still wishing for one more sip of coffee, and being that awake before 8:00 just wasn't natural to me.

As I walked her to Home Room, I noticed she had a smile on her face that was something more than her usual cheery personality—like there was something she knew and wanted to tell really bad.

"OK...What's up with you this mornin'?"

She tossed her head to move her bangs out of her eyes, and leaned over to whisper in my ear, "Coach Little's not gonna be here today—or for the rest of the year. Daddy told me at breakfast."

I couldn't believe there was any way we could be so lucky. Her blond hair bounced when she nodded to assure me she was telling the truth.

"You remember Daddy askin' you about what all went on in practice, an' the changes that got made, an' how Coach kept sayin' you'all were a bunch-a losers? Well, I found out you weren't the only one he talked to, and Daddy waddn't the only one askin' questions.

"Danny's brother an' Brad Main, an' several of the old players talked to a lot of people. They put it all together an' figured out Coach Little didn't have a clue about how to run a football team, or how to deal with players, or 'bout most anything else. Daddy an' Rocky paid a visit to the School Board people, an' from what Daddy said, the Board fired him."

The first bell rang, signaling the five minute warning to get to class, so I told her we'd talk later, not to say anything to anybody till we got it checked out, and I ran to get to Home Room.

As soon as I walked in the door of Home Room, Will asked me if I'd heard Coach Little was gone. I had time to say Carrie Ann had just told me when the second bell rang and we had to get in our seats. I was busting to know more, and luckily we didn't have to wait long. We no more than got sat down when Principal Webster came over the intercom and said for all the seniors to report to the cafeteria.

On the way there Will repeated essentially the same thing Carrie Ann said, and told me he'd talked to Rocky and answered pretty much the same questions Mr. Mallory had asked me. So it looked like they sure enough had done their research on this before they went to the School Board. There wasn't any word about a replacement yet, and we all wondered on it, but nobody had any answers.

The senior class members settled in around the cafeteria tables, talking amongst ourselves while Mr. Webster introduced a guy from Josten's Jewelry Company that was set up to take class ring orders. He also announced we'd be having class pictures made on Tuesday of the next week, so we could get prepared.

I probably needed to get a haircut before the pictures, but it was the class ring order that particularly interested me. I'd actually been thinking about a ring. I wasn't much on wearing jewelry, and what I really wanted was a college ring. But having something to offer to Carrie Ann, to show her how I felt and that she could have next year while I was away, was something I'd thought about.

The next several weeks went by fast with all the stuff that was going on. Several afternoons a week, Carrie Ann spent meeting with the Prom Committee. She took over Danny's old job and got put in charge of the refreshment committee, and since I'd already asked her about walking with me in the Prom Promenade, she enlisted one of the other girls in her class to be at the gym while we were doing the walk from town to the school.

I continued to work a couple of days a week at the Jail, cleaning up all their paperwork. Sitting at the desk in the back of the office gave me the chance to overhear a lot of things, and every once in a while, I caught snippets of talk about a drug investigation that was going on. Nobody was saying anything to me outright, but I overheard enough to know something was happening.

The last of January, Mary Beth got a bunch together and did a birthday party for Carrie Ann, and on the last Saturday night of the month we went to the 'Jim-Tones' dance at the Lodge. Then we got the whole crew back in February for a Valentine's party in Amy's basement.

The Sunday paper on the day after Valentine's, ran a story giving Gallup Poll results on what people were thinking about the war in Viet Nam. The poll said 55% of the American people still supported what the President was doing, and opposed immediate withdrawal of our troops. But 35% of the people were in favor of withdrawal, and that number was up from the 21% that wanted us out back in November.

The next Thursday, news reports told about the acquittal of the Chicago Seven on Riot Conspiracy charges. They were the seven guys that got arrested for causing all the upheaval at the Democrat Convention back in '68 in Chicago. They did get convicted of the lesser charge of Inciting a Riot, but that charge didn't carry much penalty, so it looked like they were going to pretty much get away with causing all the trouble they'd stirred up.

Then, at the 'Jim-Tone's' dance the last of February, we had our own short war. Well... it wasn't much of a war, because Will made short work of it when he squared off on Wally Lawson.

Big Wally showed up right after the 'Jim-Tones' started their last set of the night, talking loud, trying to hang on some of the kids that were standing in the back of the room by the entrance doors, and seeming to be a little unsteady on his feet. His arrival was kind of hard to miss.

Me and Carrie Ann, Danny, Jenny, Amy, Randy, Will and Mary Beth were about mid-way in the room, closer to the amplifiers set up in front of the band, when they struck the first notes of the "Lovin' Spoonfull's" hit, *Good Lovin'*. We were fixing to step out on the dance floor, when Wally put his hand on Mary Beth's shoulder, pulling her away from Will toward the dancers.

I caught a glimpse of the shock on Mary Beth's face as Wally spun her around, and out of the corner of my eye, saw Will, coiled tight like a rattlesnake, ready to strike. Apparently Randy and Danny saw it too, and the three of us moved quick to get between

Will and Wally, taking Wally by the arms and escorting him through the crowd and out the door.

What we didn't see was Will following right behind us.

Once outside the door and into the parking lot, we turned Wally around, demanding to know what he was thinking. But Will didn't waste any time. With his fists balled, in a quiet, steady voice, Will got right up in his face, and told him he'd heard some of the things Wally had been saying about Mary Beth.

I thought that was it, but Will took a step back to get a little more leverage, and hit Wally in the stomach. As Wally bent over from the first blow, Will brought his arm around in an upper-cut and smashed his fist into his face—and it was all over. Wally crumpled like a paper sack—and with hardly a glance back, we all walked back in the door, acting like nothing out of the ordinary had happened.

FORTY-FOUR

We didn't see much of Wally for a few weeks, and none of us thought much about it. Most all of us had heard through the grapevine, some of the things Wally had been saying about Mary Beth. Things like how she was flirting with him, and coming on to him were pure bullshit, and at first Will just blew it off as the rantings of a blow-hard. But when a few of the lewd remarks Wally was making about what he was going to do, got back to us, every single one of us completely understood Will's motivation.

And too, there were a few rumors around that Wally was dabbling in drugs. Something like that would account for him being bold enough—or stupid enough—to go for Mary Beth at the dance. And if that's what it was, it explained why he was louder than usual, and why he looked to be staggering around that night.

To tell the truth, we didn't think much anything about it. We all thought Wally got exactly what he deserved. But I was more than a little interested in the rumors about the drugs, since I knew the Sheriff's Office was looking into that kind thing. I kept my mouth shut about what I'd heard at the Jail, and I kept my eyes open at school.

Dogwood winter set in the first week of March, but we could already see signs that warmer weather was on the way. Usually that involved wind and storms, but it wasn't anything we hadn't had before.

Tuesday morning, the Senior Superlatives, voted on by the teachers, were announced. As most of us expected, Will and Mary Beth were picked as "Mister and Miss LHS." Danny got "Most Unpredictable" and Amy was named as "Most Likely to Succeed."

On Thursday, we had Career Day for the seniors, and the school brought in recruiters from a bunch of colleges, trade schools and some of the factories that were hiring high school graduates. And along with them, came a couple of military recruiters—one from the Army and one from the Marine Corp.

Each bunch set up at tables in the cafeteria, right after they got it cleaned up from lunch, and the seniors got dismissed from fifth and sixth period classes to talk to 'em. Danny spent considerable time with the girl from Hiwassee College, where Rocky and Katy went, talking about their baseball team. And the fact that she was really cute didn't hurt.

Will and Mary Beth talked to Hiwassee too, but I also spotted 'em talking to the guy from Maryville College and the recruiters from U.T. Knoxville. And Amy talked the ears off of the guy from Emory & Henry, mostly because that's the place where poor ole Randy was going.

I tagged along with Danny for a little while, and picked up some pamphlets on Hiwassee. Then I looked over the stuff about U.T. Knoxville and talked to the guy from East Tennessee State. I knew both UT and ETSU had ROTC programs, and if I could get in, I figured maybe I could get Uncle Sam to pay for my college. But me and a couple other guys spent the majority of our time talking to the recruiter from the Army.

Master Sergeant Dory was all dressed out in his pressed khaki uniform, spit shined shoes and had all sorts of ribbons and decorations pinned to his shirt. When he found out I was just 17, he lost a little interest, but he told me I could still enlist if I could get Mom and Dad to sign off on it.

With a shooting war going on, the Army wasn't the most attractive option for me. But it was still one way I could go. And the military was kind of a family tradition in Dad's family. I figured one way or another, the Army was where I was going to wind up, and if college didn't work out, I had that to fall back on.

When the bell rang, signaling the end of school, I gathered up all the material to take home to look over and talk to Dad about. I was walking across the parking lot to the Corvair, not paying a lot of attention to what was going on, when Paddy Leary pulled up beside me.

"Cubby… Ya got a minute…."

"Sure Paddy. What's up?"

"You told me one time if I ever wanted to talk, you'd listen."

When I nodded, he told me to get in. Since I wasn't on any kind of schedule to get to the Jail, I opened the door, settled in and he drove out of the parking lot, lighting a cigarette from the car's lighter. I asked for and got one of his cigarettes, and sat waiting as he drove.

"Cubby… I seen ya talkin' to the Army recruiter. An' if you're thinkin' about joinin' up, I want to be sure you know what you're gettin' into."

I looked over at him, but he kept his eyes on the road, taking a few seconds to choose his words.

"I figure you watched all the war movies an' heard all the stories 'bout fightin' the Germans an' the Japs in World War II. Growin' up, I was the same way, hearin' 'bout what all our guys done, an' how whuppin' the enemy made the world safe again.

"But nobody ever said nothin' about the bad stuff. It ain't like what you think it is Cubby. There's more to it than wearin' a uniform an' marchin' around. There's some really bad shit that goes down, that nobody's gonna wanna tell ya.

"Since I got back, I've been watchin' you an' the rest of the kids in school. My bet is there ain't none of ya ever been too far away from here. An' I'd bet that your home is a pretty nice place to go to. Some place where ya feel safe an' people care for ya. You really ain't had a whole lot of bad things happen in your life.

"War's the total opposite of that. I don't think 'Nam is any different from war any other time. But it's our war, an' what goes on there ain't nothin' like what the movies or the stories are like. You see things you can't even imagine, an' they'll teach ya to do things ya never thought ya could do... The people that are supposed to know what's goin' on, ain't got a clue... An' that's the kinda shit that gets people killed.

"I'm tellin' ya... it does somethin' to ya. Some guys handle it OK. But some of 'em lose it completely... They come apart at the seams an' they stay drunk or zoned out, just to make it through the day, tryin' to hide from what all they seen or what all they done...

"I 'uz raised up in a situation a whole lot worser than you, an' I seen a lot of bad stuff when I 'uz a young'un. An' I didn't handle none of the stuff I seen in 'Nam too good. To tell ya the truth, except for the first week, I stayed stoned 'bout the whole rest of the time I was over there."

Paddy paused for a second, and flipped his cigarette out the window before he went on.

"Just from knowin' you... I'm thinkin' you're one of the good guys. You ain't never had hard times. You've got a good home an' a good family. An' to tell ya the truth, from what I see, you ain't one of 'em that would handle it too good.

"So, ya need to think long an' hard 'bout what you do."

By the time he finished, he'd circled the block behind the school, and pulled back into the parking lot. Paddy pulled into a space next to my Corvair and turned off the ignition.

"Paddy... I appreciate you tellin' me this. But to tell ya the truth, I really don't know what I'm gonna do. Joinin' up right after high school's just one option I've got. If I had my druthers, I'd like to go somewhere I could maybe play football. But I've got to figure out how to pay for it an' ROTC might be one way to do it. But I've got a lot to think about before I make any decision."

He nodded his head. "Just remember what I told ya when you're decidin'."

I got out of Paddy's car, wishing I'd asked for another cigarette, and watched him drive out of the lot. I think he was doing his best to warn me off from joining up, and I could tell it took a lot for him to open up that way. It wasn't like we were good friends— just speaking friends. But Paddy must have felt like it was something he had to do... and I really appreciated him for it.

Taking everything into consideration, I did have a lot to think about. My days in high school were quickly coming to an end, and I had to make some decisions about the rest of my life. Going on to college was pretty much a given, and would get me a 2-S, student deferment from the draft. But where to go and how to pay for it was what I had to decide.

And somewhere in the mix, I had to figure out where Carrie Ann fit in.

FORTY-FIVE

———————

On Tuesday of the next week, I'd just walked in from work at the Jail, when the phone started ringing. Like always, Amy never said hello or anything else, charging right in.

"What're ya doing?"

"I just walked in the house. Whadda ya need?"

"Come get me. I need to talk to ya." Then the phone clicked in my ear.

I put my letter jacket back on, checked to be sure the car keys were still in the pocket, and went right back out the door.

As usual, Amy was waiting outside, with her arms hugging her chest against the chill, and she ran to get in the Corvair as soon as I pulled in the driveway.

She slammed the car door shut, checked to be sure the window was all the way up and then reached to turn up the fan on the car's heater.

As far as I knew, everything was going pretty smooth, and I couldn't figure out what was so important to talk about that we couldn't say on the phone. But I didn't have to wait long.

"Cubby, I got a call from Angel this afternoon."

"Aw, shit..." I could feel the bottom drop out of my chest. "What's she wantin'?"

"She waddn't callin' 'bout you. I think she's moved on, so you can pretty much put the seal on that chapter of your life. I think she's a little sorry for what happened between the two of..."

"Hell fire, Amy! What'd she call about...?"

"Oh... I thought you'd want to know about her..."

I glared over at her as I turned right onto the Oak Creek Road.

"She was callin' to see if I knew Paddy..."

"What the hell is she wantin' to know about Paddy for?"

"Well... If you'll listen for a second an' not bite my head off..."

"OK... I'm sorry. Go on..."

"Angel said they're havin' some problems with kids takin' pills at her school, an' word is that Paddy's the source for whatever anybody's lookin' for. She said she thinks the shit is about to hit the fan there, an' they're hearin' there's some kind of joint operation between the two counties to make a bust pretty soon.

"I thought we needed to warn Paddy off, if he's really the one doin' the supplyin'. But I don't see him much, an' when I do, he makes a bee line to get away from me. I thought you might be able to get in touch with him."

I'd thought a lot about Paddy, and what he'd told me a few months back when I'd run out of gas and hitched a ride back to Lincoln with him. And how he'd put himself out, to tell me what he did, trying to warn me off when he thought I was going to enlist. I knew he hadn't had the easiest time of it, and he had a lot of rough edges. And, doing what he'd done to help me, looked to me like he was trying to get past it, and I wanted to help him.

But, if he was the source of the drugs that were starting to get into the schools, that wasn't the right road. If he was the local dealer, he was directing traffic on a highway to hell.

I'd seen first-hand some of the people the Deputies brought in the jail, all strung out on uppers, or practically in a stupor from taking downers. And at first, the mellow demeanor of the ones stoned from smoking grass was almost funny. But when the same names and faces kept turning up, letting drugs take over their lives, it wasn't funny anymore.

"Amy, you need to stay away from Paddy. If I get the opportunity, I'll talk to him. But if he's into this the way Angel says, we've gotta stay out of it."

Amy turned in the seat with a shocked look on her face.

"Damn Cubby… I thought you and Paddy were friends…? I thought you'd want to help him?"

"Amy… I'd really like to do somethin' to help. An' I promise if I get a chance, I'll talk to 'im. But there's right an' there's wrong. If Paddy's doin' wrong, warnin' him to lay low, ain't gonna help, if that's all he's gonna do. He's got to do the right thing. That's what I'll talk to him about—when I can."

She sat back in the seat, thinking as we drove back into town. It wasn't in Amy's nature to take somebody else's counsel and let them control a situation. But on this one, she was stumped. I think down deep she knew I was right.

When we pulled back into her driveway, I looked over at her. "You're just gonna hafta trust me to handle it this time."

I guess she must have agreed, because she nodded and went back in her house.

On Tuesday the next week, the Army released the results of an internal investigation confirming that officers and soldiers, who knew about the My Lai Massacre, hid the information and did their best to cover it up and keep it from the American people.

What happened at My Lai, had to be a mission gone horribly wrong. I kept thinking there had to be some explanation, some justification for the whole thing. This was American soldiers we were talking about. There was something bad wrong with everything that was happening.

Baseball started the first week of March and we spent time traveling with the team to watch Danny play. They had so many games, the month was gone before we knew it.

We ended up the month going to the 'Jim-Tones' dance at the Lodge again. Because of the problems the month before, our little group stayed close to one another, but we didn't see hide-nor-hair of Wally, and it turned out to be a pretty good night. The music was good, spending time with our friends made the night go too fast, and there was still a little nip in the air that made holding someone special very close as we said goodnight, a really nice experience.

April started off with the government sticking their nose where it most likely didn't belong, when the President signed federal legislation banning cigarette ads on TV and radio. Apparently they didn't trust people to make up their own minds. "Big Brother" had to tell us what to do.

Meetings to finalize all the little things to be done for the Prom kept Carrie Ann busy, and the only time I got to see her was on the weekends. Since we were seniors, and already had our turn organizing last year's Prom, all we had to do was get dressed and show up.

I'd asked Carrie Ann to be my date earlier, ordered her a corsage so I wouldn't forget it, and went with Danny and Will to Duggan's Clothing Store in downtown Maryville to get outfitted. I got a nice gray suit and Will picked out a navy one with a vest. But Danny insisted on getting one with a wide pin-stripe, black and white wing-tip shoes, a black shirt and a light gray tie. It made him look like a skinny gangster, but he liked it.

They started putting up the first of the decorations on Monday before the Prom, which was set for the 18th. Me and Danny stopped in to see how everything was coming along, and it gave me a chance to see Carrie Ann. All the juniors were hard at it, so we didn't stay but a few minutes.

On the way home, WNOX radio news gave the results of a new Gallup Poll just released, that showed the country's approval of the conduct of the war had dropped from 55% to 48%, and folks disapproving had gone up to 41%. It looked like America was sure enough, losing faith.

But it was the next news story that caught my attention. That afternoon, Paul McCartney told the world about the break-up of the Beatles. Their music had led the British Invasion and when they appeared on Ed Sullivan's Show in 1964, it probably had a big part in healing some of the wounds the young people were still dealing with after President Kennedy's assassination.

For the rest of the weekend, rock-'n-roll radio stations across the country played the 'Fab Four' sounds we grew up with.

On Monday, the networks all issued Special Bulletins to tell us the oxygen tank aboard the Apollo 13 spacecraft had exploded. They'd blasted off from Kennedy Space Center the Saturday before, and one more trip to the moon seemed to be going along fine, until Mission Control heard the calm radio transmission, "Houston... We have a problem."

The whole country sat on pins and needles for the rest of the week, as the astronauts made repairs, sling-shotted around the moon and headed right back home. You could almost hear the entire nation exhale in relief, when they safely splashed down in the Pacific Ocean—on the day before the Prom.

FORTY-SIX

It hadn't rained on Prom Day in over ten years, and in 1970, the prediction was for a warm day with clear skies. That morning, I met Danny at the Shell Station and we cleaned up both our cars. I'm not sure why, since we'd be leaving 'em in the church parking lot and walking in the Prom Promenade. But we did it anyway.

After that, I made a quick trip to the florist and picked up Carrie Ann's corsage. When I got back home, I called Will to coordinate the time to meet at the church so we could all walk together.

Will said Mary Beth had talked to Amy and they'd decided we'd all meet at 6:30. He'd already talked to Danny, so all I had to do was let Carrie Ann know what time I'd pick her up, and get dressed. Simple enough.

When I called, Carrie Ann told me to be at her house a little before 6:00, because her Mom wanted to take some pictures with her new Instamatic Camera. So, at ten minutes of, I was standing on her front porch, with the corsage box tucked securely under my arm. I was getting ready to knock, when Mr. Mallory opened the door and ushered me in, with a huge grin on his face. I didn't have to wait but a minute to see why.

When Carrie Ann walked into the room, it was like all the air was sucked out of it. She was stunningly beautiful in an emerald dress that came just below her knees, and perfectly matched her flashing eyes. She had told me to get a corsage that would go with a green dress, and the yellow roses surrounded by white ribbon was a perfect accent with her blond hair. I couldn't take my eyes off of her.

We took several minutes taking pictures, and everybody left—me and Carrie Ann to meet the rest of the gang, and her Mom and Dad to meet my parents at Dadaw's house, where they could watch the procession from the front porch. The rest of our bunch was already in the parking lot when we got there.

Mary Beth was as usual a knock-out, and Jenny and Amy looked really nice. But my eyes were glued to Carrie Ann. I couldn't believe she was really with me, and I'm sure my pride showed as we joined in with the rest of the Senior Class, slowly walking down Main Street to the school, speaking and waving to all the folks gathered on their porches and in the front yards along the way.

I couldn't help but smile as we passed Dadaw and Mamaw's house, and we waved at my Mom and Dad and Mr. and Mrs. Mallory. Mrs. Mallory snapped a couple more pictures as we passed, and Mom was standing on the porch steps, wiping her eyes for some reason. I'd really dreaded the Promenade, but doing it with Carrie Ann holding onto my arm, made all the difference. When we got to the school, I was kind of sorry it was over.

That night was like a dream. The gym was all decorated in the school's red, white and blue colors, and Carrie Ann's committee outdid themselves on the refreshments. They had tables set with trays of little biscuits and country ham, bowls of chips and a big bowl of boiled shrimp. And there were mounds of fresh fruit and cookies of all kinds. Me and Will searched for brownies, but never found any—so we figured this year might turn out OK.

We ate some, talked and laughed a lot, and danced to dang near every song. We even got a group picture done by the photographer they'd hired to do shots of each couple.

Like they'd done for the past couple of years, 'The Air Notes' from Maryville were booked to play, since Jimmy Dawkins and a couple of the other 'Jim-Tones' were in our class. And like before, 'The Air Notes' didn't disappoint.

They played a lot of Motown, and a few of the newer hard rock songs that we'd been hearing on the radio. But they dipped back and did a lot of the old songs too.

At one point during the night, Amy reached over and punched me in the side, leaning close so I'd be able to hear her over the music.

"This is a lot better than last year!"

I grinned at her, and bent down close to her ear.

"The night's young yet. You've still got time to proposition me!" She leaned back and laughed.

"Ain't gonna happen, ass-hole! I told ya then ya missed your chance!"

A little after 10:00, just as the band was coming back from taking a break, Paddy Leary quietly came through the door. The brunette on his arm was wearing a tight, dark red dress that I figured she'd had to use a shoe-horn to get into. Paddy had pulled his long black hair straight back in a pony-tail at his neck, that fell down the back of a dark colored sport coat. His white shirt was unbuttoned down his chest and the gold chains around his neck bounced with each step.

He stopped just inside the door and looked around, nodding to me when he saw me looking, and I nodded back. When the music started, he and his date, stepped to the back edge of the dance area, and gyrated to the song. And when it ended, Paddy took the girl by the arm, and I watched as they walked back out the door.

By 11:30, we were starting to wear down, and knew the night was coming to an end. 'The Air Notes' announced their last song, saying goodnight, and hit the first notes of The Platters, *Only*

You. Carrie Ann put her arms around my neck and laid her head on my chest. Our bodies again fit together like Lincoln Logs and I inhaled the scent of honeysuckle with a hint of baby powder like it was a drug.

She was soft and warm, and as I held her, the words of the song echoed what I felt inside, and I softly sang along:

> *Only you, can make this change in me,*
> *For it's true, you are my destiny,*
> *When you hold my hand, I understand,*
> *The magic that you do,*
> *You're my dream come true, my one, and only you.*

The Prom for the Class of '70 came to an end. We gathered copies of the programs for the girls to save for their memory books, and as a group, slowly walked back up Main Street to the Church parking lot.

It was past midnight when I stopped the car in front of Carrie Ann's house. I didn't want the night to be over. The new spring buds of leaves on the trees in her front yard, hid the glare from the streetlight. And I guess we thought the leaves hid us from view of the rest of the world.

But only for a few minutes… a wonderful few minutes.

She held onto my hand as we walked to the front porch. At her front door, we held each other close, and the feel of her made me wish for a time when there were no good-byes. With every particle of my body, I wanted time to stand still… for just a little longer.

FORTY-SEVEN

We were almost to the end of twelve long years that all of a sudden, were neatly wrapped into a memory. If I closed my eyes, I could still see Danny on the morning we started first grade, with a new burr haircut, rolled up jeans, short sleeve Hop-Along Cassidy print shirt and a book-satchel hanging off of his shoulder.

And there was Will with his hair slicked back wearing dirty Keds high-tops, Amy squinting through her cat's-eye frame glasses trying to see the blackboard, and skinny Mary Beth, in a dress, patent leather shoes and turned down white socks.

Twelve years had changed the way we looked, and the way we looked at the world—but not the way we looked at one another. For some reason, we had been drawn to each other from the beginning, and after all that had happened, we were still together.

We only had about four weeks of actual classwork to go before it would be over, and we'd most likely start drifting apart, each of us going our own way, carrying with us pieces of our past.

Will and Mary Beth had decided to go to the University in Knoxville; Danny had accepted the offer of a half-scholarship to play baseball at Hiwassee; and Amy was intending to go off to the Methodist school in Virginia where Randy was.

But I was still undecided.

I'd applied to Hiwassee, thinking I'd follow Danny, kind of like I'd always done. And I also put in an application to East Tennessee State, mainly because of their ROTC program. But I wasn't settled on either of 'em. Whatever I decided, I was going to have to figure out some way to pay for it.

There was always the option of joining the Army, staying in a few years and let Uncle Sam pay for college later. But with everything going on in the world, there might not be a later. Paddy had about convinced me of that.

Then there was Carrie Ann.

The thought of leaving Lincoln and being away from her, and missing her senior year was almost more than I could stand. I wanted to be with her all the time, to smell the honeysuckle, to put my arms around her and feel her body pressed up against mine, to feel the touch of her lips, to trace the freckles across her nose, to lose myself in her green eyes.

We'd talked about our future only a little since we'd started dating again, and decided on nothing. But in the next few weeks, it was something I had to know.

On the Monday after the Prom, Nixon's news conference was on TV, and the whole country heard his promise to withdraw 150,000 troops from Viet Nam over the course of the next year.

After all that had happened, could it really be so?

Two days later, kids in colleges and schools across the country, celebrated the first "Earth Day," calling for conservation and getting back to the basics of living. A lot of what I read about, sounded like the way folks were still living here in the mountains. But I figured anything that would protect this place that I dearly loved, and bring people back to a more simple way of doing things, had to be good.

The days leading up to graduation came and went in a blur. On Wednesday, both the year books and our class rings came in. Will didn't get to wear his class ring a whole day before it wound up on a chain around Mary Beth's neck. But the rest of us sported the new hardware around for a while longer.

Our year books were a thing of beauty, with a red LHS Crest on a navy blue cover, and inside, the pictures told the story of the past year. In the senior section, they had an entire layout of us from first grade, all the way through. I guess they wanted to show the world how far we'd come.

The pictures of the senior class turned out pretty fair. The girls, of course, looked great. And even Danny and Will's pictures were presentable. Mine wasn't anything to write home about, but I guess it was OK.

As soon as we got the books, we put our name in the front, so we could hopefully get 'em back, and started handing 'em around to all our classmates to sign and write a little something.

I reserved the last page for Carrie Ann, hopefully to write something special… something just for me.

On the same day the rings and yearbooks arrived, 30,000 U.S. troops and 50,000 South Vietnamese troops, attacked across the Cambodian border, invading 20 miles into the neighboring country.

They said it was to destroy supplies and clear North Regular troops and Viet Cong operation bases that had been deviling our guys. The North Vietnamese fighters had been able to hit our bases and then run back into Cambodia laughing at us, since the politicians wouldn't let our guys follow back across the border. So, going in to clean out the hornet's nest actually made sense from a military point of view.

But telling us they were bringing our boys home and getting out of Viet Nam, and then invading the country next door, actually widening our involvement in the war, looked to be the exact opposite of what we'd been hearing. It left the whole country confused and feeling betrayed. It looked like Nixon and the Pentagon Brass were talking out of both sides of their mouth.

And the worst was yet to come.

After the Cambodian invasion, all kinds of people grabbed their signs and took to the streets and college campuses across the country. At a school in Ohio, some of the more radical protesters took over the ROTC building and set it on fire. To restore order, the Governor called out the Ohio National Guard. But when protesters started name calling and throwing rocks, the soldiers fired into the crowd of students.

That day—at Kent State University—four young Americans were killed, and eleven wounded—by Americans...

That day, we made it official... we'd completely lost our minds.

Back when we were in the Primary grades, May Day had been a day of celebration and something we looked forward to. Twelve years later though, trying to tie up all the loose ends, and making sure everything was done so we could graduate, kind of built up the pressure on some of the kids in school.

A lot of the seniors had grades that got 'em exempted from taking final exams. That wasn't exactly the case for me and Danny. He'd screwed up his mid-terms in Senior English, so he had to take that final. And I was carrying a high "C" in Geometry, so I had to sit for that test during the last week of the month.

Even if we blew the finals completely, we were still going to graduate, since we both had a high enough average to finish out the classes. We just didn't get exempted from taking the final tests. And that meant we weren't going to get out of school early, like some of smarter ones would. But it really wasn't a big deal to us.

There was always a few that had a hard time with school, and they were going to have to pass final exams to see if they would graduate. Some of 'em really got all worked up over it. The stress of it all made some chew on their fingernails, and a few went on eating binges. And there were a few that turned to other ways to calm their nerves.

We all knew there were things out there that could help take the edge off. Drugs could be had, but I really didn't know where they were or who exactly had 'em. Either they were keeping them away from the people we were around, or we were just plain ole blind to what was going on.

Rocky and the guys at the Sheriff's Department couldn't get a handle on it either. I knew from what I'd overheard at the Jail, an investigation had been going on for a while. They had their suspicions of where the stuff was coming from, but as far as I knew, they couldn't pin anything down enough to do anything to stop it.

None of the deputies ever directly asked me if I knew anything about drugs being in the school, and I never volunteered any of the rumors I'd heard. And I especially kept a tight lip on the rumor Angel had called Amy about. I didn't know anything for sure, and there was no way I was going to say something that serious about anybody, without having concrete proof.

And besides, Paddy Leary hadn't ever done anything to me. Matter of fact, he'd gone out of his way to try to help me.

I knew using drugs was a highway to hell. I could see the evidence of it coming in and out of the Jail in what little time I was spending there. Like everybody in school, I'd heard stories. But the plain fact was, I didn't know anything for sure—so I kept my mouth shut.

In those last few weeks, there was talk of a couple of students walking around with their eyes glazed over, zoned out on pills, or sneaking out between classes to toke on a joint. But I thought it was just talk.

I didn't actually see any proof of it, and I don't think any of our bunch did. One of the girls in Danny's Chemistry class passed out and fell off of her lab stool, and some said she was on something. But nobody really knew for sure.

After Kent State, the whole world came out to protest. There were demonstrations against the invasion of Cambodia, protests against our troops still fighting in Viet Nam, and riots over the killing of innocent civilians—and the killing of innocent students.

In a press conference on Friday, President Nixon tried to defend his decision to widen the war by invading Cambodia. And he repeated his commitment to bring home 150,000 of our guys by spring of the next year.

But it didn't stop the protests. And it didn't stop the anger. And it didn't stop us from feeling that we simply couldn't trust the leaders of our country to tell us the truth. America was tearing itself apart, right in front of our eyes.

FORTY-EIGHT

The last week of May, and for a lot of the senior class, the last week of high school, was pretty much a non-starter. Those of us that had to sit for final tests, took 'em on either Monday or Tuesday. But the smart kids who had a 90 average or above, got exempted and didn't have to show up at all.

The rest of the students had to be in class till Friday, but the absolute last day for the seniors was Wednesday. By then, we were supposed to have all our books turned in and lockers cleaned out. Then we were off on the Thursday and Friday before graduation, which was gonna be on Saturday the 30th.

They'd been letting all the seniors off a couple of days before graduation for several years. The reason we heard was so we'd have time to get ready for the ceremony. But the real reason was to keep some order at the school. Seems idle hands must really be the devil's workshop, and a lot of things kept happening when the senior class had to sit through the last few days of school with nothing to do.

The decision was made to put the seniors out to pasture a couple of years after Rocky graduated. That was when the guys in shop class got together with the guys from the football team, and took the tires and wheels off of the Principal's '60 Dodge Dart. They say, with all of 'em working together, they pulled the wheels, set the car up on blocks, stuffed all the parts in the back seat, and were back in class fifteen minutes after they started.

Right after that was when the last Principal quit the school and Mr. Webster was appointed to the job. And the next year, they started letting the seniors have the last few days off.

Mary Beth, Amy and Will got exempted from all their finals and got out of class all week, except for Wednesday when we turned in our books, cleaned out lockers and then went through graduation practice. But since I'd screwed up Geometry and Danny messed up his English mid-term, we both had to take finals in those classes the first of that week.

On Saturday night, I spent the evening with Carrie Ann, getting tutored on all the stuff I needed to pass the geometry final. Just being with her made it hard to concentrate on the curves and angles she was trying to beat into my head, and I did my best to change the subject of study to her curves and angles. But she pretty much managed to keep me on track, and I got enough short-term learning in my head to pass the test coming up.

After church the next afternoon, I tutored Danny to get him through the English final he had to take. Since I wasn't distracted by all the cuteness and smelling the honeysuckle and baby powder, it didn't take near as long.

After I finished with Danny, we all met for the Baccalaureate service at Lincoln Baptist, and listened to Preacher Mason give his standard, "...the world is filled with evil..." sermon. We'd heard before about how we were going to be tempted by the devil when we left home to go on to school, and how we had to be strong and resist it. But to tell the truth, there was more than a few of us that were kind of looking forward to finding out just what he was talking about.

At one point, Preacher Mason mentioned the deadly combination of "drinking and wild women." Just thinking about it, Danny moaned real loud in anticipation, and I had to hide my face to keep from laughing. Carrie Ann almost broke my rib when she elbowed me on that one. But we got through it without anybody getting seriously injured.

Afterwards, we took our sweet time on the trip back to her house, and we took a little longer, saying goodnight on her front porch.

As I was driving through town, heading home, I passed the parking lot at Wilson's, and spotted Danny and Will sitting on the tailgate of Will's pick-up, talking to a few other guys in our class. Since it was still early, I pulled in to join 'em.

We decided on a whole lot of nothing for a while, and one by one, the rest of the guys left, leaving me, Danny, and Will to close up the lot. But right as the three of us were starting to leave, we saw Paddy Leary's tan Pontiac go by. He drove to the next intersection, made a U-turn and pulled in the lot next to where we were standing.

Paddy propped his arm up on the window, and lit a cigarette before he asked, "What's up guys?"

Will grinned as he opened the door of his truck and told Paddy we'd just finished solving the world's problems and were fixing to head home. I saw him glance over at Danny as he walked by to get in his Chevy, but neither of 'em said anything else before they drove off.

Paddy had just got there, and I didn't want to be rude. Besides, I really wasn't in any hurry, so I stuck around for a few minutes making small talk.

"Where were ya tonight, Paddy? Preacher Mason had a pretty good sermon for Baccalaureate."

"I ain't much interested in hearin' none-a that kinda stuff. I just wanna get through this week an' get the hell outta here."

"Not stickin' around are ya?"

"Nah… Ain't nothin' for me here no more."

He took a drag off his smoke, flicked the ash from the end, then snorted, hocked and spit over his side-view mirror into the parking lot while I stood there leaned up against my car. I thought this might be the perfect time to talk to him, like I'd promised Amy I'd do, since it was just the two of us.

"To tell ya the truth, I was kinda surprised when you come back here anyway. I'm just curious, Paddy... Why did ya come back to Lincoln? I mean... If ya don't like it here, why'd you come back after ya got outta the Army? You still got family here?"

He flicked the cigarette butt out onto the asphalt, not far from where he'd spit, and then ran his fingers through his black hair, pushing it off of his forehead before answering.

"Got a brother over in Oak Creek. But I've only talked to 'im once since I come back. I reckon Dad took off not long after I got signed up an' left for the Army. We ain't got no idea where he is.

"So no... family didn't have nothin' to do with it."

He paused for a second as his eyes followed a car that went by on the street in front of us.

"Fact is, I didn't have nowhere else to go... When I got back stateside, I took the GED at Fort Campbell, 'cause they told me I could get more disability pension if I had a high school diploma."

It was the first I'd heard of any disability, so I asked.

"I didn't know you had a disability?"

"Yeah... I got a piece of shrapnel in my ass that's pressin' on some kinda nerve. They can't take it out without cuttin' somethin' that's important, so..." and his voice trailed off for a second, like he lost track of what he was saying. Then he suddenly turned back to look at me.

"Any way, the GED people said I graded out 'bout mid-way in the senior year-a high school, an' all I had to do was sign up somewhere an' get the graduation paper. This was the only place I knowed of where I could do it. Once I got the high school papers, I figured I could move on to somewhere else an' start over... Do it right this time, an' not have all the baggage."

He didn't say how he got shrapnel in his ass, but I figured since he was getting some kind of disability from the Army, it had to be from something that happened in the war. I'd never thought much about what my opinion was of Paddy, but after hearing he'd been wounded, whatever it was before, my opinion of him went up.

At that point, it looked to me like the perfect time to mention the rumor Amy had told me about.

"Paddy… I figure me an' you are good enough friends, that we can talk, private like… just between us."

He looked at me and nodded, so I went on.

"I ain't said nothin' 'bout this to nobody… but I think there's somethin' ya need to know…"

I took a deep breath and charged ahead.

"Word is that you're the connection if somebody's lookin' to score a few pills, or get their hands on some grass."

He turned his whole body around in the car seat to look straight at me, and his eyes narrowed and got mean looking. He knew I was working part-time at the Jail, so I guess that's why he asked, "Did ya hear that from the law?"

"Nope… That rumor come from somebody away from here… An' I ain't said nothin' to nobody at the Jail. I wanted to talk to you."

He continued to eye me, thinking about what to say, or probably whether to say anything at all.

Finally, he must have decided to trust me… or something… His face softened and as he started talking, the tone of his words were different from his usual self.

"I ain't sayin' yea or nay to what you're askin'…

"I'll admit, I ain't never been exactly on the right side of things. But I seen in the Army that things can be different… Like, if I was to change my ways, they could be different for me. Maybe I could turn it around, an' start over. It's one of the reasons I want to get my high school papers. I've watched all of ya, an' to tell the truth, I'd like a chance at havin' what you've got—what all you guys've got."

Paddy reached up and punched in the cigarette lighter on the dash, then pulled a pack of cigarettes from over his sun visor, shook one out for himself and offered one to me. The dash lighter clicked and he pulled it out, lighting his smoke first and then holding the glowing lighter out the window to me.

"Paddy... I've got no idea how deep you're into whatever it is you're into, an' tell the truth, I don't wanna know. The only reason I said anything was 'cause you've been straight with me on things. An' I figured you oughta know the word that's gettin' around.

"But if you're lookin' for a way to make some changes—ya know Danny's brother's a vet. I know he's the law an' all, but he spent time in 'Nam, so he'd most likely understand where you're comin' from. If ya wanna change things, did ya ever think about talkin' to Rocky...?"

Paddy eyed me for a minute while his mind worked over what I was saying.

"Hell Paddy... I can set it up with Rocky to talk to him, confidential like. You wouldn't have go anywhere near the Sheriff's Office to talk. I'm sure he'd meet somewhere private."

His gaze never left my face and I saw the corners of his mouth curl up. But I couldn't tell if it was a sneer or a grin.

"Cubby... I don't think that's anything I want to have any part of right now...." and his voice trailed off as he looked around the parking lot. Then he turned back, and looked up at me again.

"Tell ya what... I'll think about it... But don't do nothin' or say nothin' to nobody. I'll get back with ya... OK?"

I nodded my agreement. Then he reached down and turned the ignition key, backed out of the parking space and drove out of the lot, turning left toward the mountains.

FORTY-NINE

Carrie Ann was one of the juniors working graduation, and she had a meeting after school on Monday to go over assignments. After we finished the Geometry final that morning, she asked if I'd come back to get her about 4:30. I told her I would and since that was the last thing I had to do except for Wednesday check out and graduation practice. I left the school and went to the Jail to see if any work was piled up for me.

I noticed Rocky was in his office doing paperwork, and it would've been the perfect opportunity to talk to him about Paddy. But I'd agreed to keep our conversation to myself till Paddy gave me the green light.

I typed a couple of reports and worked on the filing, and then hung around in the dispatch room for a while, until it was time to go back to the school. Carrie Ann had a couple of tests the next day, so I didn't stay long at her house, and I spent the rest of the day at the Shell station, talking to Danny.

I slept in Tuesday morning and then watched Danny change the oil in somebody's car at the station till it was time to get Carrie Ann again. That night we met Will and Mary Beth at Wilson's, and occupied a booth for most of the night, talking.

Wednesday morning, I picked up Carrie Ann a little before 8:00 for our last ride together to high school. The rest of the students had to finish out the week, but since all of the seniors were cut loose after doing a run through of graduation, that morning the parking lot was full. Will and Mary Beth pulled in the lot behind us, and we ran into Amy, Danny and Jenny just inside the door.

With the gang all assembled, we took our last stroll through the hall to Home Room. I could feel everything coming to an end, just like when you know a story is wrapping up and the end of a book is coming.

In a way, I was looking forward to the end of one volume and the beginning of a new one. But I felt kind of bad about some of the things I'd be leaving behind. When it came time for Carrie Ann to go to her class, I held onto her hand for a few seconds longer, trying to stop time for just a little while.

In home room, we answered the roll, turned in our books, and then walked to our lockers to wait for the final inspection. After that, we all made our way to the gym, where they gave out the caps and gowns. The guys had blue robes and the girls were wearing white. All of us had red mortarboard caps with a red tassel that had a plastic silver colored "70" attached to the knot.

Principal Webster and a couple more of the faculty ran through the basics of the graduation ceremony, telling us when to sit, when to stand, and when to walk across the stage. Danny asked about practicing the 'secret handshake' for when they handed us our diplomas, and as usual, got a laugh from everybody… Well, Amy was a little disgusted with him, but the rest of us laughed.

With that done, several of us went to Wilson's for lunch, and sat around talking till time for school to be out. A little before 3:00, I drove back to the school to wait for Carrie Ann.

Thursday was the last day of finals for the rest of the school, and Carrie Ann still had her English test to go, so we didn't spend a lot of time together on Wednesday. She called me about 7:00 to ask a question about Robert Browning's poetry, that she expected to be on the test. But we didn't talk long.

I slept in the next morning, finally hauling my butt out of bed a little after 9:30. After a couple pieces of toast and a shower, I went looking for Danny, and found him sitting on the drink cooler at the service station, sipping on a RC cola, watching the cars go by on Main Street. He looked so chilled out, I joined him and we did absolutely nothing for the better part of an hour.

Sometime around noon, Mr. MacMahan hollered that the phone was for Danny. When he answered, he put his hand over the receiver and whispered to me that Amy had finally tracked us down, wanting to know if either of us was planning on saying anything that evening at Class Night.

I watched as his face lit up with a grin when I shook my head at him, and he told her, "Hell no. You're the class President, so you're all on your own."

We could both hear her cussing as he reached over and pushed down the button, hanging up the phone.

Both the Baccalaureate service at the Church and the Graduation Ceremony on Saturday were put on by the school system, but tradition was that the class get together for one final 'class meeting' and re-hash their twelve glorious years of school. Generally they'd give out a program with a class history, and talk about teachers they liked and didn't like, and such stuff as that.

There was only forty-eight of us in the Class of '70 that we knew for certain would be walking across the stage to get a diploma, so we only had to use a little part of the cafeteria. A couple of the girls had done some decorating with a few pictures, and some red, white and blue streamers, to try to hide the cafeteria look, but it really didn't work.

At 6:00 sharp, me and Carrie Ann walked in the cafeteria door with Will, Mary Beth, Danny and Jenny. As we were going in, we met Paddy coming out. We all greeted him, but he singled me out and said he wanted to talk to me for a second. So I sent Carrie Ann in with the rest to stake out some seats for us.

"What's up? You're not leavin' are ya?"

There wasn't anybody close enough to hear us, but he looked around, to make sure.

"I thought I wanted to do this—to come here tonight—but really, it ain't for me. I feel like a fish outta water in there... I plain ole don't belong.

"I need to ask ya for a favor. I got notice that there's some paperwork back at Fort Campbell I've gotta finish on the pension stuff, so I'm headed over there. But I'll be back for the graduation Saturday...

"I've been thinkin' 'bout what we talked about the other night, an'... well, I think it might be time for me to try to make some changes. I was wonderin' if your offer on talkin' to the Sheriff, an' see if you can set up a meet, was still on the table?"

I looked at him to be sure he was serious, and from the look in his eyes, could tell he was. So I told him I'd take care of it and we'd talk at graduation. He mumbled thanks, turned and walked on to his car.

Since she was the senior class President, Amy presided over Class Night, reading from a script she'd been working on, and all things considered, I have to admit she did a pretty good job.

She hit all the high points, talking about what the world was like when we started, the fear we all felt over hearing the Cubans had missiles pointed at us, and the moment frozen in our memory when the news bulletin came over the school intercom about President Kennedy's assassination.

She noted the year our schools were integrated and we discovered that underneath the first layer of skin, we were all the same. She talked about future promises lost when Dr. King and Bobby Kennedy were taken from us.

And she talked about the ball games, the dances, and the protests, skipping over the mess that happened with Gerry Don and the Prophet's Revival that went so wrong. All the while, Jenny Wilton, who was operating the slide projector, was flashing pictures up on the wall over her head.

I saw Will stiffen a little when a slide of Danny and Mary Beth back in the old days, came up. But when Mary Beth put her arm through his, and patted him on the leg, he relaxed again.

With Carrie Ann beside me, I sat in dread through the whole program, hoping against hope there wasn't a picture of me and Angel anywhere in the mix. Thankfully, if there was one, Amy or Jenny culled it, and we finished out the night without any problem.

One more day…

FIFTY

On Friday, they had the last day of school just to be able to show they'd been there, so the school system could collect from the state. Students were going to be dismissed at 11:00, so going was actually a total waste of time.

But since Carrie Ann was determined to have a perfect attendance record, she had to be there. And it gave me a little time to run by the jail while I waited for her to get out.

I wasn't exactly sure how to tell Rocky what Paddy had asked, so I started from the beginning: about how we got to know Paddy, what happened when we were freshmen that got him sent off to the Army, and how he helped me out when I ran out of gas. I went through Paddy's warning to me when he thought I was wanting to enlist, and ended up with our conversation in the parking lot when I offered to set up a meet. Rocky mostly listened, asking questions only a couple of times.

When I finished, the High Sheriff of Andrew County sat quiet for a minute, leaned back in his desk chair with his fingers steepled in front of his face, like he always did when he was thinking. After a spell, he sat up, opened the drawer of the desk and pulled out a file folder full of papers, arranging it in front of him, before looking up.

"Cubby... I appreciate you tryin' to help, but this ain't one of the smartest things you've ever done. Matter a-fact, messin' in this coulda been downright dangerous for ya." He paused for a second to let it sink in.

"What I'm about to tell you is confidential, an' I'm trustin' you to keep it to yourself. You can't even tell Danny any of this… OK?"

He waited for me to nod my agreement before he went on.

"We've been keepin' tabs on Paddy Leary since he got back in town. As soon as he was discharged, I got a call from the Army givin' me a head's up that he was probably comin' home.

"Paddy was wounded while he was overseas, an' by the time he got outta the hospital, he was hooked on the pain pills they were givin' him. An' apparently he's still takin' whatever pills he can get, either legal or illegal.

"We've got reports that he's been spotted in Knoxville, Johnson City, an' a couple of times in Blount County with some pretty rough characters that are known drug dealers. He's associated with the kinda people that wouldn't hesitate to cut your throat if they thought they had half a reason. An' he's a suspect in a couple of incidents in Knox County where kids who were buyin' drugs, got robbed and beat up pretty bad.

"So far, they hadn't been able to get anybody to give a positive ID, but it's just a matter of time before it all catches up with him.

"Right now, he's gettin' a little pension money from the Army, but not near enough to pay for what he needs, so we think he's supportin' his habit by sellin' some of his supply off to other folks, an' doin' some strong-arm work for dealers he's workin' for.

"Like I said, up to now, we hadn't been able to catch him with anything or tie anything to 'im for sure. But we will…

"Now, if what you're tellin' me is true, maybe there's a good side to Paddy, an' he might be lookin' for a way out. If that's the case, I'll talk to him—see if we can get him in a rehab program to get him cleaned up. An' if he'll give up some information, maybe we'll be able to get back to the source of where this stuff is comin' from.

"But don't kid yourself... Paddy's a dangerous character. He was raised up mean, he's got a hair-trigger temper, an' he acts most times without thinkin' what the consequences might be."

He leaned back in his chair again, and looked straight at me.

"Paddy's not stupid. He's probably figured out the noose is gettin' tighter, and he's lookin' for a way out. But what you need to understand is that junkies, hooked on drugs, will do anything to get what they need. They'll lie right to your face, and do it so convincingly you'll believe 'em.

"I'm hopin' he's bein' sincere on this, an' not pullin' a con to give himself a little more time."

Rocky took a deep breath and thought for a second.

"OK. You seem to have some relationship with him. You tell Paddy I'll meet with 'im. But he needs to know it's gonna be on my terms. I won't be by myself. I'm not stupid enough to walk into somethin' like this without back-up. An' once you tell him—I want you to steer clear of him.

"Between now and whenever I talk to him, if we catch him in possession, or sellin' any of his stuff, all bets are off. We'll take him an' anybody with him into custody."

We talked on for a few more minutes, and I told Rocky what Paddy said about having to go back to Fort Campbell to finish up some paperwork, but that he was going to be here to go through the graduation ceremony. He told me again, to tell Paddy he'd meet with him next week, but after that, to not have any contact with him. Rocky said it in such a way, I knew he was dead serious.

When school let out at 11:00, I picked up Carrie Ann and we met Danny, Amy, Will and Mary Beth at Wilson's for lunch. We had the afternoon free, so we made good use of it.

It was a beautiful late spring day, and when Mary Beth suggested we take a ride up to the lookout off the road to Winter Cave, we jumped at it. It was one of the clearest days any of us had ever seen and the view would most likely be one we'd remember forever, so the six of us squeezed into Danny's Nova and headed for the mountains.

The radio was tuned to WNOX till the ridges blocked off the signal, so we changed over to the 8-Track for music. Amy wanted to hear the tape of the Platters Greatest Hits, but Danny wanted to listen the Stones, so they argued over it for a good ten minutes while the rest of us listened to the static crackle of the radio and the roar of his Cherry Bomb muffler. But since Danny was driving, and Amy was stuck in the back seat with Will and Mary Beth, Danny won out.

It took almost twenty minutes to get to the turn off, and Danny drove up the old logging road as far as he could go, then we hiked another fifteen minutes up to the lookout.

We weren't disappointed by the view. The air was so clear we could see dang near all the way to the Plateau. It was a work of art. Ridge after ridge of blue-gray mountain tops rolled across in front of us, with the horizon finally dissolving into a bank of clouds coming in from the west. The handiwork of God was awe-inspiring, and we sat silent on a rock outcrop and watched the sun slowly slide down behind the clouds.

None of us wanted to leave, but before it got too dark to see, we gathered all the stuff we'd brought with us and headed back to where we'd left the car. But not before Will turned and kissed Mary Beth and I kissed Carrie Ann—and Danny and Amy made fun of us for trying to commemorate a moment of magic.

Danny did his best to rush us on the walk back saying he didn't want to have to drive back down the mountain in the dark. But he waited till we were all safely in the car, almost to the main road before he mentioned that he really wanted out of there so he wouldn't run into the ghost of the girl that got murdered on up the road to the Cave.

Of course Amy didn't have any idea what he was talking about, so Danny launched into a half made-up description of the murder, acting like he was in on all the information from the Sheriff's investigation.

As we went around a curve and I reached for the dashboard to steady myself in the seat, Danny got to the part in his story about the murdered girl not having anything in her pockets except a poster for a rock concert in New York.

All of a sudden, I got the uneasy feeling I'd heard it all somewhere before.

The girl's body had been found just a little before all the whoop-la about the Woodstock rock concert. And I'd heard somebody say something about having "a good concert."

Puzzle pieces started to fall in place... I didn't have any proof of anything. It was just a gut feeling that maybe I knew something that nobody else knew...

The only thing the murdered girl had on her was a poster for a rock concert, that I'd bet anything was for Woodstock. And the investigators had guessed she was probably one of the hippy hitch-hikers that we'd see on the roads from time to time.

The night I ran out of gas, Paddy had said something about picking up a girl that was hitch-hiking, trying to get to a rock concert in New York. He said he'd set her out in Knoxville. And he'd told me she'd spit on him, and called him a baby killer when she found out he'd just got back from 'Nam.

And then Rocky had lectured me on what we all already knew—that Paddy had a hair trigger temper. And we'd all seen what could happen when he flew off the handle—it was like he didn't have any control at all.

The puzzle pieces in my head looked to be fitting together perfectly.

But then I thought about what Paddy had told me about the war, and how he'd gone out of his way to warn me off when I talked to the Army Recruiter at Career Day. And how from the look on his face, and the sound of his voice, I really thought he was sincere about trying to change things, and get his life back on track, and do the right thing.

From what Rocky had said, Paddy was sitting on the edge of the cliff now. And if I went to Rocky without any proof, and told what I suspected was a connection to the girl they'd found up near Winter Cave, I could possibly be pushing Paddy off the edge.

From the time I could sit up by myself, I'd been schooled to know the difference in what was right and what was wrong. And I knew in my heart, the right thing to do was to tell Rocky what I thought I'd figured out.

But at the same time, I'd learned that loyalty to family and friends was one of the highest obligations anybody could have. There wasn't any doubt I had a lot of faults. But disloyalty wasn't one of them.

I didn't get a lot of sleep that night, struggling with the question of what to do. But finally I came to the conclusion that there was only one right thing to do. Good had to win over the bad. To keep my mouth shut in this situation would be wrong.

This was a decision I had to make all on my own. I'd never told anybody what Paddy had said to me on the ride into Lincoln.

And to my knowledge, there wasn't anybody else that knew what I did. I had to do what I thought was the right thing.

At 8:30 Saturday morning, I called Rocky, met him at the Jail and told him what I thought I'd figured out. He called in Brad Main, his Chief Deputy and had me repeat the whole thing to him, and then had me write it down on paper before I could leave—again with a warning that I was not to have any further contact with Paddy.

As I left the Jail, I heard Brad tell Happy Sims to get notice out statewide, to be on the lookout for Paddy Leary.

FIFTY-ONE

———————

The graduation ceremony was set to start at 2:00 and take about ninety minutes. Carrie Ann was one of the ushers, so she had to be there early. We'd already agreed that I'd stay after the ceremony and help her finish up, then we'd have the rest of the day to do whatever we wanted.

Officially, the ceremony was the last thing, but the 'Jim-Tones' had rented out the Lodge, and put out flyers that they were going to have a Graduation Dance starting at 7:00. Dang near the whole class of '70 said they were intending to go, so we were all really considering the dance to be the final ending for our year.

I was for certain sure that telling Rocky what I knew, or at least what I thought I knew, was the right way to go. But that didn't keep me from feeling that I'd somehow betrayed Paddy's trust. Maybe he was really trying to make a change in his life, and he'd asked for my help. But right was right and wrong was wrong.

Whatever happened now, it was done, and there wasn't anything I could do to change things.

The members of the graduating Class of 1970, began gathering a little after 1:00 in the cafeteria where we'd met just the night before, and where we'd congregated for the last four years. We all had our graduation gowns and mortarboard caps, some still in the boxes, and some, like Amy and Mary Beth, pressed and on hangers.

The girls made sure their hair and makeup were perfect before draping the robes around their shoulders, and the guys stood around and made fun of the girls. After all the time we'd been together, nothing much had changed in twelve years. But we were all coming to realize that this was actually a pretty big deal.

Just before 2:00, Principal Webster stepped in the door and gave us the high-sign to start lining up. After a few minutes of nervous jokes and a little confusion, we marched in the gym to take our seats.

When I came in the door, Carrie Ann was standing there with a hand full of programs, doing her thing as an usher. All we could do was exchange smiles as I passed by in line behind Amy. As we walked down the aisle between the rows of chairs, I saw Mom and Dad, sitting with Danny's Mom and Dad. They all had a smile on their faces, I reckon, surprised that either of us had actually made it this far.

I looked around, expecting to see several uniformed deputies watching to see if Paddy was going to make an appearance, but the only law evident was Rocky, sitting on the stage with some of the other county officials.

Preacher Mason opened the show with a prayer, and Mrs. Hunter, the choral director, led everybody in singing the national anthem before Principal Webster stepped to the podium and officially welcomed the crowd. He gave a short talk about how important it was to get an education, and then he must have crossed his fingers when he told the crowd what a joy it'd been to work with the members of our class over the past four years.

Our Commencement Speaker was some big wig from the State Assembly, who was more interested in telling us what all he'd done in Nashville, than he was in sending us out into the world. We squirmed and daydreamed through twenty minutes of talk about the good ole days, and how he and his cronies were working hard for us.

Five minutes into his speech, we pretty much tuned out, listening only for him to wrap it up.

After thinking he'd never stop talking, it was finally time to hand out diplomas and on Principal Webster's command, we all stood up and walked to the edge of the stage, waiting to hear our name.

In alphabetical order, the name of each graduate in the class was called, and it wasn't long before Principal Webster leaned close to the microphone and read, "William Boyd." Will walked up on the stage, accepted his diploma and with a tip of his mortarboard, walked to the other side and back to his seat.

After a few other names were called, it was our turn.

"Amy Higgins." Amy started up the steps, walked to the podium, took her diploma, and walked across to the steps on the other side. She had just stepped down on the floor to return to our seats when Mr. Webster called out, "Abern James."

Amy stopped dead still, and turned around with a huge grin to look at me. I could hear the murmur of everybody in the gym, wondering who the hell "Abern" James was, and red faced, I quick stepped across the stage, took the offered diploma, shook hands, and moved as fast as I could to get to the steps—where Amy was standing, waiting on me.

"A-bern?"

I leaned close to her ear, whispered for her to kiss my ass, and gave her a little shove toward our chairs. Then just as we got to the entrance of the row of chairs where we were sitting, I heard Principal Webster call, "Padraic Leary."

Me and Amy both turned and saw Rocky step up to whisper something in the Principal's ear. He set the diploma aside, looked back down at the list he was reading from, and continued calling more names.

"Daniel MacMahan" was called about the middle of the pack, with "Mary Beth Rivers" and "Jennifer Wilton" ending out our group. Once we were all back standing in front of our seats, Mr. Webster said the magic words, we all changed the tassel from one side of our caps to the other... and all of a sudden, it was over.

There was applause from everyone in the gym, hugs all around, and a few tears from proud parents. Principal Webster called on Preacher Mason to close out with a prayer and then pronounced the graduation ended.

Amy elbowed me in the side to shove me out of the way, and scooted down to the end of the aisle where Randy was waiting to give her a hug. I turned to look for Carrie Ann, but she was talking to her parents, so I found my folks in the crowd and threaded my way through to them.

Danny was already there, talking to his Mom and Dad, so both of us got hugs from our Moms and handshakes and back slaps from our Dads. Then we went hunting for the girls. I found Carrie Ann first, and got a big, long, hug. I got so wrapped up in the feel of her that I lost all track of where Danny went.

We hung around for a while, talking to one another and getting a few pictures made. Amy's Mom got several pictures of the five of us that started together in first grade, and a few snaps of all the couples together. And Carrie Ann's Mother took a couple of pictures of the two of us standing together. But after a while, the crowd started to thin out, and everybody began leaving.

I stayed with Carrie Ann to help pick up the papers left on the floor, and put up some of the chairs. As I was folding one of the chairs, I spotted Rocky walking across the floor, heading in my direction. I met him half way.

Standing in the middle of the gym, Rocky smiled, held out his hand and said, "Congratulations..."

I thanked him quickly, and got right to the point.

"What's happened with Paddy?"

"That's what I came to tell ya..." He paused for a few seconds and looked around to be sure nobody was close enough to hear.

"We got word to the MP's at Fort Campbell to be watchin' for him, an' to hold him if he showed up. They called back pretty quick to let us know Paddy already got there, finished up whatever it was he was doin' an' left before they got our call. We'd notified the Highway Patrol the same time we called the MP's, so they had a description of his car an' plate number too.

"Since we thought he'd be here for the graduation ceremony, we had ever'thing set to pick him up when he showed. But just before I left to come here, the THP office in Crossville called.

"From what they could see, Paddy was driving east on Highway 70, an' was about five miles this side of Sparta, when he lost control an' hit a tree.

"It was a single car accident so nobody saw it happen, but the Trooper said from the length of the skid marks, he musta been going pretty fast. It looked like he might've swerved tryin' to avoid hittin' a deer they found not far from the accident."

I looked at the Sheriff when he paused, waiting for him to continue.

"When he hit the tree, his head musta hit the windshield. The Trooper on the scene, said it looked like the impact snapped his neck. He was dead when they found him."

FIFTY-TWO

———

There wasn't much anything else either one of us had to say. Rocky told me the Troopers were going to go through the wrecked Pontiac with a fine tooth comb and he'd be getting a complete report on the accident. He'd already gotten a search warrant and sent a couple of Deputies to the trailer where Paddy was living to see if they could find anything. And they were going to look for his brother's address or any information on where his Daddy might be so they could get the notifications made as soon as possible.

The bottom line was that we'd probably never know what all Paddy had been involved in, and that included whether there was any connection to the girl found on the road to Winter Cave. The investigation was ongoing, but Rocky said he really didn't expect to get a lot of answers.

I sat in the bleachers and watched the clean-up crew for a few minutes while Carrie Ann finished up. There wasn't anything for me to do, but sit and wonder about it all.

On the short drive taking Carrie Ann home, I was wrapped up in my own thoughts, still thinking about everything that had happened. I guess I must have been a little too quiet. As I turned onto her street, she turned down the radio and asked, "What's the matter, Cubby? This oughta be a happy day for ya…"

For some reason, I needed to tell Carrie Ann what had happened, and it dawned on me how much things had changed. In the past, when I needed to talk things out, it was Danny or Amy or Will that had to listen to me. But all of a sudden, their counsel or approval wasn't what I wanted. What I wanted now was for Carrie Ann to tell me I'd done the right thing.

Word about Paddy's fate would get around. That's the way it was in a small town, and I'd tell the rest of the bunch what I thought I'd figured out when the time was right. But right then, I needed Carrie Ann's understanding and approval. What she thought, was the most important thing to me now.

We sat in the car in front of her house and I told her everything, beginning with what Paddy had said when I rode back to Lincoln with him. I conveniently left out the fact that I was coming home from a date with Angel when I ran out of gas, but that was the only thing I left out.

I told her what Paddy told me about the Army and about the horrors of war, and how he'd tried to warn me off when he thought I was going to enlist. And I told her what he'd said about trying to straighten out his life.

Then I told her how our trip up to the Lookout and Danny's story about the murdered girl had triggered things in my memory that tied it all together. And I told her that I'd truly struggled with it, but came to the realization that the right thing to do was to lay out what I knew, and let Rocky handle it all.

By the time I finished, Carrie Ann agreed that the circumstantial evidence was damning, but unless there was some evidence to back everything up, that was all it was—a lot of things that pointed in one direction—but no real proof of anything. She said she understood the conflict I felt, telling Rocky my suspicions.

I sat quiet, waiting for her judgement. The late spring sun had warmed up the interior of the Corvair and through the open car windows I could hear birds singing as they watched us from their perch in the trees that surrounded her house. After a few minutes, she reached out and put her hand over mine, and told me she thought I'd done the only thing I could do... the right thing.

Then she leaned over, kissed me and said to pick her up at 6:00 so we could get something to eat before the dance.

When we walked into Wilson's, Danny, Jenny, Randy and Amy were already there and Will and Mary Beth came in right behind us. Word had already spread about Paddy, and most of the conversation over burgers and fries had to do with stories we'd either heard, or things we actually knew about him. It wasn't the time to say anything about what I'd suspected, so neither me nor Carrie Ann said anything about what I'd told her. That night was for remembering the good times.

As we were walking to our cars to go to the dance, Amy took me by the arm and pulled me off to the side, out of earshot of the others.

"I kinda get the feelin' from some of the looks you an' Carrie Ann were givin' each other, that there's more to this story you ain't tellin'."

I opened the door of Randy's car so Amy could get in, and said, "Not now Amy. I promise I'll tell ya. But not tonight. Tonight's our night."

The dance had already started when we got there, and the eight of us joined what looked to be the entire graduating class on the dance floor. The music was loud, with multi-colored lights flashing to punctuate the beat of rock-'n-roll.

Those not on the dance floor were congregated in little groups, and their shouts and laughing fought to compete with the amplified sound coming from the band. It was obvious we were determined to have one last fling before we had to confront whatever would come tomorrow—and for the rest of the tomorrows in our lives.

By 10:30, we'd been on the floor for dang near every dance and were just about exhausted. The 'Jim-Tones' out did themselves that night, playing a mix of old and new songs, both fast rock-'n-roll and slow romantic tunes. I danced a few times with Amy, Mary Beth and Jenny, and Carrie Ann danced with the other guys, but we stayed close enough to find each other for all of the slow songs.

When we held each other, the feel of her shape against me, the tickle of her hair against my cheek and the smell of honeysuckle and baby powder became overpowering. I knew with all my heart that I wanted to spend the rest of my life holding her close. But I could feel the darkness of the coming year's separation, creeping over me like a fog.

Just before 11:00, Jimmy Dawkins stepped to the keyboard and announced they were dipping back into the past for the last song of the night. Then he played the opening notes to the old ballad the King had covered so well, *Fallin' in Love With You.*

Carrie Ann put her arms around my neck and I hugged her tight to my chest. Usually, I was the one who sang, but this time I heard her voice, softly singing:

> *...Shall I stay, would it be a sin,*
> *If I can't help, falling in love with you.*
> *Like a river flows, slowly to the sea*
> *Darlin' so it goes, some things, are meant to be...*

The song was over way too soon. I wanted it to last forever, and I wanted there to be no doubt in her mind how I felt. I drove really slow on the way to her house, and we talked about the future, about me leaving to go to college, and how being apart would be a test.

I held her hand in mine as we walked from the car to her front door, and once there, she turned, put her arms around me and laid her head on my cheek. We stood there for a long while, and as we held each other, with my hands behind her back, I removed my class ring from my finger. Then I took a step back and held it out to her.

Carrie Ann looked at the ring, and her green eyes glistened when she looked up at me. She slowly reached out and took the ring from my hand, held it in hers, and looked at it for a few seconds...

Then she reached for my hand and placed it back on my finger...

"Cubby... I can't take your ring. I'm not saying I don't want to be with you. Maybe someday, but now's not the time..."

I know she could see the confusion on my face.

"Think about it for a minute. Neither one of us has been out in the world. We don't know what might be out there for either of us. I can't say right now that this is all there is. An' I don't know how you can say that either.

"We've got a lot of things to do in the next couple of years. And to tie either one of us down now wouldn't be right. You're goin' away to school an' there's gonna be things you'll wanna do. An' I'm sure there's gonna be other girls you'll wanna go out with. An' I've got another year here, without you around, an' there'll be things I'm gonna wanna do.

"It wouldn't be right to tie either of us down."

I started to protest, but she put her fingers on my lips to stop me, before she went on.

"You mean more to me than anybody right now... But I can't make the kind of commitment you're askin' me to make. Someday it might work out that we'll be together... But tonight's not the night."

I could feel the catch in my throat and the tears beginning to form in my eyes. I bit at my tongue to keep from completely breaking down in front of her.

I didn't know what to say or do, so I stood there, as she slowly traced my lips with her fingertip.

Then she moved her hand around to the back of my neck and pulled me to her, and our lips met, softly at first… and then with a passion I'd never felt from her before.

I wanted to be with her forever, and I wanted her to know it. But she didn't want the same thing. I was crushed and I felt like the bottom had dropped out of my world.

But there was no way I was gonna let her know it.

I could feel her shape and the touch of her lips on mine, and the warmth of her body pressing against me. It was a passion I would carry with me for the rest of my life.

After a while, we stood back from each other. As I struggled to get my breath, Carrie Ann turned, went inside… and I drove home, with a hole in my heart once again.

I slept in the next morning and skipped church.

How could I have mis-read so badly my relationship with Carrie Ann? I didn't have any doubt that I loved her, and for the life of me, I couldn't understand why she didn't feel the same way. I'd laid out my heart to her—again. And again, I'd had it handed right back to me.

Maybe I really was a fool. Maybe I was just lying to myself when I thought she really cared about me. The rejection hurt, and the more I thought about it, the madder I got. Not really at her, but at myself.

I loved her more than anything in the world…

But how many times was I gonna let her play with my feelings for her? How many times could I let myself be led around like a love sick puppy on her leash?

Hell… I was somebody worth being with… I was a good person… I deserved somebody that loved me…

A little after 2:00, I heard the phone ring, and Mom told me Amy was calling. I didn't want to talk to her, but I knew if I didn't, she'd keep on until I did. So I took the phone, covering the receiver with my hand while I stretched the cord into my room so we could talk privately. Once I got the door closed and said hello, as usual she charged right in.

"Carrie Ann called an' told me to call ya. She said you offered her your ring an' she didn't take it, an' she's afraid you're gonna go off the deep end or somethin'. She said the time waddn't right, an' I'm gonna tell ya, I agree with her.

"Now Cubby, you know how I hate to tell ya what to do with your life…"

"Shit-fire Amy, when did ya start NOT tellin' me what to do?" I interrupted in mid-sentence.

"Well, OK… So maybe I do stick my nose in your business. But dammit Cubby. Somebody's gotta steer ya in the right direction."

I had to admit that most everything she'd ever told me, turned out to be what I actually should have been doing all along, but I caught myself before I said it out loud.

"Cubby, we're flat-out not old enough to tie down completely. We've got a-ways to go before that time comes an' we've got a lotta things to do between now and when we tie down to somebody forever.

"Carrie Ann told me she thinks the world of ya. An' she really does care for ya—a lot. But she just can't tie herself down, an' she don't want to tie you down right now… Maybe someday it'll happen… But not now.

"Hell Cubby, we're leavin' Lincoln for school in a couple of months. We've got a lot ahead of us."

Amy paused to get a breath, and I took the opportunity to tell her that I'd been up most of the night thinking about it all, and still couldn't understand what had gone wrong. I admitted right out to her how I felt, and that I was more mad at myself than I was at Carrie Ann for letting her jerk me around. I had to admit that we were awful young, and I knew we had a lot of things facing us. But it still didn't change how I felt about her.

We talked on for a few minutes, and Amy worked it around to where I pretty much realized that Carrie Ann had probably done what was right for both of us. I still didn't like it, but I knew deep down, she was right.

When I finally said it, I could almost hear Amy smile over the phone line, smug in her knowing she was most likely right on the money again.

We talked on for a few minutes about her and Randy, and she confirmed that she'd been accepted to the school in Virginia where he was going. She told me, Randy had gotten the call to preach, and she was going to go support him every step of the way.

Somehow, I couldn't get the image in my head of Amy being a Preacher's wife, but I guess stranger things have happened. Then she turned the subject back to me.

"Have ya decided where you're gonna go to school?"

"Yeah… With the way things are goin' with the war now, I'm thinkin' ROTC might not be the smartest way to go, just to get my schoolin' paid for. An' I've been keepin' Danny's ass outta trouble since we was little. I talked to Hiwassee an' they say they'll get things worked out financially for me, an' me an' Danny can room together. So, I signed the papers to go there a few days ago."

The line went silent for almost a whole minute, and I wondered if we'd been disconnected. Then I heard Amy breathing on the other end of the line.

"Uh… Cubby? I hadn't told ya, 'cause I figured it didn't make any difference, but I got a call from Angel about a week ago, an' she was askin' about ya. The football player she threw ya over for, started goin' out with one of their cheerleaders, an' she's not seein' him anymore. She sounded kinda disappointed when I told her you an' Carrie Ann were pretty tight. But she told me somethin' I think you oughta know...

"Angel's gonna be goin' to Hiwassee in the fall too."

My memory flashed back, and in my mind's eye I could see the long dark hair, her mysterious eyes crinkled in the sunlight, and for some reason, I reached up and rubbed the tip of my nose.

I felt a pang of guilt about it... or at least I think it was guilt. But the memory was still there.

Well hell... The future just might get pretty interesting after all.